KT-509-642

'I'm asking you to marry me.'

Yance leaned back in his chair and smiled. 'I have a great deal to offer.'

China kept her calm. 'What would that be, besides security, which I don't need?'

'What if I told you that security is what I want from *you?*'

'Your son,' China said into the silence that followed, and Yance nodded.

Sitting very still, China contemplated the man before her. 'Why this sudden impulse to give Trace a mother he probably doesn't want?' she asked. "Besides, you don't know anything about me.'

'But I know your father. Your father says you have an honest, caring nature, and, most important, you're loyal.' Yance gazed at China. 'My own father thought you were something special, too,' he said quietly. For a long moment he stared at this woman, whose very essence was made of laughter and femininity. And she was no stranger…

Dear Reader

Welcome to August's fabulous line-up and what better way to start than with superstar author Nora Roberts! Her famous family **The MacGregors** are back. In *The Winning Hand*, Darcy Wallace goes from being a pauper to a millionaire in an instant—and runs into seductive Robert MacGregor Blade. There's more from this author to look forward to this year—look out for *The MacGregor Grooms*, expected in October!

This month we're also starting a delightful new trilogy, **Prescription: Marriage**, with *From House Calls to Husband*. Three nurses vow *never* to marry doctors— but find it hard to keep their word... And Barbara Bretton brings us a heroine who falls for her pilot after a plane crash!

Tiffany Santini is trying to stop powerful lawyer J.D. from playing 'knight in shining armour' in Lisa Jackson's *A Family Kind of Girl*. And another determined heroine won't let a *Prenuptial Agreement* stand in the way of true love. Finally, catch up with those **Big Apple Babies**, in the last part of the series from Jule McBride.

Happy reading!

The Editors

Prenuptial Agreement

DORIS RANGEL

™ SILHOUETTE

SPECIAL EDITION®

For Pat Hoppe,
whose generosity of spirit is only equalled
by her generosity with praise.
Thanks, Cousin.

DID YOU PURCHASE THIS BOOK WITHOUT A COVER?
If you did, you should be aware it is **stolen property** as it was reported
unsold and destroyed by a retailer. Neither the author nor the publisher
has received any payment for this book.

*All the characters in this book have no existence outside the imagination
of the author, and have no relation whatsoever to anyone bearing the same
name or names. They are not even distantly inspired by any individual
known or unknown to the author, and all the incidents are pure invention.*

*All Rights Reserved including the right of reproduction in whole or in part
in any form. This edition is published by arrangement with Harlequin
Enterprises II B.V. The text of this publication or any part thereof may not
be reproduced or transmitted in any form or by any means, electronic or
mechanical, including photocopying, recording, storage in an
information retrieval system, or otherwise, without the
written permission of the publisher.*

*This book is sold subject to the condition that it shall not, by way of trade
or otherwise, be lent, resold, hired out or otherwise circulated without the
prior consent of the publisher in any form of binding or cover other than
that in which it is published and without a similar condition including
this condition being imposed on the subsequent purchaser.*

*Silhouette, Silhouette Special Edition and Colophon are
registered trademarks of Harlequin Books S.A., used under licence.*

*First published in Great Britain 1999
Silhouette Books, Eton House, 18-24 Paradise Road,
Richmond, Surrey TW9 1SR*

© Doris Rangel 1999

ISBN 0 373 24224 7

23-9908

*Printed and bound in Spain
by Litografía Rosés S.A., Barcelona*

DORIS RANGEL

loves books—the feel of them, the smell of them, the sight of them. And she loves talking about them. She has collected them, organized them, sold them new and used, written them, taught others to write them, read them aloud to children and published them. History, philosophy, science, satire, Western, romance... She loves reading it all. In her home, books are the wallpaper of choice.

B.C. (Before Children), Doris worked for the Peace Corps in the Philippines and was bitten by the dreaded travel bug. Since then, she's been prone to abandoning her three grown or nearly grown urchins in order to wander the roads of mediaeval Japan, Regency England or modern Australia, all for the price of a paperback. What a bargain! But she admits someday she hopes to breathe in the frigid air of Antarctica first-hand, and personally traverse a hanging walkway among the treetops in a rain forest. Someday. In the meantime, her fictional characters do the wandering, little knowing they carry her piggyback.

Other novels by Doris Rangel

Silhouette Special Edition®

Mountain Man

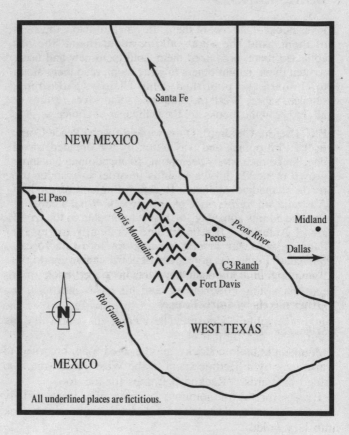

Santa Fe

NEW MEXICO

El Paso

Davis Mountains

Pecos River

Midland

Pecos

Dallas

C3 Ranch

Fort Davis

Rio Grande

N

WEST TEXAS

MEXICO

All underlined places are fictitious.

Prologue

Using a thumb to push his Stetson to the back of his head, the young cowhand studied his cards morosely before laying the hand facedown on the scarred top of the bunkhouse table. "I'm out. These cards jus' don't like me a'tall. Y'all can fight it out."

Across the table a stocky middle-aged man, browned to warm teak by a lifetime spent in the West Texas sun, also folded his cards. "Reckon that goes for me, too."

Except for the monotonous buzzing of a frustrated fly batting against a window screen, the bunkhouse sank back into lazy quiet.

Blackjack Kerrigan stared at his own cards and ran a roughened palm over his jaw to hide growing excitement. In all his years playing bunkhouse poker, it was probably the best hand he'd ever held. A sure 'nuff winnin' hand, likely. But he'd have to raise the pot to know for sure.

Trouble was, he didn't have anythin' extra to raise it with.

Slowly, he, too, folded his cards and placed them on the table, but fixed an unsmiling eye on the remaining card player who'd made a small movement.

"Don't be hasty now, Yance. I'm thinkin'."

Blackjack scraped his chair back as he left the table, but went only as far as the screen door where he stood quietly, peering out into the bright autumn sunshine.

From his place at the table Yance Chisholm watched the grizzled, bandy-legged little cowhand, smiling slightly with the first humor he'd felt in a while.

It had probably been a good fifteen years, since Yance had been around the old man, but he'd swear Blackjack hadn't changed a bit in all that time, his pithy, drawled comments and cantankerous ways still as full of vinegar.

Blackjack was a "character," even for this part of Texas where characters were the rule, not the exception. Moreover, Kerrigan was a man known for his impeccable honesty, his hard work and his absolute loyalty to whoever was his boss at the time.

"C'mere," Blackjack called.

A year ago Yance might have taken exception to the old man's tone, but that was a year ago…a lifetime ago. Now he merely pushed away from the table to stride across the room and stand obligingly beside the small, straight-backed figure. There was, after all, no need to prove to Blackjack who was boss. Both of them knew that while Blackjack was and always would be his own man, Yance, as owner, was undisputed authority on the C3 Ranch.

"I'm puttin' up China Dare," Blackjack said brusquely. "Do you accept?"

Yance looked to where the old man, with a curt nod, had motioned. Some distance across the packed earth in front of the bunkhouse stood the corral. In it was Blackjack's mare. Nothing about the horse marked her as exceptional, but Blackjack was known to take her everywhere with him as he traveled the southwestern ranches, going wherever and doing whatever temporary ranch work was needed.

Hell, he didn't want the old man's horse, Yance thought tiredly. "There's only thirty dollars in the pot," he said, striving for tact. "She looks like she's worth far more than that."

Blackjack snorted and swung to face the younger man who towered over him. "Damn right she's worth more'n that. You can't put a price on what China Dare's got, son. That'd be like tryin' to put a money value on courage or honesty...or love. China's full o' those and more. Nothin' special for looks mebbe, but if you're the man I think you are, then you know looks don't count for much no ways in the end."

Yance said nothing, trying to think of a way out of this that wouldn't hurt the old man's feelings. He turned his attention back to the mare and noticed a girl in the corral feeding something to the horse. As he watched, she wiped her hands on the seat of her jeans...with a nice fit across her trim bottom, he noted absently...then reached up and patted the horse's neck. The mare bobbed her head a couple of times and, when the girl turned to walk to the fence, gave her a playful shove in the back.

The corral was too far away for Yance to see the girl's features, but something about her movements made him think she was laughing as she turned and patted the horse again before continuing to the fence, the horse docilely following her every step of the way.

Slipping through the bars of the corral, she then climbed up to sit on the top rail. Sunlight glinted off a single thick dark honey blond braid.

"Is that your daughter?" Yance asked in an effort to gain time. He knew it was. He'd heard somewhere recently that the girl traveled with Blackjack even though her mother had died last year. Sissy, he thought she was called, though the teenager at the corral didn't seem to fit his vague recollections.

Yet how easily time slipped away, lost irretrievably in the pressing necessities of day-to-day living. He frowned. Trace, too, would be a teenager in a few short years and badly in need of a strong guiding hand.

"Stepdaughter, but she might as well be mine. She was just a baby when I married her ma." Blackjack snorted again before adding in a gruff voice fooling no one, "Got too much loyalty for her own good, that girl. Gallivantin' around is no life for a single female, but she thinks she's got to look after me. Says she likes travelin' and she can do her drawin' anywhere. When they was passin' out the lovin' and carin', she musta snuck around and gone through the line twice."

The old man moved irritably, as if ashamed of his small show of emotion. "Well, you acceptin' China in the pot or not, boy?" he asked, brusquely getting back to the main topic of discussion.

Yance sighed and looked again at the horse, noticing as he did so that his son, Trace, had climbed up on the corral fence and sat beside the girl. "Yeah," he said without enthusiasm, "I'll accept her."

As he turned back to the table he noticed the men seated there were both fighting to keep their faces noncommittal, one of them shooting him a curious look. Behind the old man's back, Yance gave a small shrug to indicate his reluctance. There was no way out of this without offending Blackjack's pride.

On a ranch this size, he thought in resignation, what was one more horse?

After resuming their places and in heavy silence, the two men spread their cards on the table.

Blackjack's shocked gaze went from his full house to Yance's four of a kind, before traveling up to the expressionless face of the younger man. Thick straight lashes couldn't quite hide the sympathy in the gray eyes.

Feeling a curious combination of loss and total well-being, Blackjack smiled slowly.

Yance saw with relief that the old man's smile was genuine. He himself fought down a sudden feeling of emptiness, wishing bleakly that he had just a fraction of Blackjack's courage.

"You're lucky, boy."

"Yeah," Yance replied, the bitterness of the word lost in the scrape of the chair as he pushed away from the table. He'd always been lucky at cards, he thought, and his luck seemed to transfer over to the similar game of business. "Lucky at cards; unlucky at love," the old saying went.

But love wasn't the issue of the moment.

Life was. Would the adage still hold?

He joined Blackjack, and both men paused in the doorway to look outward toward the corral.

The girl and Trace had disappeared, and the mare stood in the corral alone, head hanging, looking lonely.

"What's your daughter going to say about this?" he asked the old man abruptly. With any kind of opening, he'd make a gift of the horse to the girl.

Blackjack chuckled. "Plenty, I reckon, but she wasn't playin' the cards." The answer effectively cut off that avenue of escape.

They strolled over to the corral to stand leaning against its bars. The mare came to them immediately, and Blackjack reached up to scratch between her ears.

"Don't think I'm doin' this lightly, boy," he said, looking at the horse but speaking to Yance. "China's the best there is, and she bred true. Her ma was a thoroughbred and she passed it on to China Dare. I don't know much about her pa, except what I've heard here and there, but that was all good." He rubbed the horse's nose.

"You're worryin' about me, son," he continued, "but

you needn't. I've been frettin' over what to do with China for some time now. This movin' around is no good for her. She needs a home, stability, a chance to be what females are supposed to be. It come to me while we were playin' cards that this would be the ideal place for her. Her gentle heart and that kid of yours were made for each other. So I sat back and let the cards decide, and this is what they come up with.''

Blackjack swung his head once to indicate a touch of amazement. ''Even with me holdin' a full house.'' He barked a laugh before gruffly continuing, seriousness in every line of him now. ''What happens between China and you won't be any of my business after today, but I expect you to treat her with honor. If you don't, you'll have me to reckon with.''

Yance acknowledged Blackjack's warning with a small nod holding no trace of condescension; nor, for that matter, any fear. Each man knew and respected the worth and potential of the other.

''But I ain't worried,'' Blackjack added. ''You'll give China a good home. I know how you treat your animals...and your folks. This is a big country, but there ain't enough people that a body can hide his personal ways. I've kept up with you over the years. Your pa and me went way back and was good friends to the end. You're a prime man for my China Dare and your boy needs her, too. An' she may not know it, but she needs the two of you just as bad. She's achin' for somebody besides me to love.''

Yance clapped the old cowhand on the shoulder. ''I'll do right by her,'' he said sincerely, touched in spite of himself. ''Come up to the Big House for a drink before you go,'' he then invited. The old cowhand had a job that would see him through the winter on a neighboring ranch and was leaving immediately.

Though Blackjack was known as a top hand, he'd turned down many offers over the years for steady employment, including one from the C3 when Yance's father offered him the foreman's job.

He liked seeing the country, the old man maintained, and apparently it was so, for even when his wife was alive and his stepdaughter quite small, he'd traveled the various southwestern ranches, the three of them living in a gooseneck trailer Blackjack hauled with his pickup. And since Blackjack seldom used any horse but his own, behind the gooseneck there was always a horse trailer.

For the past ten days he'd worked the fall roundup on the Chisolm Ranch, but he and Yance hadn't come into direct contact until this morning when Yance arrived on the ranch in time to distribute paychecks and greet personally the extra hands hired especially for the gather.

Unable to leave Midland until the last possible moment, Yance missed out on the grueling work the roundup entailed, but many of the hands, Blackjack among them, had lingered long enough to fill him in on the personal details that wouldn't show up in the manager's or foreman's report. These details included large amounts of gossip, opinions and jokes too good to be missed.

It was the first time in years a Chisolm had not been present at a major gather and Yance felt as if he'd let his heritage down in some way. Until recently, he'd never truly realized how many of the important things in his life hinged on his being physically there.

The two men walked across the scraggly ranch yard toward the Big House, a sprawling single-storied structure with a long, wide front porch facing an imposing view of the encircling Davis Mountains.

After thoughtlessly taking the porch steps three at a time, Yance had to suppress a twinge from outraged muscles as he held the screen door open for the older man.

"Still feelin' the effects of that plane crash, are you, boy?" Blackjack commented. "You need to stay home for a spell, I reckon, and get yourself back in shape."

"I plan on it," Yance drawled, smiling thinly, and led the way to the study.

The small but spacious room was a comfortable blend of masculinity, utility and comfort. "Looks just like it did when your pa sat behind that desk," Blackjack commented approvingly as Yance took a bottle of bourbon and two glasses from a cabinet. "I hear tell you're not bad as a long-distance ranch boss. That's high praise for someone who ain't even in the country half the time and a striplin' at that."

This time Yance's smile reached his eyes, causing Blackjack to wonder why the humor, so obviously a part of the younger man's nature, had been seldom seen this day. Rumor had it that the Chisolm business interests were in flux and Yance was coming back to the ranch to stay awhile.

Well, he had troubles, financial probably, but like any man worth the name, Yance was keeping them to himself, the old man thought approvingly. Let him stay on his ranch for a while with his boy and China Dare. Before long, whatever was wrong would work itself out. Blackjack knew for a fact the C3 was stable, and the C3 was heart's blood to a Chisolm.

"Hardly a stripling. I'll be thirty-eight next birthday."

Yance's dry voice brought back the older cowboy's wandering attention. Blackjack grinned. "As I said, a mere striplin'. Wait till you're my age, son. Anybody under sixty is still a youngster."

Again, the answering smile merely curved the younger man's mouth.

"Long life and good health," Blackjack saluted abruptly and tossed off the smooth Kentucky whisky.

Yance's hand jerked, causing some of the whisky to spill onto his fingers before he, too, tossed off the drink.

"Boy…" Blackjack began on a small, puzzled frown, but the phone jangled imperiously. Just as well, the old man thought. He'd been about to step into another man's business. "You go ahead and answer that, son. I'm sayin' goodbye to you, and you pass it on to China Dare. No sense me gettin' her all riled. Just tell her I love her and did it for the best."

The two men shook hands with a hard, brief clasp as the phone rang again. Blackjack jerked his hat on his head, and Yance picked up the phone, nodding in farewell as the cowboy left the room.

He gave the call only part of his attention. It was business, highly important to one of his executives on the other end; trivial to Yance who, daily, was finding the only things important were his son and the colors of sunrise against far mountains.

The rumors were wrong about him selling off major Chisolm holdings, though he'd sold most of the smaller ones. Over the past few weeks, however, he'd set about delegating all decision making for the remaining holdings to hand-picked subordinates. After this morning, if John Peters would get it through his head, the only business Yance personally controlled was the ranch that had been in his family for five generations. With the C3 having a ranch manager, even that control was indirect.

With ranching frequently in economic semicrisis, the C3 was often little more than a tax write-off for the Chisolm financial structure. Long ago, with what money he could scrape together, Yance's grandfather bought shares in several industries when he'd realized how an extended West Texas drought could mean monetary disaster if there was no other income on which to rely.

But ranching remained the heart of the Chisolm interests, no matter where else they had financial ties. It was tradition that the sons grow up here, just as his was doing; and for a Chisolm, the C3 was the only place that was truly home.

Vaguely, Yance heard Blackjack's rig bouncing over the

rocky drive. The sound grew louder as it approached the
Big House, idled a moment, then drew away. Puzzled, unable to fathom why Blackjack would drive out of his way
to the ranch house, Yance walked to the window and
peered through the old-fashioned wooden blinds, the phone
still to his ear. The window faced toward the corral and
Yance was just in time to see the old man's pickup and
trailer as they headed toward the dirt ranch road leading
to the highway.

His hand, still holding the phone, lowered slowly as he
stared out the window with unbelieving incredulity.

A one-horse trailer bounced behind the gooseneck
hitched to Blackjack's truck. Quite distinctly Yance saw a
brown tail waving from it before dust obscured his vision.
To verify what couldn't possibly be true, his gaze swung
to the corral. It was empty.

Raising the phone to his ear, Yance broke into the
speaker's dialogue with cold precision before striding to
the desk and dropping the receiver onto its cradle. Then,
putting both hands on the desk, he leaned on his arms and
inhaled deeply. He felt as if Kerrigan had just punched
him in the gut.

Dammit, he'd won that horse! No, he didn't want it;
would have given it back had there been a way. But for
Blackjack to arbitrarily take the horse was incomprehen-
sible.

No Western man of Blackjack's generation welshed on
a bet; not many did in Yance's generation, for that matter.
In this part of Texas, honor was still as important to a
cowman as the fit of his boots. Nor had he ever heard
otherwise where Kerrigan was concerned. As the old man
said, everyone knew everyone within a three-hundred-mile
radius in this sparsely populated country, either personally
or by hearsay. Hell, just last year Blackjack had been pall-
bearer at Steve Chisolm's funeral!

As incredulity wore off, anger rushed in. On top of everything else, he'd been worrying for weeks over the possibility of his son being cheated out of his inheritance. For Blackjack to blatantly cheat him, Yance Chisolm, out of a nondescript two-bit horse was the final straw.

Had the old man assumed age gave him special license? Not hardly, Yance thought bitterly. Not damn hardly!

Sweeping up one of the whisky tumblers, he hurled it across the room in a rare display of rage. There was, however, no pleasure in the resulting explosion of splintering glass.

The exertion left his still-healing ribs aching, and he lowered himself into his desk chair with a grimace. Get a grip, Chisolm, he told himself. Since when did tantrums solve problems?

But bitterness still lay over his features when the study door was pushed cautiously open and the anxious face of his son peered around it.

"Somethin' fall, Dad?"

Yance chuckled, his face clearing at once. "No. I lost my temper and threw a glass at the wall. Pretty dumb, huh?"

Trace grinned at his father. "I'll say. Now you have to clean it up. What made you mad?"

Pushing away from the desk, Yance stood and came around it to ruffle his son's shock of straight black hair, knowing the boy hated the gesture. "My business, partner," he said firmly, and laughed as the boy ducked away from the teasing hand on his head. "You're kinda quiet out there, son. What are you up to?"

"About four feet," Trace replied and giggled in his turn when his father rolled his eyes in mock despair at the old joke. "Nah, we're in the tree house playing Crazy Eights," he answered Yance's question. "Catch you later, Dad." And he whirled away, obviously anxious to get back to the game.

On his way to get the broom and dustpan, Yance heard

the back door slam and smiled reminiscently, wishing he could turn back the clock and join his son for the afternoon. He'd built the tree house himself when not much older than Trace, and knew from firsthand experience the somnambulant creak of branches against its planking on warm days such as this.

He swept the glass fragments together and bent down to whisk them into the dustpan. How many lazy afternoons had he spent in that tree house, lying on its rough boards with his hands behind his head, daydreaming and finding animals in the clouds? He, too, had been an only child and knew what it was to make his own entertainment.

Trace was so damned alone now, but this was nothing compared to what it might be if…

The boy's words finally jelled. *We're in the tree house.* We?

Striding down the central hall, Yance arrived at the back door just in time to hear Trace give a yell and giggle. In the same instant he saw his son leap from the platform in the tree, catch a lower branch in a fair imitation of Tarzan, and swing to the ground, immediately running around the house and out of sight.

Right behind him, copying his yell, his giggle, his leap, swing and run in a blur of jeans and dark blond braid was Blackjack Kerrigan's daughter.

Yance opened the door and stepped out, but the two had disappeared. What the hell was going on?

Pivoting, he strode purposefully back down the hall and pushed the front screen door partly open just as the girl came flying around the corner hot on Trace's heels. She made a final lunge, caught the boy from the back and around the chest, lifted him off the ground with Trace squealing in rapturous delight, and twirled him round and round as though drunk on warm fall sunshine.

At last the two collapsed into a breathless laughing heap, then lay on their backs in the sparse grass of the front lawn, giggling together as they caught their breath, the tops of their heads pointing toward the front door.

Yance gazed at them, his anger arrested by a twinge of envy at their youthful ability to take the gift of the day and make it their own. Gradually the giggling died away, but he was too far away to hear anything but the low tones of their desultory conversation. He saw the girl extend one arm and with a slim finger make drawing motions in the air, and realized with a touch of amazement that she was tracing out cloud pictures.

Instinctively he glanced upward to see what animal she found in the sky, but his eyes encountered only the roof of the porch. Pulling himself together sharply, he opened his mouth to summon the pair and find out why the girl hadn't left with her father.

Before he could do so, however, she sat up, her attention riveted on the spot where Blackjack's pickup and the trailer had been parked. Immediately scrambling to her feet, she turned to Trace and said something while absently dusting off her behind. The boy shrugged and they both turned toward the house.

The man watching them started slightly.

This was no girl coming toward him, but a woman in her middle twenties. Tall, strongly boned and well proportioned, her breasts pushed against her T-shirt to accent a slender waist in her well-worn jeans. She wasn't truly pretty, with high wide cheekbones bearing a dusting of freckles, brownish green eyes, a distinct jawline, and her mouth, free of lipstick, wide and slightly square.

Yance's eyes narrowed to slits, and his gaze took on a dangerous glitter not unlike sunshine on a gun barrel.

The girl smiled at him as she trotted up the same steps that earlier left him puffing. His answering scowl didn't so much as faze her.

"Hello, Yance," she greeted him cheerfully…just as if she'd known him for years. "Do you know where my father is?" She paused. "Remember me? I'm China Dare."

Chapter One

"**I**'ll be damned."

China's eyes widened at the drawled words, her friendly smile wavering under the onslaught of blatant hostility glinting from cold gray eyes. Never slow, her mind acknowledged and dismissed the curvature of the chiseled mouth in the man's equally chiseled face.

Though she hadn't seen him since his father's funeral, where she'd spoken to him only briefly, this reception certainly wasn't what she expected. She'd been prepared to enjoy becoming reacquainted with Trace's father. Though Yance Chisolm was now more a part of the West Texas business community than its ranching community, he'd grown up on the C3. His roots were here, and he'd insisted his son's roots be here, too.

Trace was such a likable well-rounded child that she'd felt sure Yance would still be as easygoing and good-humored as he'd been in his youth. Yet the man in front of her radiated tightly leashed rage.

Why was he so angry? He looked as if he'd like to strike her, the steel eyes holding her mesmerized and immobile.

"Whose cases, Dad?"

Trace's words blessedly broke the spell and the unyielding gaze released her to turn in the direction the boy indicated. China, too, followed the grubby pointing finger, and she caught her breath. Those were her suitcases and easel!

Before she could utter a sound, an acid drawl cut into her astonishment.

"Apparently they belong to China Dare."

The tone was venomous, but China was allowed no time to take it in as Trace hurled himself into her midsection, wrapping his young arms around her in an enthusiastic bear hug. "You're staying with us, China? Su-*per!* Why didn't you say? I'll take your bags in." And he whirled around to pick up the largest case.

"Hold it!"

The command came simultaneously from two adult throats, one on a high squeak, the other on a note of authority demanding no argument.

Trace froze and gazed at his father's unsmiling face for a long moment before turning slowly away, his shoulders hunched in defeat. "I'll be in the tree house," he mumbled resignedly and walked with dragging feet down the steps and around the house as China and Yance watched his small dejected figure in silence.

Determined to get to the bottom of the situation, China turned back to the man standing beside her, implacability radiating from every livid inch of him.

"Your eyes should be blue," he said.

The incongruous words caught her off balance again so that she stared up at him in astonishment.

"With a name like China Dare your eyes should be blue," Yance explained with chilling mockery. "Green ones don't fit the name."

"Hazel," she corrected, fighting to make sense of a conversation tending toward the absurd.

"Green. Blackjack said you weren't much on looks."

If he hoped to disconcert her further with that kind of statement he wasn't going to succeed. China grinned. "Blackjack thinks any female without four legs is lacking something," she acknowledged, adding with assumed patience, "Yance, can we quit playing cut and thrust? Just tell me where my father is and why my things are here."

But instead of answering, the man before her leaned his large body against the front door frame and crossed his arms over his chest, insolently allowing his gaze to slide over her from the top of her tousled head with bits of grass still clinging to it, to her long narrow feet encased in a pair of calf-high Apache moccasins.

China's face burned. But two can play this kind of game, she thought angrily. And she'd spent a few years observing the game being played by the best. As coolly as he, she looked the tall rancher over from north to south with blatant appraising eyes.

Not for worlds would she betray how impressed she was. An older generation would call Yance Chisolm a fine figure of a man; her own would call him sexy as hell. Narrow hips, broad shoulders, a strong neck supporting an arresting face too angular to be handsome but nevertheless possessing something that called to every feminine instinct China possessed.

One glimpse of the laughter lurking in the knowing gray eyes, however, had her fighting those instincts immediately. Her gaze dropped to his surprisingly utilitarian Western boots. No exotic animals died for their skins to walk the earth on this man's feet. Slowly her fascinated gaze traveled up the stone-washed Levi's lightly hugging legs and thighs, but so lovingly that…

Yance didn't move, continuing to lean against the door frame with assumed negligence, but he felt as if the woman caressed every portion of his anatomy her green-eyed gaze traveled over. Certainly he was being given his own back in spades, he thought with reluctant admiration, but damned if he'd let her have the last word.

"Blackjack put China Dare and a full house against four of a kind and thirty dollars," he said laconically, his face never changing expression.

China gaped at him, her mouth opening slightly in amazement before turning irrepressibly up at the corners. "You're kidding!" Yet no one knew her stepfather better than she, and she believed every word.

She began to chuckle softly, shaking her head. Blackjack obviously thought he'd found a man for her at last. To wager her in a poker game sounded just like him.

Her stepfather had been telling her for months that she needed a husband, this time around a Western man who would take care of her the way Blackjack thought a woman should be taken care of. Since she wouldn't find one for herself, he must have taken it on himself to find one for her. The old man was probably patting himself on the back for his shrewdness at this very moment.

"Just wait till I get hold of that chauvinist," she said, half ruefully, half humorously. Then she tipped a puzzled face up to the man before her. "But why in the world did you let him get away with it?"

Yance straightened, humor and the last vestiges of anger warring over his features until humor won, chasing away the harsh lines as his mouth curved upward.

China felt the force of that crooked grin right to her knees.

"I thought China Dare was a horse," he admitted, obviously trying to keep from laughing as he made the outrageous statement, but with her immediate howl of laughter it was a lost cause.

Somehow, without either of them knowing quite when it happened, they were sitting side by side on the front porch steps, laughing into the warm autumn sunshine until their sides ached.

"Oh, the ignominy of it," China said at last when she could get her breath. "No wonder you were angry. How disappointing for you."

"Oh, I wouldn't say that," Yance replied softly, his gaze on the far mountains in speculative concentration. "I believe you're just what I need, China Dare." And the gaze shifted to her with the same fixed intent it had given the mountains.

All laughter had completely disappeared from his face, and China's eyes widened at the dreadful look of purpose that took its place. She knew now why Yance Chisolm was known as "The Hawk" in Southwestern business circles. Every instinct told her this was a man who wouldn't give up once he saw what he wanted.

And for some reason, he wanted her!

Not sexually. It wasn't lust she saw in the steady gray gaze, nor even desire. He wanted her, but not for the purpose a man usually wanted a woman. She refused to acknowledge a traitorous niggle of disappointment.

She then realized that Yance sat so close beside her that she felt the warmth of his body, smelled the faint musky odor of horse, the remains of a subtly spiced aftershave, and an indefinable something else that was the essence of the man. Her skin prickled. The side of her body nearest Yance Chisolm seemed to have grown a whole new set of sensory receptors.

He gave a soft sudden laugh, and for no reason at all her heart started a crazy knocking in her breast.

Leaping to her feet, she rounded on him angrily. "You can take that smirk off your face right now, cowboy. This isn't the Middle Ages. It's not even the Old West anymore. Human life, even lowly *female* human life, can't be bartered or used as betting material by two outdated males who should know better."

"Would you have Blackjack cheat on a bet?" Yance asked mildly.

China flushed but stuck her chin out. "Damn right I would. It was a bet he had no business making."

"But I accepted in good faith," Yance argued, all amiable innocence.

She snorted. "Too bad. Now where is Blackjack, and if he's already left can you have someone take me to him?"

Her eyes searched the empty ranch yard restlessly, as if expecting her stepfather to immediately appear from one of the quiet outbuildings standing still and somnolent in the bright sunlight. It was almost noon.

"Blackjack is well on his way to the Gilmer's Quad X and…no."

Whirling to face him, China found that Yance, too, had risen and now stood with his fingers tucked into the back pockets of his jeans, his features bland as he watched her.

"No?" she asked with deadly sweetness.

For the first time, she noticed the deep lines cutting grooves into his face on either side of his nose and mouth. They looked out of place somehow and made him look years older. They also gave him a look of uncaring cruelty. Feeling the first stirrings of panic, China fought them down.

"No, I will not have someone take you to him. And if you ask one of my men anyway, and he agrees, tell him to gather his gear while he's at it because he won't be working here anymore."

China had no doubt at all that Yance Chisolm meant exactly what he said. If she went to one of the C3 hands, the cowboy would probably agree to take her to Blackjack even knowing he'd be fired. Western men were notorious pushovers for damsels in distress. But once the fall roundups were over, winter jobs were hard to find and she didn't want putting someone out of work on her conscience.

Shrugging, she lifted her head proudly. "So I'll walk,"

and she turned on her heel to strike out for the dirt road leading to the highway eight miles away. Once she was there, someone would give her a lift and she could always drive Blackjack's truck back and get her things.

Yance silently watched the woman's straight retreating back, the graceful sway of her hips as she walked. She didn't hurry, but her steps were purposeful, with a swinging stride that ate up the distance. She walked like a woman who enjoyed her body's movement, and sunshine, and living. The eight-mile trek might be no more than a pleasant stroll. But she was hardheaded enough to crawl it on hands and knees if she had to, he'd bet.

This woman, as Blackjack had known so wisely, was exactly what he needed; what Trace needed.

When she was almost out of earshot, he called out just loud enough for her to hear. "Blackjack told me you had loyalty and love to give."

China stopped. Slowly she turned around, her head still at its proud, stubborn angle. "So?"

"So I need that," he replied evenly.

"Why?"

But Yance didn't answer, only looked back at her over the intervening space.

She felt as if she'd been touched.

Without being aware of it, she walked toward him a few steps, then stopped again.

"Why?" she repeated.

He merely shook his head, the cool gray gaze never leaving her face, and she knew that if she wanted her answer she would have to go to him. Sighing in resignation at her own weak curiosity...and stupidity...she began walking.

When she drew abreast of him, Yance, too, turned back. Side by side, they walked silently to the house, up the steps of the porch, past her suitcases and in through the front door.

A touch on her elbow guided her into the study. Yance waved her toward a chair and took a seat himself behind his desk. She noticed a fine film of perspiration across his upper lip.

As if aware of her scrutiny, he swiveled his chair around and reached into a lower cabinet situated behind the desk. When he faced her once more there was a yellow legal pad in his hand. The perspiration was gone.

"I have a business proposition for you, Miss Kerrigan," he said evenly. "Without putting too fine a point on it, I need…"

"Smith."

He stopped, disconcerted. "I beg your pardon?"

"Smith," China repeated. "Blackjack never got around to legally adopting me. I'm China Dare Smith."

The gray eyes remained studiously bland, but she saw a sudden radiation of laughter lines around them. "Go ahead," she said kindly. "You can laugh without hurting my feelings. I think the name's kind of a joke myself, with it being such a mixture of the exotic and the mundane."

Yance didn't laugh but his eyes kept their warm humor. "And what is your opinion of the name Chisolm?" he asked.

Tilting her head a little, China gave the question thought. "Western, of course," she replied after a moment, "and historical. The Trail and all that, although I understand the family connection is tenuous. But it's a strong name. It suits you."

"Chisolm Oil and Gas, Chisolm Savings and Loan and all that?" he mocked.

"Hard, uncompromising, getting your own way with little regard for others and all that," she countered evenly, angered by his cynical assumption that she was impressed by the Chisolm wealth.

Had the man strayed *that* far from his upbringing? Though she couldn't say she liked him after this morning's events, she hadn't heard of Yance Chisolm being over-blown with his own importance. Yet unlike his father, apparently he could only see his relationships with others in terms of his assets.

"Sometimes circumstances force one to be that way," he said as if reading her mind, and watched her intently.

"Only if you want more than you should have," she replied, her eyes staring back into his with steady defiance. "You want, and you think that gives you the right to demand. Money gives you no rights. I think it only gives you responsibilities."

The grooves cutting into Yance's face grew even more pronounced. "I agree, and it's those responsibilities that I want to talk with you about. Do you think China Dare Chisolm sounds any better than China Dare Smith?"

After taking a deep breath to stem a near uncontrollable exasperation, China managed to say tightly, "Will you please just get to the point? In all probability, I have a long walk ahead of me and I want to get on with it."

"That is the point, Miss Smith. I'm asking you to marry me." He leaned back in his chair and smiled, but again it was only a token curvature of lips, its meaninglessness reflected in his flat gray eyes. "You'll notice I said asking, not demanding."

"No," China answered composedly. "Is there anything else, or may I leave now?" *Miss Smith.* He didn't remember who she was at all.

"No?" Yance repeated, but without apparent surprise. "That's your answer?"

She nodded.

"Not very flattering, but then I doubt handing out flattery is one of your weaknesses. I would appreciate your giving my proposal further consideration, however. Take it for honesty if not modesty when I say that I have a great deal to offer."

China kept her face deliberately without expression. "What, besides the obvious?"

"Most women would be satisfied with the obvious."

"Yance…"

He sighed. "All right. You're not most women. Still, security is nothing to thumb your nose at."

"Yance," China repeated in the patient tone that said he was a slow student in a fast class. "I've been illustrating children's books for several years. I'm very good at it. I make enough money to meet my needs and still have enough left over to play a bit. Like *most women,* I don't need to marry security—I'm perfectly capable of earning it myself."

"But what if I told you that security is what I want from *you?*"

"Then you've got rocks in your head. I may earn enough to be comfortable, but it comes nowhere close to paying off Chisolm IOUs."

She paused abruptly, eyeing his bland features. "But that's not the security you're talking about, is it?"

Slowly Yance shook his head, a small half smile curving his mouth as he watched her consider.

"Trace," she said into the silence, and he nodded.

Sitting very still, China silently contemplated the man before her. "You don't strike me as the kind to ask a woman you met little more than half an hour ago to marry you just to give Trace a stepmother," she said at last. "Melodie has been dead for years and your son is well past the clinging-to-mommy stage. Why this sudden impulse to present him with a mother he probably doesn't want?"

"When I know the facts, I make most major decisions in less than half an hour," Yance countered.

She raised a skeptical brow. "In this case you don't know the facts. You don't know me or anything about me."

"But I know Blackjack Kerrigan, and Blackjack has a reputation any man could envy. My father trusted him enough to offer him the job of ranch foreman," Yance replied evenly. "You can take Kerrigan's word to the bank, as the saying goes. And Blackjack says you have courage, honesty and a loving and caring nature."

He paused. "More important, Blackjack says you have loyalty."

"The man is my father, Yance," China said dryly. "Certainly he thinks I'm wonderful. But you have to know that taking someone else's word, no matter how much it can be trusted, is not reason enough to ask a stranger to marry you."

Yance pushed away from his desk to stand at the window and look out at the still ranch yard. He saw Trace sitting on a small boulder with an elbow on his knee and his chin propped up with his palm, the other hand tapping a short stick halfheartedly against the rock's surface. The boy clearly waited to be called indoors.

"Blackjack's word is all I have, China," he said quietly, and watched his son suddenly toss the stick as far as he could, then use both grubby palms to hold up his chin.

He turned back to the woman sitting in front of his desk. The placement of the chair was that of a supplicant, he thought inconsequentially. Even with bits of grass in her hair, straight, proud, no-nonsense China Dare Smith sat in it like a queen slumming.

Thrusting his fingers in the front pockets of his jeans, Yance assumed a lounging position at the window, half leaning, half sitting on the low sill. God, he was tired.

"And I'm out of options," he added flatly.

With his back to the sunlight, China couldn't see the man's face clearly but at his tone, something within her turned to ice.

"You need to explain that."

Yance nodded but thought a moment before beginning on a note of slow rumination. "I'm an only child."

The bald, softly spoken statement was so far from what China expected that she gaped.

"And my father and mother were both only children," he continued with a small shake of his head, as if the simple words set forth a rare and revealing fact. "My grandfather had a brother, Great-Uncle Thomas, who is still living. He's quite elderly, of course, and lives in Indiana, as do his two children. I've never met my second cousins. Or is it first cousins, twice removed? At any rate, I've never met them."

Though not following his train of thought at all, China remained quiet when the sentence trailed away into thoughtful silence, sensing a great sorrow that she didn't understand and the man's need to tell his story in his own way.

"My wife was also an only child," he said, his tone growing more brisk. "Her parents, Trace's grandparents, used to have the Kelleston ranch before it went under. You may know them. They live in Pecos now."

At his inquiring glance, she nodded. "Melodie and I were the same age and ran around together some when B.J. worked in this area. I was at art school in New York when you married and finishing up there when she died. There was no way I could make it back for the funeral. Her death was a shock."

Yance studied the toes of his boots.

"It was a shock to us all," he said. "No one expects a woman to die in childbirth in this day and age. We didn't know she had a bad heart."

Yet Melodie's sudden death taught him nothing, he reflected bitterly. Certainly he'd not had the foresight to clearly plan for his own demise.

He frowned, rubbing a massaging knuckle over his nose. What seemed the answer to a prayer less than an hour ago now seemed an act of lunacy when he tried to explain it. He recognized that asking China Dare Smith to marry him was an idea born of desperation…and he'd built a large part of the Chisolm financial structure by capitalizing on the acts of desperate men. Some would say "The Hawk" was getting his comeuppance.

Pushing away from the window, he resumed his place behind the desk and looked at the woman across from him. Best drop this now while he still could. There had to be a better way, and he'd find it if he didn't back himself into a corner.

"You've done a great job with Trace," China said warmly before he could speak. "He's one of the most well-adjusted youngsters I know. Uncle Steve said he was a natural born people person."

Yance allowed himself to be sidetracked. "Uncle Steve?"

"Your dad," she explained. "You don't seem to remember, but he claimed me as his unofficial goddaughter."

Yance shook his head. "Once I left home, Dad and I maintained separate households except here at the ranch. He talked about a little girl sometimes, but your name is unusual enough that I think I'd remember it."

"Your father called me Sis or Sissy," China told him, her eyes crinkling with a blend of wry humor and remembered affection for a man who'd been like a grandfather to her. "A name like China Dare was just too exotic for an old cowman to spit out, he said."

She stopped, realizing again that she knew far more about Yance Chisolm than he knew about her. "I've been friends with Trace for a long time, too," she informed him quietly so that he would know. "I saw him often when he stayed on the ranch with your dad."

"I remember a Sissy," Yance said slowly. "Dad thought you were something special."

"I thought he was special, too," China said softly.

For a long moment Yance stared at this woman who had known and loved his father, who knew and played with his son, whose very essence was made of laughter, he'd bet, yet who possessed the earthy femininity of a Norse queen. And she was no stranger.

The fist that had clutched his gut for a month, loosened.

From beneath her lashes China flicked a look across the desk, only to have the look intercepted and held fast by a pair of gunmetal gray eyes. The very air between them seemed suddenly to hiss and crackle just beyond the range of hearing. When she sucked in a startled breath and the smoky gaze dropped to her slightly parted lips, China forgot to breathe.

"Dad, I'm *hungry.*"

The moment shattered as they both shifted a grateful focus to the boy standing in the doorway.

Trace, finding himself with more attention than he bargained for, looked wary a moment before saying defensively, "Well, I am. It's noon. Ever'body's eating but us."

"Then why don't you go eat with the crew at the bunkhouse?" his father asked reasonably.

"But I want to eat with you and China." The boy's tone was plaintive, sounding as downtrodden by an uncaring world as only a ten-year-old can.

China stood. "I'm hungry, too," she said brightly. "Since I've been abandoned on your doorstep, as it were, what are you going to feed me, Yance? And with the story of that poker game probably the main topic of lunch conversation, I'd appreciate not being invited to the bunkhouse."

Trace looked interested. "What story?"

"I'll tell you about it another time," Yance told his son quellingly as he, too, rose to his feet. "Let's raid the refrigerator. Mabel promised to save something from last night's barbecue, since we weren't here for it."

China helped Yance and Trace load the kitchen table with barbecued brisket, ribs and chicken, beans, potato salad, garden salad, pickled okra and jalapeño corn bread. "Where is Mabel?" she asked casually.

While the microwave zapped the meat and corn bread, Yance poured three glasses of iced tea. "With the gather over, she and Chad are taking a two-week vacation. Their son and daughter-in-law have a new baby and the proud grandparents left for Oklahoma bright and early this morning."

He found discussing mutual friends with this woman disconcerting. Things had been much simpler when he thought of her as a stranger. For some reason, the thought of marrying her had seemed easier then. Hell, the thought of *not* marrying her had seemed easier then.

China nabbed a green olive. "Another one? Doesn't that make number five?" She laughed. "Tommy Chadwick never did do things by halves."

"Wow. Five kids! D'you think you'll ever give me a brother or sister, Dad? It gets kinda lonesome bein' an only child, y'know."

From the look of pure mischief on his face, Trace's question was far from serious, and as he noisily dug in the drawer for knives and forks he didn't see the look that spasmed across his father's face. But China did, and the pain in it seemed to score across her own heart.

Yet the look was gone so quickly that she wondered if she'd imagined it when Yance replied easily and with the age-old parental refusal to be goaded. "Live with it, pard. And don't forget the napkins."

Talk about weird, China thought in amazement some moments later. She'd been lost in a poker game…or won, depending on the point of view…then abandoned by her loving father to the tender mercies of a man angry because she wasn't a horse who then proposed marriage. And did she bop the man over the head with a baseball bat as any other red-blooded American girl would?

Heavens no. She joined him for a pleasant lunch, exchanging tidbits of ranch gossip and discussing the current drought as a ten-year-old chip off the old block with more charm than even a Chisolm should have bounced worn-out jokes off the two of them.

Later, they were equally harmonious in getting the kitchen back to the pristine order in which Mabel Chadwick had left it. China watched Yance, a dish towel decorating one shoulder of his Western shirt, put a plastic cover over the container of remaining potato salad. What was it about a man doing kitchen work that made him so darned endearing? she wondered. Personally, she couldn't stand kitchen chores of any kind.

"Sam and Cully are checking the stock tank in High Meadow this afternoon. Why don't you see if you can ride along?" Yance suggested to his son as the boy put the last of the cutlery in the drawer.

Trace's face lit up. "High Meadow tank? D'you think they'll go swimming?"

"Maybe. But you *ask,* pard. You can go only if they say it's okay."

"Yes, sir," the boy called over his shoulder, heading for the front door and obviously not worried in the least. The hands on the C3 had been letting him trail after them as long as he could remember.

He was back in the house almost immediately and trotting toward his room, saying as he rushed past, "Great minds think alike, Dad. Cully was on his way over to get me. He said to get my trunks and a towel."

As the boy came barreling back through on the return trip seconds later, Yance reached out a long arm and hooked it around his son's midsection. "Walk in the house, Trace, and tell Cully I said thanks."

At those last words Trace, who'd obligingly slowed to

a rapid walk, stopped and turned around to send his father a puzzled look. "Thanks for what?"

But Yance only laughed at him. "Cully will know."

Trace rolled his eyes. "Oh." Then the mischief slipped from his face as he sobered. "You'll be here when I get back, won't you, China?"

"No," she replied, but her answer collided with Yance's.

"She'll be here."

China shot him a hard look.

For a moment Trace gazed at the two of them before he walked over and gave China a hug, his young face serious. "I hope you stay for a while," he told her, "but if you can't…well, I'm glad you had lunch with us, anyway."

"I'm glad I did, too," China replied, hugging him back. This boy played dirty pool, more so because his affection was genuine.

She watched Trace as he left the house, his second exit noticeably lacking the exuberance of the first. Then she turned to the boy's father. "I'm leaving now," she said firmly, adding before he could speak, "and no, I won't marry you. You don't need a wife just to give Trace a mother. He's a bright, articulate, warm and loving child. A mother couldn't do it any better than you and Uncle Steve have done."

"Thank you," Yance said quietly, genuinely appreciative of the compliment, yet his smile was rueful. "But you can tell he misses having a woman in his life."

"Oh, pul-leeze," China appealed to the ceiling, fed up suddenly with an emotional string pulling that, as far as she could see, made little sense. "These are the nineties, the era of single-parent families. Even you, Yance, stayed with your father when your parents divorced. How old were you? Nine? Ten?"

"Ten," he agreed. "But I also spent a lot of time with my mother until she died a few years ago."

"I didn't know she was dead. I'm sorry. Did she ever remarry?"

His response was clipped. "She was a woman who didn't like marriage."

"Maybe I am, too," China shot back.

Eyebrows lifted, Yance sent her a questioning look. "Are you?"

Damn. "No," she replied grudgingly. "I just never found the right man who thought I was the right woman."

"I think you're the right woman."

That strange something sizzled between them again.

Unconsciously China took a half step before she caught herself. She laughed, a sound totally lacking in humor. "For what?" she asked bluntly. "Wifehood or motherhood?"

Good question, Yance thought dazedly. He hadn't known himself he was going to set this up again. Hell, he thought he'd changed his mind about the whole harebrained scheme. Now suddenly he was maneuvering like it was still a viable plan.

For a moment he felt sick. Was this brain damage?

All the more reason to get things taken care of as soon as possible.

He rubbed the back of his neck tiredly. "Both, I guess. I didn't finish presenting my case, did I? Shall we go out on the porch? It's cooler out there. Would you like another glass of tea?"

There was nothing in the courteous tone to prove it, yet China could swear there was a touch of pleading in Yance's voice. "Nothing for me, thanks. I'm still full of lunch," adding against her better judgment, "Sure, let's sit on the porch awhile."

But she had enough sense not to sit next to the man on the bench swing hanging there, choosing instead a wooden rocker. Sitting anywhere near Yance Chisolm did strange things to her common sense.

She fought back a laugh of self-derision. Who did she think she was kidding? Just being on the same ranch with him sent her equilibrium into a spiral dance! For a moment she rocked the old high-backed chair for all it was worth.

Unaware, Yance lazily pushed the swing back and forth with one boot planted on the porch railing, The chain holding the swing to the roof moaned a low sad screak with each push.

Off in the distance a meadowlark trilled, but the couple on the porch sat quietly, each reluctant to bring up the topic on both their minds.

China's rocking evened out to match the rasping of the swing, until she realized her chair was the only one making noise.

Her gaze swung from its fixation on cloud shadows playing over the mountains to the long-legged figure in the swing.

With one foot propped on the porch railing and the other on its floor, Yance Chisolm was sound asleep. An arm rested on the armrest, the flaccid fingers of his hand lightly grasping the chain, the other hand lying loosely on his thigh. He was slumped slightly so that his head rested against the back of the swing.

So much for sexual awareness, China thought. Wasn't she just scintillating company, though?

Tilting her own head back, she examined the man's sleeping face without compunction and consciously continued her slow rocking, knowing the monotonous sound of the rockers on the wood floor was sleep-inducing in itself.

With his eyes closed, Yance looked tired to death, she thought, the vigor that was so much a part of him seemingly drained from his body.

Yet even in sleep there was still something about the man that mesmerized her, that caused her fingers to tingle with the simple desire just to draw the line of his nose.

Straight and delineated it was, in fascinating counterpoint to a mouth sensually curved at bottom, no-nonsense arced on top. Hard cheekbones, soft sweep of lashes; slashed devil-brows, angelic hairline.

A face full of contradictions calling loudly now to the artist in her; a face that from the moment she saw him this morning whispered to the woman in her.

Wife and mother, he'd said.

How wife? As in mate…or as in spouse? As in someone to stand beside him in a receiving line, or as in someone to lie beside him in his bed?

Her rocking stilled abruptly. China stared again at the cloud patterns mottling the sweep of land before her, but saw only her own naked body tightly clasped in strong brown arms as eyes of gunmetal gray gazed smilingly into her own.

She laughed. Yeah, right.

"What's so funny?"

With a startled gasp, she jumped. "Nothing." Pushing herself out of the rocker, China stood jerkily. "Yance, it's late and I need to leave. I…"

"This is how it is," he interrupted, not giving himself time to pick and choose his words. *Tell it straight out, Chisolm, before she walks off and leaves you, damn her.* "I need surgery, and it's dangerous enough that I want someone I can trust to take care of Trace."

I fell asleep right in front of this woman, he thought, for a moment the terror of leaving his son without protection threatening to engulf him. *Asleep, for God's sake, in the middle of the damn day like a tired old man.*

China slowly sank back into the rocking chair, appalled at the words, appalled at the look on Yance's face as he'd uttered them.

He sat stiffly erect, glowering now out over his ranch as if he hated it, as if he wanted nothing more than to pound something or someone into the ground. The tired, worn look might never have been. Vigor and vitality underscored the anger in every line of his strongly sculpted body.

Sick? This man couldn't be sick.

"What kind of illness do you have?"

"It's not an illness," Yance replied bitterly. "It's fallout from the plane crash I was in last month. No one can be sure of the outcome and I don't want the possibility of leaving my son without a guardian. Chisolm Technology, Inc. and all that," he added with a biting ironic reference to their earlier conversation. "And a hell of a lot more. Too much more. And there's Trace. Ten years old. Warm, loving and generous just as you said, but maybe burdened with an inheritance that will call to every vulture in the country."

He caught himself and slowly uncurled his fists. That might not be all of it but it was close enough to make a sane woman run for the hills, he thought tiredly.

So let China Dare Smith give him that level-eyed look of hers before she started her proud hike to the highway. He'd given it his best shot. No, he wouldn't make her walk, not when he knew he would run like hell away from this scenario himself if he could. Maybe in the round-trip to take her to the Gilmer's ranch and Blackjack he could come up with a plan B.

But if plan B was so damn simple, why hadn't he been able to come up with it in the last four weeks?

"Yance, I don't know anything about high finance. What makes you think I can protect Trace's interests?"

He laughed abruptly, surprising them both. But then, she'd surprised *him*. She should be running by now.

"You don't have to know anything about high finance. I've got my business affairs locked up tighter than the old maid's girdle. Even Trace can't wheel and deal till he's twenty-five."

Standing, he swiveled so he could cock one hip on the

porch railing in front of the swing and look at China directly, taking it as a good sign that she hadn't said no yet.

"What I need is someone to act as Trace's legal guardian should anything happen to me—someone to be a buffer between my son and anyone who might try to use him to gain control of the Chisolm consortium," he explained earnestly. "I need someone who will live with him here on the C3, who will be a parent and make sure he grows up with a sense of values and that sense of responsibility you were talking about."

He sighed. "I need a person with stability in Trace's life with enough common sense to see that he doesn't become just another too-rich kid while making sure no one steals his source of income."

"What about Melodie's parents?" China asked. "Wouldn't the Havilands be the logical people to take over guardianship? After all, they're Trace's grandparents."

Instead of answering, Yance commented dryly, "I thought you knew the Havilands."

"I do, though I haven't seen them in several years. The last I heard, Dusty had a hardware store in Pecos."

"You're behind the times," he told her with no expression. "My father-in-law had the hardware store, all right, soon after he lost his car dealership. He bought the dealership after he had to sell the ranch, if you remember. Since the hardware store went under, Dusty has owned and lost a restaurant. Right now, he's trying his hand at running a truck stop."

"I'd forgotten the famous 'Haviland touch,'" China said slowly. She grimaced. "I guess I see your problem."

"Don't get me wrong." Yance's smile was faint. "Dusty and Laura love Trace and are indulgent grandparents. Sometimes too indulgent. But neither of them has any business sense nor any idea of when to leave well enough alone. Dusty would probably think he's doing Trace a favor by trying to break the locks I've placed on the Chisolm pie cupboards. I don't think he could, mind you, but Trace's guardian will have a powerful lever. I need my son to have someone in his life who will not only *not* use that lever but who won't allow anyone else to, either.''

He straightened away from the porch rail and China's artist's eyes followed the graceful fluidity of the movement.

''There's another thing we need to discuss,'' he said.

She didn't like the look on his face. Everything they'd ''discussed'' so far had left her reeling. Her expression turned wary. ''What?''

''What's in it for you.''

Chapter Two

China looked at him blankly. "What's in it for me?" Reality hit. "Oh. Yes. Uh, what *is* in it for me?"

"A great deal of money. Other than that, not a whole lot."

He was being deliberately prosaic and she was grateful for it. Focus on the mundane, she thought. She couldn't possibly make a rational decision if she focused on the emotional issue of this vital man in a hospital.

Rational decision? Was she crazy? Steal a line from the First Lady and just say no, for heaven's sake!

But of course she didn't. "Why marriage, Yance? Why not simply appoint me Trace's guardian should anything happen to you? Why tie all of us in such legal knots?"

"Because the more knots I tie, the less chance there is for anyone to unravel them to get to Trace," he replied grimly.

She'd been studying her knees, afraid to look at him, afraid he would read the pity for him in her face. Wanting to move, wanting to go to him and wrap her arms around this strong man who was trying so desperately to protect his son, she stood jerkily, but only walked around to the back of the rocker to grip its corners tightly, her action effectively making the chair a barrier to a gesture she knew he wouldn't tolerate.

How he must hate doing this.

"You can't have thought," she said a little desperately. "You haven't had time to think, Yance. Don't you realize that by tying all these knots to protect Trace, you're tying yourself as well? In less than an hour after you met me, you proposed marriage. Who will protect *you* if I'm not who or what you think I am?"

If her hands hadn't clasped the back of the rocker so hard she would have wrung them. She wanted to scream at this man, call him every kind of idiot.

"Is that a yes?" Yance asked mildly, watching her fingers flex in frustration on the rocker's corner knobs. He wore a small satisfied grin that she hated.

"No, it's not a yes," she snapped. "If this is the way you handle the Chisolm holdings, cowboy, I'm surprised you've anything left of your own inheritance. What do you know *for sure* about me that makes you think I can keep unscrupulous people from using Trace if…if you're not here?" Then added for good measure, "And not take you to the cleaners once everything turns out all right?"

"I told you earlier," Yance said patiently. "Blackjack said you have courage, loyalty and honesty."

"And I told *you*," China replied with patience just as false, "Blackjack is my doting father."

Yance lifted a brow. "You mean Kerrigan lied to me?"

Studying him for a long silent moment, China finally asked, "Yance, do you know any perfect women?"

When his short soundless laugh answered the question, she shot him a look of triumph. "Blackjack thinks I'm perfect."

He laughed outright then before nodding to concede the point. Rolling his broad shoulders, he stood. "What d'you say we move around a bit, China Dare? Take a walk, maybe. Then you can fill me in on why you wouldn't make Trace a good mother and me a good wife."

Wondering what he was up to and not sure she trusted the polite invitation, China reluctantly agreed and walked with him off the porch. But as they left its cool shade and stepped into the early-afternoon September sunshine, she halted.

"It's too hot," she complained innocently and glanced at the man beside her. "Why don't we sit in Trace's tree house instead?"

That should give him a clue, she thought. CEOs wanted the mother of their children to have their Nikes firmly planted on the ground. And while she might call Yance Chisolm "cowboy" now and then, he was a long way from being just another good ol' boy.

But Yance, all amiability, merely agreed to her suggestion.

Once at the foot of the old pecan tree towering above them, however, China suddenly stared up at him appalled. It was so easy to forget this vigorous man wasn't in the best of physical shape. "I'm sorry," she blurted. "I didn't think. Of course a walk is fine."

"Race you up," he said, and leaped to catch hold of an overhead branch.

China was right beside him, going hand over hand through the branches as fast as she could go, knowing that to use the ladder boards nailed into the trunk would only slow her down. All her life she'd never been able to resist a challenge.

But when she arrived at the platform high in the branches of the old tree it was to find Yance already there, kneeling on the plank flooring and holding out a hand to hoist her the rest of the way up. He was breathing heavily, but then so was she, and she lay on the boards panting as she tried to catch her breath and laugh at the same time.

"Oh, you're quick," she acknowledged on a gasp.

Yance, too, lay on his back, his eyes closed but satisfaction playing over his face. "I know all the shortcuts," he said complacently.

She laughed again and the two of them lay on the weathered old planks companionably as their breathing evened out.

"I love tree houses," China said at last.

"Um."

She lazily rolled her head in Yance's direction and saw that his eyes were still closed but a smile gently curved his lips. The man had the most kissable mouth north of the Rio Grande.

"You asleep?" she whispered, to get her mind off it.

The smile stretched into a grin. "No. Now tell me what a bad woman you are, China Dare."

Abruptly China turned her head back so that she could stare up into the tracery of overhead leaves. "I didn't say I was a bad woman. I said you don't know me." She took a moment to pull her thoughts together. Again she'd forgotten why she was sharing this small island among the branches with Yance Chisolm. The man had a way of making her forget a lot of things.

"I've been married before," she said abruptly.

Though Yance didn't move, somehow his stillness intensified.

"To a man with a small daughter," she added, determined to get it said and stop this charade once and for all. "He...he didn't think I was much of a mother." Nor much of a wife, either, she tacked on silently.

"Why not?" Long ago Yance had learned to listen with more than his ears. It was the secret to his knack for business dealings. Now he sensed the pain behind China's halting statement. However, if he knew that another man had questioned her maternal abilities, he himself would be a fool not to find out what was behind it.

"Well...I like to play, you see. My work involves being able to get down to a child's level. It's a level I find fascinating as well as comfortable."

Wanting to laugh at the defensiveness in China's tone, Yance pursed his mouth consideringly. "Hmm. Y'know, I kind of like playing myself," said the man whose aching ribs had taken a beating racing up a pecan tree just moments ago. How long had it been, he wondered, since he'd romped with Trace the way China had been doing earlier? The desire for laughter faded.

Too long.

China was aware of Yance's amusement. Frank had also apparently been amused when he'd unexpectedly brought home a business associate one afternoon, and the two men found China with Leanne inside a tent made of sheets in the middle of the living room floor. Later he'd been livid.

"And I don't believe children should have to make straight A's," she tacked on, the statement unknowingly challenging. He wanted her to teach three-year-old Leanne her letters, Frank had said, not teach her to sing nursery rhymes and make up stories from picture books.

"I guess I don't, either," Yance replied slowly. Education had its place, of course, but the wide world itself was a formidable classroom; a classroom he'd ignored the past few years, concentrating instead on Corporate Procedures 2000.

"I'm not a very good cook." That had been an important issue with Frank.

"I have a cook, China, who suits me just fine. I don't need another one."

"I hate to keep house," China said firmly.

"My cook-housekeeper, both here and in Midland, shovels the place out regularly," Yance countered. He grinned at the branches swaying with the afternoon breeze above them, pleased with himself and the world for a moment. "I think we'd probably rub along quite nicely, China Dare," he said, his tone the essence of geniality, and waited.

"But I'm an artist," China argued, her voice dropping to a desperate huskiness as she realized that the person she was arguing with most was herself...and they had yet to cover the key issue. "I work whenever the light is right or I'm on a roll. Sometimes I work all day."

"Sometimes I do, too."

At yet another matter-of-fact reply, China puffed out a sigh, her mind blank. All right, not blank, just completely blanketed with what neither of them were mentioning.

Slowly she rolled her head in Yance's direction, to find his gray, knowing gaze ready for her. For a long, silent moment they stared into the depths of the other's eyes, each caught by what they saw there.

Each wary.

"I don't want to sleep with you." Her words a whisper, soft as leaf rustle.

"Don't you?" His words no louder.

China sat up with a jerk.

But Yance sat up just as fast. "And anyway, who's asking?" he added coolly before she could open her mouth. "Look," he continued in that same controlled voice. "You have some pretty lame excuses for not marrying me. I know a few better ones. Let me help you out here." He folded his legs Indian-style.

Unconsciously China followed suit, and leaned forward slightly to listen.

Yance smiled inwardly. China Dare was just the person for his Trace. She proved it every time she opened her mouth. Could he convince her of it by not trying to convince her of it?

"Number one," he said, lifting an index finger.

She nodded.

"I'm not asking for short-term commitment here. I want a marriage that will last until Trace is eighteen. Even if I come through this operation okay, it's been more than brought home to me that if I get broadsided by an ice-cream truck three years from now and sent to my just reward, there will still be no one to take care of my son's interests if I don't do something about it beforehand. Therefore, I'm asking for the next eight years of your life."

Eight years! She'd thought he was looking for someone to marry just until the results of his surgery were known.

"Number two. There's a slim chance you might have an invalid for a husband, one mentally or physically incompetent."

China couldn't speak, but she kept her face carefully dispassionate.

Yance saw the compassion in her eyes, however. To remove it, he held up another finger. "You look younger, but if you went to school with my wife, you must be about thirty. The next eight years represent practically the last of your safer childbearing period."

He froze. Oh, God. What was he asking of this woman? Running a hand over the top of his head, he allowed his fingers to drag through his hair, tugging a little. "I'm sorry about that," he said gruffly, but refused to concede even to himself. "Maybe we can work something out."

China didn't even nod. She just stared at him. The compassion was gone, and her level green eyes a careful blank.

"Number three." He cleared his throat. "Four. Whatever. You don't love me and romance is important to a woman. Hell, it's important to us all. I don't love you, either. Could you love Trace?"

"Who couldn't love Trace?" she replied, and Yance felt the urge to put his head on her breast and weep.

But he only answered, "Lots of people," and smiled a bit. "He doesn't believe in making straight A's, either."

Her mouth turned up in an answering smile but he sensed it was as meaningless as his had been.

"Number six..."

"Five."

He shot her a look. "Five. A point you've made several times. You don't know me. You met me only a few hours ago. I could be a serial rapist or a con artist or—"

"Actually, I do know you," China broke in.

Yance gazed at her, arrested. "Sorry," he said ruefully. "I don't remember."

"Probably not. I was in elementary school when you were in high school. I remember the summer you were chasing after one of the Rankin girls. Cynthia Rankin, myself, and a couple of others were typically nosy little girls and did a lot of spying on big sister and her boyfriend. Roberta ran us off but I recall you being a little pink around the ears."

Yance felt as if he were a little pink around the ears now. He remembered Roberta Rankin. Still saw her now and then. They'd learned a lot from each other.

"And I was at your father's funeral," she added quietly, "and spoke to you there."

"Again, I apologize. There were so many at Dad's funeral, and I guess I was still in some sort of shock. His death was sudden, you know—just one minute here, the next gone."

But his dad had been prepared for all that, Yance thought, unlike himself who'd acted as if abrupt endings only happened to other people. Oh, he had a will, all right. It left Trace everything. There were also a couple of hefty insurance policies...as if his son needed more money.

Like the good businessman he was, he'd updated his will several times, but always with the subconsciously blind belief that it was a token gesture to good manage-

ment. The will always named the Havilands Trace's guard-
ians in the off chance anything happened to his own father.
Not until after his father's death and Yance was abruptly
forced to confront his own mortality, did he realize just
how empty and how dangerous that will was. What it actually left his son was standing in a mine field alone.

Strange how he'd never realized the emptiness of his
life, Yance mused. He had power, he thought, and found
out in the two and a half minutes it took for a small plane
to fall from the sky and bounce across a wheat field just
what good it was.

He'd thought he had friends, and he did, but when he
tried to think of one he'd trust to raise his son, he realized
that not one of those friends had any idea of what being a
Chisolm was all about. Ranching friends understood the
ranching half; business friends understood the business
half. None had a clue as to the whole.

But of the two, when it came down to it, the part he
most trusted was the ranching half. Nor was it, after all,
one of his own friends he finally chose to act as guardian
to his son, but one of his late father's. Or at least, that
friend's daughter.

"As to any hidden vices," China continued, unaware of
Yance's drifting thoughts and studying a paint stain under
a fingernail, "if you've become a con artist, you've managed to keep it pretty quiet. You must have forgotten what
it's like trying to keep dirty linen from being aired in the
West Texas ranching community. I'm surprised no one
knows about your upcoming surgery. Everyone heard
about the plane crash, and the word was you came through
it with bruises and lacerations but nothing major."

"That last is still a question," Yance said briefly. "Not
even the doctors know for sure. At any rate, I camouflaged
the issue by not trying to stop rumors about changes going
on in the Chisolm financial structure." He grimaced.

"Once I'm in the hospital I imagine it will all be out in the open."

"What *is* wrong?" China dared to ask.

"I'd rather not go into the details until I know whether you're in this with me or not. Number six," he resumed briskly. "I'd be getting everything and you'd be getting damn little."

"Lots of money," China reminded him.

He nodded.

"And power," she added deliberately. "If anything happens to you and if I want it badly enough, you know and I know I could probably loosen a few knots."

His face shuttered. "Number seven. This is really a stupid plan."

China nodded slowly in agreement. "Got a better one?"

"No." Yance straightened to square his shoulders, grimacing slightly at the pull on his ribs. Stupid kid stunt, climbing a tree just because a pretty woman dared him with a look in her eye he couldn't resist. And in spite of the pain pill he'd taken before lunch, his head hurt.

"So what will it be, China Dare Smith? Will you marry me?" He didn't know what he hoped she would answer. If she said no, he was again left without any kind of plan for Trace's safety.

If she said yes, he knew he would carry it on his conscience to his grave.

"I'll think about it," she said.

A week he gave her. And China warned him to use that week for careful thought, as well. If he came up with a better alternative to his problem or if she decided she wanted no part of his mad scheme, then there were to be no hard feelings on either side.

Arriving at the Gilmer's ranch after Yance returned her to Blackjack, she gave her father a sharp piece of her mind…to which he was singularly unrepentant…but she didn't tell him about Yance's proposal.

In all honesty, she'd probably decided before even climbing down from the tree house.

Blackjack wanted her settled, she told herself, so she'd settle. As much as any naive cowboy, she'd always been a sucker for anyone in need. And there was Trace, a child alone and vulnerable. Tall, broad men with crooked grins and gunmetal gray eyes had absolutely nothing to do with it.

But eight years? Well, maybe everything would be all right. She and Yance might learn to love each other and the marriage then become a real one. Such things happened.

Her stomach flip-flopped.

Such things happened in fairy tales. And also maybe she would be a widow in the same month she was a bride. Don't forget that.

She waited the full week before calling Yance to tell him she'd do it. Yance then set up an appointment for her to meet him at the C3 the following day.

An *appointment?* That was her first clue.

When she arrived, he courteously led her into his office, and offered her a soft drink. Trace was at school, Yance said briefly, and handed her the Prenuptial Agreement to read.

That was how she thought of it. In capitals.

She read it through, sort of, sitting in Yance's quiet office on one side of the desk while he sat on the other. It was a bloodless document that left her feeling the same way. As he'd warned, she wasn't getting much out of this marriage but a whole lot of money and the responsibility of being Trace's sole guardian should anything happen to the boy's father.

Make that a *whale* of a lot of money; a breathtaking

amount, probably why she had to fight for breath as the damn document shook in her hand.

Yance had even provided for the possibility of her meeting another man and falling in love sometime in the next eight years. No, there could be no divorce, or remarriage in the event of Yance's death, until after Trace was eighteen, but there was no objection to a discreet affair.

The word *discreet* was defined. Naturally.

The next part made her want to laugh; made her want to fold her arms on Yance Chisolm's cherry-wood desk, lower her head to them and weep.

Should she become pregnant through this affair she could give the child the Chisolm name, or her own name, or her lover's name but the child or children would inherit only through her. Chisolm money would support and educate any such children but China's offspring through this supposed liaison would never have access to Trace's inheritance.

There was more of the same. Much more.

After a while she simply stopped reading and stared at the sheets blankly, flipping through them as if she actually took in the printed words. When she reached the last page, she lifted a chilled face to the man seated across the desk.

"The only point in any of this is to take care of Trace," he reminded her quietly.

She nodded, unable to think of a thing to say.

Yance waved a hand toward the papers in front of her. "Take the document with you," he said, "and let a lawyer look it over. Add to it if you want, or make adjustments. I'm sure we can come to agreement."

As if it sat on a spring, China bobbled her head again.

"Be certain you know what's in there before you sign anything," Yance added sharply and left his chair to come around the desk and stand beside her. "I don't want you going into this with your eyes closed or expecting anything that just can't happen."

China stood then and took the papers from the desk to make a production of folding them neatly so that the blue cover sheets allowed none of the white pages beneath to show. After placing the folded sheets carefully into the side packet of her purse, she looked up into Yance Chisolm's face witlessly, unable to think of a single polite banality to get her out of the room and out into the open air.

Finally, she blurted, "I have to go now. I…I have things to do this afternoon."

Yance touched her arm. "Are you all right?"

"Of course I'm all right," she said sharply. "I just have to go."

He walked her from the house to place her in the cab of Blackjack's old pickup. From the rearview mirror she saw that he stood in the ranch yard staring after her until she rounded a curve and dropped from his sight.

When China read the agreement again that afternoon, she was calmer and this time read it with the same attention she gave to any contract. There was no need for a lawyer, in her opinion, because what she read was an agreement to tie her life into the legal knots Yance promised, while at the same time providing for her interests and personal freedom as much as possible.

She wondered if Yance realized that his formal agreement was at least fifty per cent devil's advocate for her defense.

There was no way in hell she would sign this thing.

Even Frank, she thought bitterly, who had a key to the men's executive washroom for a heart, had not presented her with a Prenuptial Agreement before they married.

Yes, she knew a great deal of money was at stake, and a child's security. Her head knew those things, but her heart remembered that Yance said he was marrying her for her honesty and loyalty. This document said such qualities only had staying power if bound between blue legal end-papers.

Dammit, she'd already been married to one high-powered businessman and the marriage had been a disaster.

He loved her for her "fairy quality," Frank had said.

China snorted softly to herself. Frank spouted a lot of drivel like that before they were actually married.

Her slightly askew vision of the world charmed him, he'd said.

Askew?

But after the wedding, he modified the word to exuberant. Her paintings were just too *exuberant* for their formal living room and it would be best to place there only the art pieces he'd bought for investment. To his credit, he did not suggest she relegate her paintings to the closet...or the waste bin...but he did hint that her own studio walls would be a better place for them. How that had hurt.

She was exactly what his baby daughter, Leanne, needed, Frank declared.

But was horrified when his new bride expected the adults, many of whom were his business associates, to be blindfolded and twirled around before batting at a huge Superman piñata at Leanne's first birthday party. That everyone seemed to have a good time was not the issue, he said darkly.

She brought laughter and color into his drab life, China heard constantly while Frank courted her.

But really, having knock-knock-joke wars with the company's VP was not conduct becoming to a business executive's wife...even though the VP was a master of the genre and won hands-down.

And it would help his career if she did less sketching at the zoo and played more golf with his associates' wives, he suggested. But please, taking Leanne with her to stroll the links was not done. That's what the new nanny was for.

When, after three years, Frank asked for a divorce, it had been a relief to them both. Nor did it help knowing Frank not only considered her a dead loss as a wife but a flake as a mother. He never came right out and said it, but he more than gave the impression that divorcing China was as much to rescue his daughter from her influence as to provide his own freedom to marry said nanny.

Frank had decreed no child-visitation privileges, although giving up Leanne had broken China's heart. It would only confuse the child, Frank said.

Now here was another businessman, even though he came disguised as a cowboy, offering marriage, offering a child to love…offering her the freedom to have as many discreet affairs as she chose, no questions asked.

Just sign on the dotted line.

No, thank you.

Yance Chisolm was a tycoon who could swallow up ten like Frank and not get indigestion. He offered freedom for extramarital affairs but would probably have a fit if she demanded freedom to be herself, as well.

Let him give his Prenuptial Agreement to another woman, China thought; one who "dressed for success" and drank springwater from a designer bottle instead of from its source. China wanted no part of him.

Tomorrow she would return Yance's legal *tender,* pun very much intended, and wish him the best of luck with someone else.

As if it were a noxious piece of garbage, China used the tips of thumb and forefinger to pick up the closely typed pages and place them in a drawer for safekeeping.

Anyway, Blackjack needed her.

Devastated following the divorce, China packed up her paintings, all that she would take, and headed west to Santa Fe to lick her wounds and give her book contracts her undivided attention. When Blackjack had his first heart problems only a few weeks following her mother's death, yet refused to give up his work and his travel about the southwestern ranches, she'd closed up her studio to join him.

For the past eight months she'd traveled with the old man, seeing to it that he ate right, and discreetly letting his friends, many of whom were his bosses, know that Blackjack needed some of the younger cowboys to take over in a few areas. Yet her stepfather was headed for serious trouble if he didn't slow down even more.

China had kept her apartment in Santa Fe, returning there frequently to take care of business and catch up with friends. Several times she'd begged Blackjack to live with her there. It was time for him to retire.

He'd flatly refused. He couldn't live in a city, Blackjack told her. Not even one like Santa Fe. He'd grown up in the open, had lived in the mountains and high plains of the Southwest all his life. And if she'd just leave him alone, dagnabit, he'd die in them. But don't count on him heading for the Great Corral anytime soon, he snapped, because he couldn't afford the casket.

With that oblique statement she'd realized that while she made more than enough to take care of them both, Blackjack was afraid he didn't have adequate money set aside to handle an uncertain future.

To the old man, dying of a heart attack on the back of a horse was preferable to dying in a city and someone else's money paying for the hospital bills. In vain China tried to convince him this would never happen and that his insurance was substantial enough to handle any crisis, even without her money. He refused to believe her. Blackjack's view of legal documents was as biased as her own.

And as silly.

Slowly China rose from the table where she'd been watering her thoughts with hot coffee and returned to the drawer containing Yance's contract. She scanned through it once, took out her ruler and drew neat lines through some of it, then penned three brief statements at the bottom.

When she returned to the C3 the following day, she arrived without an appointment and unannounced.

Standing on the porch, she knocked softly on the screen door. The interior of the house beyond held an empty quiet, but as she was about to turn away Yance appeared, wearing beltless jeans slung low beneath an indecently erotic belly button…and nothing else. His face looked soft and sleepy, his hair rumpled.

"I'm sorry. I should have called first," she said, knowing the statement for the lie it was. Neither the artist nor the woman in her was the least sorry. Yance Chisolm in dishabille was deliciously sexy. Should she paint what she saw standing before her, she knew there'd be no trouble selling the portrait to a calendar company.

That's if she could part with it. This man was Mr. January to the nines; the man with whom any woman might dream of beginning the new year. Wonderfully Freudian.

"No, come on in," he replied, his voice still husky from sleep, and he pushed the door open for her.

This time he led her to the living room before excusing himself to put on a shirt. When he returned, he'd not only added a starched white shirt, but belt and boots as well. With his hair combed and face washed, the only thing he was ready for was business.

And why not? Hadn't she dressed for business, too, in her straight, black skirt, silk turquoise blouse and midheel court shoes, with her hair twisted into a thick chignon at the back of her neck? Appropriate dress for a Prenuptial Agreement, she'd told herself, slapping makeup on for the first time in a month.

When Yance offered coffee she accepted, then waited

in the living room as he made it, instead of joining him in the kitchen as she would with any of her friends. After all, she was only going to marry the man. She didn't know him well enough to be his friend.

Even from its hiding place tucked away in her purse, with its blue legal overleaves, the Prenuptial Agreement seemed like some witch doctor's piece of voodoo, sucking the life from her and killing spontaneity and laughter. She'd be glad to get rid of it.

When Yance returned, he carried cups, saucers and a carafe on a tray. He placed it on the coffee table, took a place on the couch beside her, and with consummate grace played host. There was even an offering of store-bought cookies on a plate.

She took a sip of her coffee and politely munched a cookie while the two of them made stilted work of the weather. Trying to pretend this was nothing but a social call, China thought gloomily.

By the time her coffee was gone, she'd run out of patience.

Placing her cup and saucer on the coffee table she announced without preliminary, "I've read the agreement and I'm willing to sign it, but I've crossed out some of it and added three clauses." Without looking directly at him, she dug into her purse and handed Yance the packet of papers.

Yance obligingly shuffled through the pages until he came to the cross outs. "I'm afraid I can't agree to this," he said quietly. "Trace must take precedence over any children you might have."

"It's a nonissue," China replied, staring the man straight in the eye, the only place she knew to look where she could hang on to her emotions. "After a bad riding accident when I was thirteen, I can't have children. It's medically documented," she added. "I can give you the name and number of the gynecologist, if you like."

Gazing back at her, Yance saw that China's head was at its highest, that her eyes did not waver from his face, that her own face was completely bland…and knew immediately how much the words she'd just spoken must hurt.

It shamed him, then, to also realize how relieved he was by them, how much they were a sop to his conscience.

"I don't need to speak to your gynecologist," he replied, yet an element of perversity made him add, "but I would still like this particular clause to remain as written. The medical establishment works miracles on occasion these days, and what is true for you now may not be true for you in the future."

China shrugged. "Whatever. It doesn't really matter, I suppose."

Returning his attention to the document in his hand, Yance scanned the rest of it, finally coming to the neatly handwritten additions at the end of his lawyer's legalese.

She saw him smile slightly before he looked up at her.

"I should have thought of the first two of these myself," he said. "Certainly Blackjack will always have a home on the C3 and any medical expenses he incurs will be covered."

Sudden humor lines radiated from the corners of his eyes but he kept his mouth grave. "And so will those of his horse, Daisy. As to the third clause, I think I should know just what subjects you paint before I agree to your hanging your paintings anywhere in the house. I'm pretty broad-minded, I think, but Trace may not be ready for something like *Nude in Blue, Number Three.*"

China gazed back at him steadily, refusing to give her sudden vision of Mr. January a peek into her brain in case she blushed. "I'm aware that some areas of art are a learned experience," she said stiffly. "However, I haven't gone into my nude period as yet," adding, "though that's not to say I never will."

"I look forward to it," Yance murmured.

Too late she saw the double meaning in her words and colored.

Beyond the gleam in his eyes, however, Yance didn't pursue it, merely adding with a short laugh, "I was just teasing you, China. You can hang any damn thing you want on the walls for all I care."

She nodded. Another man who thought her art was a hobby, she thought resignedly.

"So we're agreed," Yance continued, turning brisk. "I'll call my attorney and have him insert your clauses into the original. Is there anything else you want added?"

She shook her head.

"And you're sure you want to do this?"

"I'm sure," she said firmly and paused. "But what about you? Did you think of an alternative?"

"No. This is it." His tone was as firm as hers. "And since you're agreeable, as soon as possible we'll both sign it in front of witnesses at my attorney's office."

Well, of course, China thought waspishly. *In front of a lawyer and all nicely notarized. Oh my, yes.* She straightened to once again look the man straight in the eye. "There is one stipulation."

An eyebrow rose inquiringly at her tone.

Her look didn't waver. "I want to know exactly what this surgery is for, what the prognosis is and what arrangements have been made."

For a moment the man's body seemed carved in stone, and when he spoke at last his voice sounded tired. "Certainly you have the right to know," he said. "I wouldn't allow you to sign anything without knowing, as a matter of fact. But after I explain, if you want to change your mind," he smiled slightly, "and I will understand if you do, I ask that you keep the information to yourself."

China fought the urge to touch his hand. "Of course."

Almost as if he read her mind, Yance rose from the

couch to stride across to the huge stone fireplace dominating the room. He didn't speak immediately, staring instead into its empty grate before turning to face her.

"I have a splinter of bone floating in my head up against the brain," he said flatly. "The doctors gave me two months to recover from the initial trauma of the crash and to get my affairs in order before they go after it. It's causing no harm right now, but they expect severe damage down the line if it's not removed as soon as possible. The removal itself might be all that's needed to return everything to normal. On the other hand, removing it might be impossible, or either the removal of it or the leaving of it might leave me brain damaged beyond repair."

The room was absolutely quiet; not even the smallest sound from the ranch yard beyond the windows infiltrated to mar its stillness.

"I don't know much about such things," China finally said. "You need to be more specific."

Yance laughed and it wasn't a pleasant sound. "I don't know much about such things, either, but that's about as specific as it gets. The doc puts it quite simply. He goes in, removes the splinter, no problem, no aftereffects. Or he goes in, and the removal procedure kills me. Or he goes in, removes the splinter and I live, but everyone, including myself, regrets the fact."

He picked up an empty vase from the mantel, examined it for a moment as if he'd never seen it before and replaced it, making sure he put it back in its exact original spot. When he turned toward the room again, his gaze settled on the peaceful ranch yard seen through the double windows behind the couch.

"The bottom line is, no one can assess at this point just how serious this little needle of bone is going to be, so I have to be prepared for any of the possible outcomes."

"You look good," China said tentatively into the silence, then felt her cheeks burn at the inanity. *Stupid, stupid words.*

He laughed his empty laugh again. "Don't I just."

"What are your chances?" Her voice was rough with pity and embarrassment.

"Fifty-fifty either way," Yance said succinctly. "Should brain damage occur, arrangements have been made with a rest home in Midland. And if death occurs, those arrangements have been made, as well."

The room was quiet a good three minutes while China examined the birthstone pinky ring her mother gave her for her sixteenth birthday and Yance examined the empty ranch yard.

"This is the time to back out," he said at last, flicking his gaze back at her.

China lifted her head, her features composed, but she swallowed hard. "No." And neither Trace nor Blackjack were a part of that one bald word.

For a long moment their eyes locked across the intervening space. Then Yance nodded once, decisively.

"Be right back."

When he returned, he carried a small, square, black velvet box with the name of one of Midland's more exclusive jewelers embossed on it. "I guessed at the size," he said as he handed it to her. "It can be adjusted if necessary, when we go in to file the agreement with my attorney."

Agreement with my attorney. China remembered suddenly just what she was getting herself into.

The ring was exquisite: a narrow yellow gold band topped with a half circle of flawless diamonds cradling three equally flawless emeralds. The C3. The dainty ring was like a fairy brand, China thought. A brand of love.

"It's beautiful," she said around a lump in her throat. Closing the box, she handed it back to him. "But no, thank you."

His face didn't change as he studied her. "Why not?"

She laughed lightly, trying to sound as if the truth she spoke didn't matter. "A prenuptial agreement and that ring just don't go together. Yance, don't feel that you have to follow the conventions in this. I don't want them or expect them. But," she added with a composed smile and looking straight into his eyes, "I do expect a wedding band. A plain one, though, please. Remember, I'm an artist and my hands are always dirty."

Pocketing the box, Yance nodded. "If that's what you want." He moved around the coffee table to take the place beside her on the couch again. "We need to get into Midland to see my attorney as soon as possible," he said easily. "Your attorney should be there, too. More coffee?"

China held up her cup and saucer and he refilled cups for both of them from the insulated carafe. "Would day after tomorrow be all right with you?"

"Fine."

"We can get the court work done for the wedding at the same time," he continued. "You can have any kind of wedding you want, you know." He held her gaze for a moment. "Money for it is not an issue."

"You don't know Blackjack," she said dryly. "No, I don't want a large wedding. Something small in front of a justice of the peace would suit me just fine."

"Are you ashamed of this?"

She jerked, stung. "Of course I'm not ashamed. It's just not that kind of wedding."

"What kind?"

"You know darn well what kind. I don't want to have to pretend I'm besotted with you in front of a bunch of sentimental cowboys. And besides, no one will expect a big ceremony. This is a second marriage for us both, after all."

Sitting back, Yance eyed her thoughtfully. "Have you told Blackjack?"

"Yes, but I didn't go into the circumstances. He has

heart trouble, Yance. I told him I would agree to this marriage only if he would retire and come with me to the C3. Other than that, he...he thinks everything is normal.'' She searched his face.

Yance closed his eyes, leaning his head against the back of the couch a moment. ''I already knew about the old man's heart, if that's worrying you. I'm delighted to have him here. He'll be good for Trace, like my dad was good for Trace. Don't think I like marrying you behind his back, as it were. He'd have my skin if he knew the circumstances, and I can't say I'd blame him a damn bit. I doubt that a cowboy with a dicey future is what he had in mind for you when he wagered you in that poker game.''

''Isn't 'in sickness and in health' a part of the ceremony?'' China reminded him composedly. ''I'll just be knowing it's a central issue *before* the ceremony, is all.''

Opening his eyes, Yance sent her a slow smile. ''You're quite a lady, sweet China Dare.''

China's heart lurched. ''I *will* have my own bedroom, won't I?'' she asked, trying to make the question sound lighter than it was meant, a small traitorous part of her hoping he would say no.

''Of course. Nor will I come knocking. Would you feel more comfortable if I stated it in the prenuptial agreement?''

''That won't be necessary,'' China replied stiffly. ''Your word is good enough.''

Yance nodded and changed the subject. ''I'll tell Trace tonight, and I have no doubt he'll be ecstatic. He's your number-one fan, you know.''

''That's because he can beat me at Crazy Eights,'' she replied, but with a pleased laugh.

''That's because you still know how to play,'' Yance contradicted gently.

Up until now China's decision whether or not to marry a man only to be his widow and give up eight years of her life to raise his son, or give eight years of her life to a loveless marriage had somehow obscured her very real doubt of her qualifications for motherhood. Now she looked up at him beseechingly.

"But mothers don't play," she said. "They join P.T.A. and things. Yance, Frank thought I was a terrible mother. What if Trace grows up to be a juvenile delinquent?"

But the man just laughed and covered her fidgeting hands with one of his own brown paws. "I've always been a good poker player," he said. "I'm banking on the fact that I'll be the one responsible for how Trace turns out."

To China, the implication was plain. Another child, she thought. So close. So far away.

Yet when she crossed the porch on her way back to the truck parked in the drive she imagined Blackjack sitting in the old rocker just as he had many an evening with Yance's father and knew that she was doing the right thing.

Chapter Three

They were married two weeks later in Midland, the small wealthy city that is unofficial capital of the West Texas oil industry. Trace was there and Blackjack. That was all.

China tried to keep things as simple and low-key as possible but Blackjack and Trace had a way of making two do the work of dozens. There was, for instance, the matter of her dress.

Blackjack, his old cheeks an unusual shade of rose, had gruffly given her a wad of bills for her "weddin' foo-foo" and China hadn't the heart to tell him she had plenty of money herself and really, her dress wasn't going to cost all that much.

With her stepfather's money, she'd bought a suit, a simple but becoming one the color of wheat. To it she added a bronze-gold silk blouse already in her wardrobe. A gold pin that had been her great-grandmother's and depicted a woman's hand holding a rosebud decorated the no-nonsense lapel of the suit's jacket, which stopped at her waist. The skirt's hem came modestly to just below her knees.

On her feet were midheel, soft-as-butter brown leather pumps that had a serious look to them but were as comfortable as a pair of old house slippers.

Surveying herself in the mirror of the motel room in Midland where she and Blackjack spent the night before the ceremony, China thought she looked…nice. Not beautiful, but then she wasn't a beautiful woman, and this wasn't the kind of wedding that demanded a radiant bride. But she'd do.

Wasn't she dressed like a woman who'd signed the final draft of a Prenuptial Agreement only yesterday?

When she joined Blackjack, he glanced at her and picked up his best hat. "Ready?" he asked, already heading for the door.

China blinked. This was laconic, even for her stepfather.

"As I'll ever be, I suppose," she replied as briefly, and caught up the brown purse matching her shoes before following him. They were early, but trust Blackjack to get her to the courthouse well before time.

Holding the door open for her, Blackjack chuckled as she went to pass in front of him. "You're forgettin' your dress, darlin'. You're gonna feel mighty silly when you get to the changin' room and don't have nothin' to wear but your slip."

"Changing…" China stared at him a moment. "B.J., there aren't any changing rooms at the courthouse. This is what I'm wearing."

Her stepfather stared back at her, his faded blue gaze holding not the slightest hint of humor. "I thought this was a weddin'," he said, "not a board meetin'. Didn't you buy yourself a dress?"

China felt like she had when she was thirteen and her mother caught her reading a copy of *Cosmo*…defensive, but not sure why.

"This is what I bought," she said now. "It's a good suit, from an exclusive shop, even if it was on sale. This isn't my first wedding, B.J.," she added softly when her stepfather didn't seem the least impressed. "I've been married before, remember."

"Is there somethin' you're not tellin' me, girl?" he asked, cutting right to the heart of the matter. "You don't look right, and you know it."

He didn't define *right,* but then he didn't have to.

"I thought I looked nice," China replied, hoping to sway him by allowing her face to take on the woebegone expression that always wrapped her stepfather around her little finger. For that reason alone, she almost never used it.

"O' course you look nice," he snapped back at her, which meant she'd gotten to him. "You always look nice, darlin'. That goes without sayin'. But you don't look like a *bride!*"

And what China heard beneath his gruffness was Blackjack's very real distress. "You're right," she said gently. "Give me a few minutes, okay?"

There had been something else on that sale rack that she couldn't pass up: a drift of green that she thought might do for a party at some time or another. Too pale a green to match her hazel eyes, but Yance seemed to like green, though that fact had nothing to do with anything at all.

When China returned, Blackjack looked her over approvingly. "Now that's the ticket," he said and cleared his throat. "You look more than nice this time, darlin'. You look beautiful. Your ma would be proud." In Blackjack's opinion there was no higher praise.

"I wish she was here," he added. "She'd approve of this weddin'. She always liked Yance when he was a boy. And he's good stock, girl. Good stock."

"I know, B.J.," China said, and wondered herself if her mother, who'd known her only child very well indeed, really would approve. She stepped forward and hugged her stepfather tightly. "I love you," she told him.

He harrumphed, as she'd known he would, and hugged her back as tightly as she'd known he would. "Save it for Yance," he said, and kissed her cheek.

China pretended not to notice when he surreptitiously wiped his eyes.

But as they walked up the courthouse steps fifteen minutes later, Blackjack suddenly stopped. "China Dare," he said, looking not at her but at the traffic passing on the street behind them, "your ma didn't love me in the beginning, but she loved me more'n enough all the resta the time we was married. And I loved her and you from the first time I laid eyes on you both." He nodded once, briefly. "I guess I thought you should know that. Now get a move on, girl, or we're gonna be late," and he hustled her up the rest of the steps before she could say a word.

Yance and Judge Soames had been talking quietly in the few minutes since Yance and Trace arrived, Trace sitting on the edge of his chair watching the office door. Clearly, his son approved of this marriage, Yance thought, as he too kept one eye on the door.

He was nervous in a way he hadn't been since his first wedding, and that was strange because this wasn't anything like the first affair, held in a packed church and followed by a party that was talked about for months. Yet he was again taking an irrevocable step, and, if not his then his son's life would be forevermore affected by it.

Did China Dare Smith really know what she held in her capable paint-stained hands?

Yet it was far too late for questions of that sort, for she and her stepfather had arrived.

Trace leaped to his feet, his face alight with excitement, while Yance stood slowly as his son's future, and perhaps his own, came through the door.

Her dress was the same hint of new green that covered desert mountains after a good, soaking rain. It drifted over her like nature's benediction, subtly highlighting her Nordic ancestry, calling whispered attention to her breasts, her small waist, the flare of her hips. She wore her hair neither up nor down but in some magical in-between arrangement, so that it was pulled away from the strong lines of her face and up off her back, yet softly haloed around her head.

He wasn't quite sure how he'd expected her to dress for this. She was the daughter of a West Texas cowboy, clearly at home on the land of her birth. That was one of the reasons he was marrying her.

But her dress spoke of more than the land and its bedrock. China wore it with total élan, like a high fashion model, he thought, walking down a Paris runway with an air that said, "This old thing?" of a dress whose cost would support a working class family for a year.

China's polish had nothing to do with the cost of her dress, however. Yance knew couture when he saw it and this wasn't it, yet her easy way of wearing the garment was totally unexpected. China Dare Smith carried herself, he thought, like a Valkyrie in nineties garb, a goddess who could wield a battle ax with one hand and weave a daisy chain with the other.

He smiled, his nervousness falling away.

"Wow, China," Trace exclaimed, "you look *bad!*"

Blackjack swelled ominously, but China laughed. "That's a compliment, B.J."

She openly surveyed the boy before her, and his father, too, but out of the corner of her eye, since she hadn't worked up nerve enough yet to look at Yance directly. "You look pretty bad, yourself," she said admiringly. "You and your dad both."

"We brought you flowers," the boy told her. "Two of 'em. One from Dad and one from me. Here's mine," and he thrust a box at her.

When China opened it, a small but exquisite corsage nestled within, made up of tiny pink roses, baby's breath and wisps of fern.

"Is the color all right?" Trace asked anxiously. "I thought you'd like pink. Girls do, y'know. But maybe," he eyed her dress with consternation, "they don't match."

"Matching is boring, kiddo," China said with a laugh. "I love contrast," and she lifted the corsage to place it on the silky shoulder of her dress, anchoring it with her grandmother's pin she'd defiantly chosen to wear anyway because it was "something old" to wear with her new dress.

"See," she said, squaring her shoulders to show off the flowers, "A lovely contrast of color and texture."

For no reason at all, when Yance chuckled, she became immediately aware of how her squared shoulders pushed her breasts into prominence. Oh, dear. But the man was stepping forward with his own box.

Inside was a bridal bouquet of pink tea roses, white shasta daisies, freesias and a feathery deep green fern. So that it was just out of sight, a narrow strip of blue ribbon was wrapped around the carry handle and tied off with a tiny bow.

Something blue, China thought, and fought the urge to cry.

"It's beautiful," she said softly, lifting her damp gaze to the man before her, looking elegant in a Western-cut charcoal gray suit.

"So are you," he replied as softly. "Would you like to borrow my hanky?" and he handed her the pearl gray silk handkerchief from the pocket of his jacket.

Something borrowed.

So she had the traditional quartet, after all. The thought made her smile a little, and she saw Yance's eyes soften.

Perhaps…

Then Yance stepped away from her. "Looks like we're ready, Judge. Shall we begin?"

"Wait," China commanded, leaving the judge with his mouth half-open. Placing her bouquet on his desk, she then carefully removed three flowers from it. Turning to Trace, she slipped a daisy into his lapel, then a freesia into Blackjack's. Lastly she added a pink rosebud and sprig of fern to Yance's lapel, feeling his gaze on the top of her head as she did so, and feeling the sheer power of the chest just under her knuckles.

Then she took her place at Yance Chisolm's side.

"We are gathered together…" Judge Soames began, and China went still inside.

In spite of the flowers, in spite of her dress, in spite of the unexpected touch of tradition, she thought, anybody in their right mind would know this for the business agreement it was. One look at the bride and groom's now expressionless faces as the age-old words were spoken would announce that to any but a blind man.

Or at least, to any but Trace and Blackjack. The two of them couldn't stop grinning, and when the brief ceremony was over, they waited so expectantly that Yance had no option but to kiss her. "We can't disappoint them," he murmured before his lips touched hers.

Afterward, Trace and Blackjack tossed rice until it covered the Judge's office floor. Instant rice, China noticed ruefully, shaking a few shriveled grains from her hair, for an instant wedding.

The ceremony had taken less than ten minutes to cover all the bases. In a marriage heading nowhere, China Dare Smith became China Dare Chisolm, instant mother, equally instant wife to a man who just might make her an instant widow in three weeks' time.

She should be miserable.

She wasn't.

And all because the groom didn't want to disappoint an old man and a young boy who thought weddings should be sealed with a kiss.

When Yance's mouth homed in on hers, China knew that what she'd just done, in her right mind and with her full knowledge, was going to be loaded with more problems than she'd bargained for. His lips touched gently, lifted gently…but oh, that in between!

How could one die and be reborn in the space of twenty seconds? she wondered dazedly.

And Yance looked as dazed as she before his features settled into neutral.

When it was over and the last document signed, the four of them stood for a moment on the courthouse steps as if they didn't know what to do next, though lunch was reserved for them all at one of the more exclusive Midland restaurants.

"Shall we all go in my car?" Yance suggested, finally taking charge, ordinarily not one to allow a moment to turn awkward. But then, this was no ordinary day. He'd just been through a ceremony that had shaken him badly. This marriage was supposed to be simply a legal move for Trace's protection, not…not whatever the hell it had been in there.

And now that it was all over, he'd had a good look at Blackjack Kerrigan's face. The man's lined features were a study of happiness, however much the old cowboy tried to hide it. That was the trouble.

Hell, Yance thought, he'd had dinner at the White House on several occasions, some of them informal. What was the big deal about sitting down to a meal with his new father-in-law, for Pete's sake?

But he knew. Having to pretend he was in love with the man's daughter, for one thing. Having to pretend he and the man's daughter had a lifetime in front of them, for another. Yance sighed. They did, he supposed, if one didn't specify the length of the life.

Trace's happiness, on the other hand, was there for all the world to see, thank God. Hopefully, if the need arose,

Blackjack would understand why the boy's father had done this thing.

Just as Yance expected, Blackjack was far too old and down-to-earth to be intimidated by the restaurant where they had lunch, and Trace was far too young. But he'd been worried about China when he'd made the reservations. He was, after all, a very wealthy man and everyone knew it.

Over the years, as he walked the sometimes precarious line between sophistication and simplicity, Yance had found that small things like restaurants could affect people in a variety of ways. There were those sophisticates half-afraid to enter a truckers' cafe, and simpler folk made nervous by fresh cut flowers on a linen tablecloth and maître d's.

But China, he was pleased to find, took the restaurant in stride, smiling at the maître d' with just the right amount of friendliness before following him to their table. She didn't gaze around her or comment on the decor, and when her meal arrived, she ate it with enjoyment and a comfortable blend of good manners and common-sense utility, all the while keeping the conversation flowing lightly and away from the questionable jokes his son and Blackjack seemed to think the occasion called for.

When the meal was over and before the coffee arrived, Blackjack suddenly raised his wineglass. "To Yance and China Dare Chisolm," he said gruffly. "Long life an' the same happiness me an' China's ma had."

Trace clinked it with his glass of sparkling juice. "Here, here," he chimed.

China stilled as her unsmiling gaze rested on her new husband. She, too, raised her glass. "Here, here," she said clearly, and meant it.

Yance had to add wine to his before picking up his glass, which he did slowly and with a small smile, and then he lifted the fragile vessel to gaze straight into China's eyes and echoed, "Here, here."

Leaning forward and sideways to reach her, he kissed his bride's cheek while his son looked on and giggled. "Here, here," he repeated huskily for her ears alone.

While his face was close to hers, China found herself wanting to reach up and touch it; and when he sat back, she wanted to reach up and touch the warm place on her own face where his lips and breath had been. She did neither.

While Blackjack and Trace drove back to the C3 that afternoon, Yance and China flew to Santa Fe to close out China's apartment.

It was Yance's first flight since the accident, and in spite of giving himself a pep talk before they boarded, he had to admit that his heart still pounded when the plane taxied down the runway and angled up into the air. After just such a takeoff had the smaller plane he'd been a passenger in come down.

But, he'd reasoned, as with falling off a horse, it was better to get back on as soon as possible.

Easier said than done.

By this time, Yance wasn't the least surprised that his new wife entered his corporate jet with the same aplomb she'd enter a city bus. Now wearing a tailored suit the color of wheat with her hair pulled into a thick chignon at her neck, she looked more like a well-dressed female executive than a Norse goddess. There was nothing about her that so much as hinted at a formidable ability to climb trees. He was finding China Dare a woman of many faces, and so far he liked them all.

Though Yance's roots in the West Texas mountains ran deep, once he left the ranch to take up his role as head of the Chisolm financial structure he often felt as if he'd become a displaced person. A man who was entertained by prime ministers, who'd briefly had a fling with the daughter of a prince, and once came close to punching out a foul-mouthed but Oscar-winning Hollywood star, he was more than a son of the soil; had to be more to hold his own in the position the Chisolm business interests demanded.

Thus he was a man who straddled two ways of life; a man of the land, but also a man of the world. Mountains eased his soul, but city life revved his adrenaline; and he was a man who needed both those things.

Early on, he'd shown a bent for figures and business and trends. His father had it, too, though to a lesser extent, but in Yance, the talent was in full flower, and he'd taken what his father began and run with it.

Still, he was a rancher, and the son of a rancher, and his son would be a rancher, too. It's what Chisolms did, first and foremost, what they were born to do. There was no way in hell he could leave that heritage behind or even want to.

Yet life on the ranch didn't fit him like a second skin as it did his father. He'd never been able to narrow his thinking to stock prices and lack of rain. Ranch gossip was interesting, all right, but so was corporate gossip. He had friends in each camp, but never a friend in both camps.

And it was the same with women. A woman of the city ordinarily became bored stiff with ranch life unless she was wide-eyed at the "romance" of it. A woman of the country was often scared stiff of the gleaming polish of the city unless she was wide-eyed at the "sophistication" of it.

As Melodie had been. However much his first wife enjoyed her life with Yance...and she had, he'd swear it...she'd still been awed by that life to the point of giggling far more than she should, drinking far more than she should, and yes, weeping far more than she should. So he'd given up the apartment in New York and taken one in

Midland, close to her folks and her old friends, and left her in it more often than not while he flew about the world to wheel and deal.

She'd been happier then, but frequently lonely.

He'd loved Melodie. Always had, always would, though he'd stopped missing her long ago. But beyond love for each other and mutual ranching friends, he and Melodie had almost nothing in common.

They'd pinned a lot of hope on the advent of Trace.

Odd, then, that China Dare, another cowman's daughter, and an itinerant cowboy at that, was as easy with the accoutrements of his corporate life-style as Melodie had never been. China had mentioned living in New York and her first husband, Frank, being an executive. Was Frank perhaps someone he knew?

He asked her.

And, sitting beside him as they flew high over the earth, she told him. She laughed.

"Frank?" China shook her head. "I doubt you know him, Yance. Frank Dellgrin is a mid-level executive cog in a very large corporate machine. We lived outside the city, in one of the trendy suburbs with other mid-level executives, and Frank commuted." She raised an inquiring eyebrow to see if the name meant anything to him.

"Can't say the name is familiar," Yance replied. "You just seem...easy, I guess, with more than I thought you would be comfortable with, not meaning any insult. Does that make sense?"

She laughed. "Not a whole lot. But I'm an artist, which covers a multitude of sins, as they say. People are people, places are places, but line and color, depth and texture are everything. Does that make any sense?"

It was his turn to laugh. "Not a whole lot."

But in spite of living in the suburbs, she knew New York, he found, and not just the tourist sites. And in spite of living a city life, she knew the West Texas mountains, and not just the tourist sites.

They talked all the way to Santa Fe, and Yance forgot completely that it was a long way down to the ground and only remembered his lifelong joy of flying.

At China's apartment, Yance saw yet another side of his new wife. She had no style, he found. No one specific style, that is, and the result was charming.

Native American pots of every size and shape literally spilled from one corner, some standing upright, others leaning drunkenly against each other, a few tipped over on their sides trailing blue and yellow corn kernels over the tile flooring.

Near the Southwestern-style fireplace a collection of antique toys were strewn about, as though recently abandoned by an equally antique child. A brightly colored Mexican serape served as a rug in front of the fireplace and on it a picture book lay open to an Arthur Rackham illustration.

Over a plain white canvas-covered couch a collection of baskets hung at various levels in a canopy, and in front of it, a wood box, scarred and mellowed with age, took the place of a coffee table.

On those walls not filled with windows, paintings and prints were everywhere, by a variety of artists in a variety of styles.

Amazingly, for all the things within it, the room held no sense of clutter. Nothing leaped out to assault the eye, but instead beckoned it to examine and enjoy, drawing one into the room, into its sense of peace.

Yance was impressed. "Nice," he said.

Sighing, China was only aware of the dismantling job ahead. She was exhausted. "We need boxes," she said tiredly and set about opening windows.

"Tomorrow, and then we'll call in professional loaders. China, I'm pooped."

At her look of immediate alarm, he added with a small smile, "It's just been a long day, don't you think?"

"Oh, my, yes," she said gratefully. "I'm not really up to handling this now, either. I don't have any groceries in the place, but there's coffee or beer or I could make iced tea."

"Coffee would be a lifesaver," he pronounced at once like the Western man he was.

The coffee was strong, as the rancher half of him liked it, and Colombian, as the executive half of him liked it. Yance sat on the couch sipping the brew appreciatively, flipping through one of the children's books, half listening to a CD of Andean flute music and wondering what the coming evening would bring. It was one of the few times in his life he was in an attractive woman's apartment without knowing *exactly* what the evening would bring.

There was no question of intimacy; they'd agreed on that however much he'd come to regret that easy agreement. But there was the question of where they would spend the night. Here, or at a hotel? Did she have room for a guest? Or would China remain here and he go to a hotel?

No, he decided at once. He and China were now a team, even if only out of the bedroom, and even if only for a possible three weeks. As husband and wife, they were in this thing together. Hadn't they just promised it? So they would begin as he meant for them to go on, and sleep in the same place, if not in the same bed. This couch was long enough for him.

China eyed the man sitting across from her, his boots propped on the wood box. Her husband now, she thought, this handsome, sexy man. But he looked tired, and he ought to have an early evening. They hadn't discussed where they would spend the night. Intoxicating thought.

Would Yance keep his word about separate sleeping arrangements, or would he try to cajole her into his bed?

And could she be cajoled?

"Do you want to stay here tonight, or in a hotel?" he asked as if reading her mind.

China jumped. "Here," she said. And hurried on before she could think of more satisfactory arrangements. "I have a guest room. Blackjack used it the few times I could get him to visit. If we stay here, we can get an early start in the morning."

"You don't have to give this place up, you know," Yance said quietly. "There's no problem with you keeping it."

"I know." China allowed her gaze to roam around the room that yesterday held so much of herself, yet none of herself today. "But it's time to move on, I suppose." Her true self now seemed to be floating in a netherworld, looking for a place to light. "Most of this stuff can go into storage."

Laying aside the children's book, Yance sat forward. "As to that," he said, "I was hoping you might loan the ranch some of your furniture."

China's head snapped up. Her furniture wasn't all that expensive, but it wasn't bunkhouse stuff, either.

"You may have noticed the living room at the Big House looks pretty tatty. When my mother moved out, she took most of the good pieces she and Dad had put together, and neither Dad nor I were interested enough in things like that to buy anything else. Besides, until now, I haven't really lived on the ranch for years." He paused. "Or we could buy new furniture for the house, if you'd rather, and leave your things in storage. You might want to set up another apartment later."

"I...I hadn't thought about changing things at the ranch," China said slowly. "It didn't seem my place."

"The C3 is your home now, as much as mine and

Trace's," Yance said matter-of-factly. "And of course it's your place." He smiled, the curvature of his lips seeming to switch on a lamp in his smoky gray eyes. "A place is a place," he then echoed her statement of earlier, "waiting like an empty lapel for China Dare's color and texture."

"Oh," China said, and felt as if the man had reached out and gently stroked her cheek. "Well, then. I…I would like to add my pieces to the C3."

When she chuckled suddenly, the rich low sound of it blending with the high trill of an Andean flute burrowed into Yance's libido.

"Every well-dressed ranch house needs a pot or two," she said with a grin.

He pretended to groan. "No wonder you and Trace get along so well. You read the same joke books. Are you hungry?"

"A little. What about you?"

"A lot. Want to order in pizza?"

Later, they sat on the floor in the living room, using the wood box to hold the pizza and beer cans, China in sweatpants, oversized T-shirt and socks, with her hair hanging loose over one shoulder; and Yance in faded denims, softened with age, an equally ancient white T-shirt with the sleeves ripped out and socks.

They lit a fire in the fireplace to use up China's few remaining pieces of wood, and now it snapped and hissed and threw off good-smelling heat in argument with the evening's fall chill.

The romance of it all was wasted on the two people before it in their sexless scruffies, China thought. She and Yance might have been an old married couple instead of a couple on their honeymoon.

"Not much of a honeymoon," Yance commented, eying China's pensive face. "Are you having regrets?"

She looked up, suddenly wary. "No. Are you?"

"No." But he was, Yance thought. The same regret he'd felt much of the day, that the few weeks left to him before he went into the hospital were to be celibate.

Celibacy hadn't mattered when he'd proposed to China, or when he agreed she would have her own bedroom; it hadn't mattered even when he'd repeated his vows with her. But when he kissed her lips following the ceremony, it had begun to matter a bit, and when he kissed her cheek in testament of his toast, it had mattered a bit more.

Now, in what had been China's home, with firelight playing over her hair, with Trace protected as much as he could protect him, it mattered a hell of a lot.

Yet he knew he wasn't going to do a damn thing about it.

It was not a question of his attraction, and he knew that China was attracted to him. But what attracted her? Yance Chisolm the man, or the fact that he might not be alive in a month?

Pity was a powerful aphrodisiac.

Looking death in the face was a powerful one, as well, he acknowledged.

And if they went forward now, would they both be sorry in three weeks' time when all was well; when pity was no longer a factor, death no longer a factor, and they were stuck with a complication contrary to what they'd both agreed on initially?

He stifled an inward groan. Hell.

"Tired?" China took a last swig of her beer. Bedtime.

Having already finished his own beer, Yance stood and began gathering debris that China took from him and headed for the kitchen. "Bushed," he said, banking the dying fire. Then he placed the fire screen in front of it.

The mighty stretch he was in the midst of stopped China, just returning from taking their trash, in her tracks. With his arms over his head and shoulders thrown back,

Yance's T-shirt rode high while his beltless Levi's rode low; the in between was the stuff of fantasy.

She swallowed.

And swallowed again later, lying in her big double bed.

Alone.

Just as they agreed, she thought. There was no comfort at all in the knowledge that—knowing her for the modern healthy woman she was—Yance promised she could have as many affairs as she wanted. How long would it take him, she wondered, to figure out that she wasn't that modern, but was most certainly that healthy? And once he figured it out, would he do anything about it?

He'd kissed her good-night.

On the cheek.

He'd even held her close for a long moment so that she heard his heart beating strongly beneath her ear, with the cheek he'd kissed pressed against the softness of his T-shirt and the hardness of the chest under it.

Texture and contrast.

She was such a glib fool.

Yance then put her away from him and strode toward Blackjack's bedroom like the good guest he was, leaving China to shower and go to her own bed.

The issue here, China Dare Smith—China Dare Chisolm—is and always was Trace. Now cut it out and get to sleep.

Which she did, after a couple of hours.

When China and Yance drove up to the ranch in the rental truck two days later, Trace burst out of the house like a cannonball. Nor was he alone. It was late afternoon, and the hands had just finished their supper and they too ambled out en masse to welcome the couple, Blackjack leading the way, grinning broadly.

Climbing stiffly from the truck, China hugged her stepfather and knew from the good-natured but ribald jokes flying around that whatever hoopla she and Yance had managed to sidetrack at their wedding was about to be made up for in spades.

She had no time to think about it, however. Trace threw himself into her midsection. "Hi-ya, Mom," he said cheekily.

China laughed, once she started breathing again. "Hi-ya, son. Have you been a good boy while I was gone?"

He rolled his eyes. "You're not serious with that, are you?" But when she ruffled his hair, he automatically ducked and got the message. "Hey, you've been around Dad too long." Reaching up, he pulled her braid, but gently, as his eyes softened into seriousness. "Welcome home," he said.

Oh, these Chisolm men, China thought. She bent and kissed her stepson's cheek. "Thank you, Trace," she whispered.

"Say, can I have one of those, too, Miz Chisolm?" one of the cowboys asked, coming forward to wrap her in a bear hug. She and Cully had danced many a mile together, and China laughed as she bussed him. She was then passed from man to man, most of whom she'd known all her life, several of whom she'd declined to know better, no hard feelings.

Yance, watching his bride being hugged and kissed by far more men than he'd been aware she knew, felt a pang of jealousy that these same men could express so openly that which he had to handle with such care.

Finally he put a stop to it by simply placing his arm around her shoulder. "Sorry, boys," he said easily. "All mine now."

Everyone laughed, but he felt China stiffen before she glanced up at him, her mouth unsmiling, her eyes puzzled. And he put a stop to that, too, by lowering his head so that she had to close her eyes or go cross-eyed, and placing his mouth on hers. Not gently this time, but not hard, either.

Soft, this kiss was, but hot, like a pillow of flame, meant to brand her lips with his; to brand her in front of his men, in front of Blackjack, even in front of Trace, as his. They could have her when he was gone, but by damn, not until.

Not until.

It was Trace's young voice that finally impinged upon his consciousness. "Hooo-eee, Dad! I thought you wouldn't let me watch X-rated stuff." And Yance lifted his head to the whistles and stomps of his men, only to grin back at them unrepentantly.

But Blackjack, who stood beside Trace with one hand on the boy's shoulder, wasn't grinning. The old man's faded blue gaze held no humor at all. It held only quiet approval, and that more than anything brought Yance to his senses. He looked down at China still under his arm, but she was leaning forward to accept Mabel Chadwick's kiss and handshake, and so he was unable to read her face.

And in a moment she was gone, following Mabel into the house, leaving Yance to set the men to unloading the truck and trying to figure out what the hell he'd just accomplished, if anything.

Because one thing was for sure, he hadn't been alone in that kiss. China's lips had been as hot as his own, and any branding that had been done had been done equally. But how hot is pity?

Back to square one.

But now that he'd had a taste, could he go back?

Perhaps he should investigate square two.

It turned out not to matter a damn. Warm, laughing China Dare turned into Chilly the Ice Princess.

Once the truck was unloaded and the living room full of boxes and the front porch stacked with furniture, things quieted down enough for China to slap leftovers on the table, since supper was served early on the ranch and they'd missed it.

Yance was hungry, and he supposed China must be, too, otherwise in the mood she was in she'd probably have gone to bed without eating. Trace, with the newness worn off their homecoming, was in the den watching television.

When another bowl made a ringing clack on the table, Yance lifted an eyebrow. "Guess with two sets of dishes now, we have enough to break," he commented, watching China out of the corner of his eye as he took cutlery from the drawer.

"I don't like being used," China said, plainly deciding not to beat around the bush and looking up to face him squarely.

If this was square two, Yance didn't like it. "Used?" he asked softly, in a tone that in a boardroom made vice presidents suddenly shuffle papers.

China was not a board member. "Used," she said shortly. "What else was that about in your front yard?"

"Whatever it was about, it was shared," Yance replied, his eyes narrowing. "And equally. Seems to me you gave as good as you got."

"Well, of course I did," she retorted. "What woman wouldn't, receiving a kiss like that? But standing in front of a bunch of leering cowboys so you could prove a point is not my idea of a good time. You only kissed me to show them you could. Don't deny it," she added. "I've been around the block with you macho Western types."

Yance mentally backed up a step. "Have you?" he said.

When her eyes glinted dangerously, he threw up his hands in a mock-defensive position. "I didn't mean that like it sounded," he said with a placating grin, adding slowly, "all right, I suppose I was staking a claim. But China, when I'm gone...to the hospital, I mean," he said coldly when her eyes widened with remembrance in that way he couldn't stand. "Or in a rest home or whatever," he added, "you'll need more protection than just an old man and a ten-year-old boy. That kiss said you're a Chisolm now and to be treated with respect accordingly."

"And where do you think I've been all these years?" China said with equal chill. "I'm more than capable of taking care of myself, and I'm Blackjack Kerrigan's daughter. Either one of those salient points earns me as much respect as I need. From everybody but you, apparently."

"I kissed you because you're my—"

"I'm your what?" China interrupted. "Property? One more of the Chisolm holdings?"

That kiss, she thought, misery feeding her anger past rationality. That wonderful, wonderful kiss that should have been given in the bedroom, with privacy, with love hovering in the air; and instead was given in front of a crowd, with no opportunity to carry it further, or even to savor the sensual sweetness that had also been a part of its message.

"To show that you're my wife," Yance said and strode from the room.

China found him on the front porch, standing in the dark near the railing, and staring off toward the far mountains outlined by the blotted stars.

"I'm sorry, Yance," she said immediately. "This is difficult for both of us. We've had a long day and we're both tired and hungry."

He didn't turn, but his low cynical laugh floated back to her. "I suppose that just about covers everything, China Dare."

"Not everything. I also overreacted. Please come inside. It's too cold out here."

"Shut up," he said softly.

She caught her breath, stunned.

But Yance turned to face her then, and in the light coming from the house behind her, she could see a little of his face.

"China," he said. "Save your pity. I'm pouting, not breathing my last. The cold is not going to kill me, and we can argue without it going to my head, as it were. For what it's worth, I'm sorry, too, but for embarrassing you, not for the kiss. The kiss I liked. And I'm warning you now, someday I'm going to give you another just like it, only better and longer. And hotter," he added, dropping his voice to a low, husky whisper, "and most definitely without an audience."

At the thought China went warm all over and was glad the light was behind her, hiding her face.

"In the meantime—" and now she heard his laughter, with no hint in it of eroticism so that she wondered if he'd just been teasing "—I'm tired," he whined in good imitation of Trace, "and I'm hungry."

But just as she was relaxing enough to chuckle with him and add her own quip, he added, "But food will have to do. Let's eat, wife."

Chapter Four

The old-fashioned living room in the C3 Big House went through a major reorganization the next day, with Yance taking charge when China held back, hesitant to touch any of its original contents. Yet when Yance had every stick of furniture in it taken out to the bunkhouse or set aside for donation to charity, China finally decided he meant what he said about wanting to use her things.

Before the two cowboys carrying it could wrangle her couch through the door, she stopped them. "Yance," she said slowly, "what's under this rug?"

He grinned at her. "The floor, probably. Perhaps a dead body or two." The two cowboys sniggered.

"Funny. What kind of floor?"

"Hell, China. I don't know what kind of floor. This rug's been down since I can remember." He walked over and peeled back a corner. "Why, it's a *wood* floor," he said in mock awe. The two cowboys snickered again.

China nailed him with a glance. "Let's see some more

of this wood floor,'' she ordered, and when he complied by pulling the rug back farther she stared at the triangle of flooring beneath it for a long moment. ''Do you like this rug, Yance?''

He chuckled. ''You're kidding, right? Of course I don't like this rug. It's threadbare in spots and I've heard that cabbage roses, even faded blue-green ones, are no longer in style. We can get new carpeting if you want.''

''No,'' China said slowly. ''I want the floor.''

China and Mabel Chadwick and one of the hands mopped and waxed the newly discovered oak hardwood floors of the living room to a rich patina before China's furniture and an end table and lamp she'd reclaimed from the charity heap came through the door to grace its surface.

By the end of the day, the room looked nothing like it had that morning, nor did it look anything like China's apartment in Santa Fe. Though made up of a blending of two households, it had become something altogether new.

A large basket from Africa now sat on one side of the hearth, and a couple of Native American baskets sat on the fireplace mantel. But the Victorian vase that had taken pride of place there since Yance was a boy still kept its throne.

Yet the deer antlers above the mantel had disappeared without regret, to be replaced with a painting of the Davis Mountains seen beyond the front porch and done by Yance's grandmother when she'd gone through her ''Grandma Moses phase,'' as she'd called it. The painting used to hang in the hall, but in the light of the living room, the vibrancy of its colors shone in a way he'd never noticed before.

Beside China's couch was the end table she'd rescued, seventies Spanish style and solidly heavy and dark. A third of its surface held the bulbous lamp of olive green glass banded with wrought iron that had always been there, but a brightly painted bowl of forties Mexican pottery now graced the end table, as well, holding a collection of children's marbles, some of which Trace contributed before Yance added a few of his own, kept tucked away in a drawer for years and forgotten.

On the other side of the fireplace sat the wood box that had been China's coffee table, at last being used to perform the job it was built for. Two redwood cubes that were once nightstands in China's bedroom took on the woodbox's former function, placed side by side before the couch in an elegance of line and form and deep rich color. To keep from scarring the floor, they sat on a couple of wool saddle blankets unearthed from the back of the barn and resurrected as accent rugs.

The couch itself was put where the couch in the living room had always been, in front of the double windows. But the faded flowered drapes that covered the windows were gone, replaced with nothing, the wood slats of the Venetian blinds that had kept out the West Texas glare since the room was built in the thirties remaining as their only covering.

Those blinds were open now, allowing the last of the afternoon sun to throw bands of diffused light over the whole.

While China was in the kitchen helping Mabel put the finishing touches on supper, Yance surveyed his living room in amazement. Wood and earth tones dominated, yet the whole had a warm lived-in quality. A professional decorator couldn't have done it better. Hell, a professional decorator couldn't have done it as well.

The room could have been featured in a country home magazine, he thought, yet it was made up of totally personal items that spoke directly to him of his family. He'd been more than willing to throw away everything in the room this morning, seeing the contents as merely worn, outdated and with little monetary or sentimental value. The uncomfortable living room had always been the least-used room in the house, with the den, added during his father's time, where the family usually went to relax.

Yet China had seen it with clearer eyes than he.

How had she known, for instance, that he'd always kind of liked the very ugliness of the old vase on the mantel, now looking almost elegant beside those baskets of hers?

Shape and texture, he supposed, smiling a little as he remembered China's favorite phrase.

Later that evening, as Yance sat on the side of his king-sized bed unbuttoning his shirt, he looked around the master bedroom inherited from his father. It would be Trace's someday.

What changes would Trace make, he wondered. Or more probably, Trace's wife?

He used the bootjack beside the bed to pull off his boots, then turned off the lamp to enjoy the moonlight coming through his window.

What kind of girl would Trace marry? And if her eight-year obligation had expired, would China be at Trace's wedding to represent the boy's family if Yance himself was not there?

The slow sluggish beating of his heart caught Yance up short, and he gave a brief, silent snort of disgust, knowing the low-level fear for what it was. Yet of all this, he thought, it was the possibility of missing his son's growing up that he felt most keenly.

There was so much China needed to know about Trace if she was left to raise him alone, and Yance had only two weeks before his operation to tell her; two weeks to fill her in on the details of Trace's schooling and the boy's medical history and insurance policies; two weeks to explain to her that Trace didn't like lettuce but loved raw cabbage, to note down Trace's clothing sizes and shoe sizes and explain to her that as the boy's father he'd refused to indulge Trace with tennis shoes that cost as much as stereo equipment.

Two weeks, he thought, to tell her where the Christmas ornaments were kept and how he and Trace usually spent Easter....

He caught himself up abruptly. Better, he thought, to think of the two weeks he had left with China Dare to see the world made new through her eyes just as she'd done with his living room.

Living room, get it? he could almost hear Trace say with delight at the play on words.

Yance chuckled, the sound of it bleak in his own ears, and maudlin.

My God, man, get a grip, he told himself disgustedly, and stood to shuck his pants. But with his hand at his zipper, he saw a white wraith pass his open door.

Speak of the angels.

When China didn't return after a few minutes, he trailed after her to see where she'd gone and found her standing at the living room door. Holding a cup of hot cocoa between her two hands, she stood with her shoulder propped against the doorjamb, surveying the darkened room that was yet illuminated by the bright moonlight.

"Any more of that?" he asked quietly.

She'd heard as well as felt him come up behind her so she didn't jump and knew now why she'd boiled more than one cup of hot water. "It's the instant kind if you're not picky," she said. "The water's still hot."

When Yance returned with his own cup, the two of them sat in the refurbished room, leaving the light off so the moonlight, flowing through the still-opened slats of the blinds could spill in bars across the floor.

China, in nightgown and bathrobe, sat on the couch with her feet in her worn-out but still comfortable house slippers propped on the elegance of the redwood cubes serving as the coffee table. Yance sat across from her in a wing chair that had been hers, and now, she thought, was theirs, wearing his unbuttoned shirt hanging loosely open over his chest, still in his jeans but without his belt or his boots.

For long moments neither of them felt the need to talk. A mockingbird, possibly a little drunk on so much moonlight, went through a portion of its repertoire somewhere nearby before starting all over again.

"Couldn't sleep?" Yance asked idly after a bit.

China sighed a little, feeling satisfied that Yance, too, didn't need any light but moonlight to go with his hot chocolate. "Didn't try," she said.

"What about you?" she asked after a moment.

"Haven't tried yet, either," he said, and she heard the smile in his voice.

China could see Yance's face clearly in the moonlight, but she chose to examine the fireplace instead. She wanted to continue to enjoy the man's company, not lust for him.

"I was thinking of all the things I want to tell you about Trace tomorrow," he said. "I should make a list, I suppose."

Slowly China rocked her face around to look at him and found that he, too, was examining the shadowed fireplace where a stray bit of moonlight gleamed off the gold trim of the Victorian vase on the mantel. China slid down a bit on the couch so that the top of her head was even with its back, took a last sip of tepid cocoa, and closed her eyes.

"Tell me now," she said, her voice even and practical.

He laughed a little. "It sounds silly, but I wanted you to know that he doesn't like lettuce but likes raw cabbage."

"I'll file that away for future reference," China said with a smile, and kept her eyes closed.

"And I want to show you tomorrow where the insurance policies are kept in case something happens to him and you need them."

"Good plan," China said.

"We use Dr. Sanders in Pecos. His number is beside the phone in the kitchen," Yance murmured. "There's an extra key to the apartment in Midland on the key ring in the desk drawer," he added thoughtfully.

"In Midland we use Dr. Price. His number is on a pad in the kitchen there, as well. Trace has had chicken pox, but other than that, he's been a pretty healthy kid. A few colds now and then, of course. When he was six, he fell out of the tree out back and broke his arm, but it healed okay and there's been no additional problems with the arm since."

China murmured something unintelligible that served to send Yance on as he talked the night away about his son…about Trace's birth and toddlerhood and young boyhood; about the boy's foibles and pranks, the boy's tendency to exaggerate and err on the side of the wild; about Trace's natural seat on a horse and his way with animals and people.

Yance also spoke about his relationship with his son. About his dreams and ambitions for his son. About the qualities he wanted instilled in his son. There was, of course, no need to speak about his love for his son.

And China listened through the night and asked a question now and then, and watched the moonlight recede from the room and take the mockingbird's song with it, and hoped that no lingering beam caught the tears that slowly washed over her face.

The room darkened, and darkened more, and suddenly Yance laughed. "It's almost dawn, China Dare. Why did you let me run on?"

With a small stretch, China covered the dampness of her answering chuckle. "Because I was taking notes," she said. "But I'm tired now. Bedtime for me." She stood, but when she would have taken Yance's mug to return it to the kitchen, he took hers instead.

"You go on to bed," he said. "I'll take these." He took

her mug, but also took the hand that had held it and placed her fingers to his lips. "Thank you," he said softly.

Back in her bedroom, China used the fingertips that still held the warmth of Yance Chisolm's mouth to swipe at tears that had begun all over again.

She awoke to the smell of Mabel Chadwick's delicious coffee and when she went into the kitchen, found Trace at the table gobbling up the last of his cereal. He looked up at her and offered a cheerful good-morning before swigging down his orange juice, pushing away from the table and carrying his dishes to the sink.

"Guess I better call Dad. He's still sacked out, and he usually takes me to the bus. Guess he forgot it's Monday."

"Don't do that, Trace," China said hurriedly as Trace went to leave the room and roust out his father. "Let him sleep. I'll take you." She paused. "That is, if you don't mind."

The boy's answering smile was full of engaging mischief. "Sure," he said. "One taxi driver's as good as another."

He returned in a flash, teeth brushed and books hitched under an arm. "Ready, Mom," he said, and grinned.

China hadn't figured out the seriousness of that "Mom" yet. Sometimes Trace called her China, but when he was feeling smart, he called her Mom. Perhaps, she thought, her stepson was just trying it out for size. She hoped he found it a good fit eventually. She kind of liked the sound of it herself.

The two of them chatted the whole eight miles to the highway and while they were sitting in the truck waiting for the bus. When it finally came along and Trace climbed aboard, he found a seat by a window and waved at China enthusiastically as China stuck an arm out the truck window and waved back.

She treasured the moment all the way back to the Big House.

The place was quiet when she entered, and when she peeked into Yance's room she saw that he was still asleep, lying on his belly with one arm outflung to strangle the pillow under his head.

He looked, she thought, altogether endearing, if one's eye didn't follow the line of his bare back to where the sheet stopped just short of interesting.

Sighing, China pulled his door closed so that no noise would filter in to wake him. She still had boxes to unpack.

But as she walked farther down the hall, she found Mabel in Trace's room, making up the boy's tumbled bed. China stopped. Nobody had made a bed for her since she was four. Clothes, including a pair of striped pajamas, were strewn over the floor of the room. A glass, with a ring of milk congealed in the bottom of it, sat on the bedside table, as well as a partially wadded potato chip sack.

"Mabel," China said slowly, "I don't mean to interfere, but do you always make Trace's bed?"

The older woman gave the spread a final pat. "Sure do," she said, and bent to gather the dirty clothes that trailed over the floor.

"And clean his room, too?" China exclaimed in amazement.

Mabel straightened, and the two women exchanged a wordless look.

"Do you also clean Yance's room?" China asked quietly.

"No. Yance makes his own bed and keeps his things picked up. I go in once a week and change the sheets, however, and gather his dirty clothes and towels to wash, the same as I'll do for you, China. That's my job and what Yance pays me for," Mabel added meaningfully. "That and cooking breakfast and supper. Lunch is on your own."

"Thank goodness you do the cooking," China said,

knowing exactly what Mabel Chadwick was trying to tell her. "I can make coffee and a fairly decent salad, boil water and operate a microwave, and that's about it. But, Mabel," she added, keeping her tone carefully noncommittal, "don't you think it's time Trace started making his bed and keeping his own room?"

"My boys did at his age," the woman agreed. "But I've been cleaning up after Trace ever since he was a baby, and no one's told me to stop."

China took a deep breath, her heart pounding with the step she was about to take. "Well, then," she said quietly, "I guess I'm telling you to stop. I'll talk to Trace about it tonight."

Again the women exchanged a silent and significant look. "Certainly, Mrs. Chisolm," the older woman said primly at last, and dipped a stiff-kneed curtsy, causing them both to giggle and adjourn to the kitchen for second cups of coffee and a gossip, that didn't, China was glad to note, include the Chisolms or their affairs.

When Yance rolled out of bed an hour later, he found China in the den surrounded by a welter of boxes and packing paper and in the act of removing a vintage toddler-sized tricycle from its nest.

"Horses eat more but they ride smoother," he said with a grin, plopping down on the couch with his mug of coffee to watch her work.

She chuckled. "Tell it to a city girl. I've been on a lot of horses that don't ride smooth at all. You know, I haven't a clue what I'm going to do with this." She shrugged. "I'll figure out something."

Using a carton opener, she then slit open another box, this time finding her collection of children's books.

"We need more shelves," Yance commented idly, enjoying the sunshine in the room, the faint fall chill in the morning breeze wafting through the open windows to pucker the nipples on his bare chest, and the sight of a woman with a rope of long honey-colored braid sitting cross-legged on his floor.

Life felt so damn good.

"My bookshelves are on the back porch," China said. "I'll put them in here, if it's all right."

"We went through this yesterday. It's all right."

But China was paging through one of the books in her lap. "I love Eloise Wilkins' illustrations," she said. "She captures children so beautifully."

Yance leaned forward to see what China was talking about, and she held out the book to him. The illustrations *were* nice, he thought: delicate, sensitive, full of wonder. He'd never paid much attention to the names of the artists who illustrated the books he'd bought Trace over the years. Yet this kind of art was China's business.

"Will you continue your own work?" he asked, slowly turning the pages of the volume of children's poetry, examining its illustrations.

She laughed. "Of course. I love my work."

"You need a studio," he said, and handed the book back to her.

"Not really. I traveled around with Blackjack, remember, so I've learned to be portable. The problem will be where to store supplies and things. A room in the barn or somewhere will work."

Yance remembered the large room she'd used as a studio in Santa Fe, full of light, a long worktable and shelves holding supplies and an assortment of objects he assumed she used as props.

It had also contained dozens of her own canvases depicting nature scenes and animals, and portraits of children of every nationality and in every activity, as sensitive as the ones he'd just looked at by Eloise Wilkins, but far more bold and bright.

The way, he thought, China herself was sensitive, bold and bright.

"I'll see what I can find for you," he said. "In the meantime, I'll have one of the boys clean out the spare bedroom, and you can put your supplies in there."

Taking a swallow of coffee, Yance looked over the sea of boxes and objects littering the floor of the den. Like China, he couldn't imagine where it all could go. "I can have this room emptied, too," he said. "That would give you more space."

Her head jerked up so she could stare at him in alarm. "Don't you dare. Your fifties wagon wheel furniture belongs here. Besides, I didn't have a den and don't have any more large pieces aside from bedroom and dining room stuff that we've already agreed to store in the attic. Don't worry, Yance. I know I have a lot of things, but I'll..."

"...think of something," Yance chimed in with her, and grinned—with humor and with relief. He liked this room, too.

And he liked it just as well when China's bookshelves were brought in and filled, not only with her collection of books but with the boxes of Trace's games that had been stacked on the floor in one corner.

Miraculously, all the boxes were emptied and all the trash disposed of, and nothing was left to put away.

The fun had come from watching China unload it all, telling her stories as she did so of what some unusual object was or where she'd found it and how. She was a natural-born storyteller with a way of hooking him into her tale immediately; and Yance listened, sitting there on the couch in the cool sun-filled room, as fascinated as any boy.

But it was a man's eyes that watched the movement of her descriptive hands; that watched China's green eyes brighten with laughter or signal a forthcoming punch line by taking on an added sparkle.

That followed the sway of her blond braid as it brushed frequently and tantalizingly across her breast.

After supper that evening, when Trace would have sunk into the television and Yance would have gone to his office to hook into a cyber world that no longer interested him, China waved a deck of cards and challenged them both to a game of Battle.

Yance went to bed later, still grinning at the sight of his son lying on his back on the floor chortling in victory and with his son's giggles still ringing in his ears. He had no trouble at all falling asleep.

But he did the next night when China chivied him and Trace out to the front lawn to lie on a blanket on the ground and stare up at a blanket of stars shining clear and cold in the evening sky and surely within touching distance. Yance was pointing out constellations when they all caught their breath as a shooting star, quick as thought, streaked across the heavens. So quick was it and in a blink gone that each of them wondered for a moment if they'd actually seen it.

"Wow, did you see that?" Trace exclaimed, and they knew they had.

"Did you make a wish?" China asked.

"Wish?" Trace said, puzzled.

Yance caught his breath. "I'd forgotten that," he said softly, and only knew he'd spoken aloud when he heard the echo of his own voice.

"Wishes made on shooting stars are even more powerful than wishes made on the first star out at night," China told Trace solemnly.

His son chuckled, probably feeling himself a little old for this but willing to play along. "Okay, I've made my wish. I wish…"

"Don't tell," she broke in, "or it won't come true."

Trace whuffed a long-suffering sigh. "Ri-i-ight." But he didn't tell.

Yance didn't tell his wish, either. And his eyes roamed over the jewel-strewn sky searching for another shooting star because he had more than one wish to make.

On one side of him his skin prickled with the awareness of his son's warm, vibrant body lying so close to his own, and on the other side China Dare's warm, sensuous body called forth an awareness of an altogether different kind.

It took China two days to remember to tell Trace about keeping his room and then only because Trace mentioned it as he sat at the kitchen table doing homework while China boiled water for a cup of tea.

"Why isn't Mabel making my bed?" he asked out of the blue.

China looked at him blankly for a moment before it came to her what he was talking about. She sighed then, feeling like she was already falling down on her mothering duties.

"I meant to talk to you about that," she said slowly. "Since your dad takes care of his room and makes his own bed and so do I, well, Mabel and I...that is, I decided you were old enough now to keep yours, too."

"Oh," Trace said. "Okay. What's nine times seven?"

"Sixty-three. You do understand that you will be making your own bed from now on, don't you?"

"Sure, Mom." He looked up at her and grinned the grin that looked remarkably like his father's.

"Before you leave for school every morning," China tacked on, trying to sound firm. "And you'll keep your own room."

"Gotcha." He switched his gaze to the paper under his hand covered with neat rows of figures. "I'm good at math," he said. "I wish English was as easy."

"What's nine times seven?" China shot back dryly.

"Sixty-three. I was testing you." And he giggled.

To pay him back, China ruffled his hair as she passed behind him on her way out of the room.

Trace's acceptance of her had been remarkably easy, she thought as she took her tea out onto the front porch to enjoy a moment of quiet before going in to help Mabel with supper. As much as she knew the boy liked her, she had expected him to be a little more rebellious, perhaps, or at least cautious with her new place in his life.

Not that she was complaining. Thank goodness, that was all. Settling into the Chisolm life-style had been made as easy for her as slipping into a warm bubble bath, and as soothing to the soul.

Blackjack was happy. His trailer was now parked permanently near the bunkhouse after he refused in no uncertain terms to move into the ranch's Big House with China. He liked his privacy, he said flatly, but added he'd stay in the house with Trace if Yance and China wanted to take some time for themselves on a trip, "or somethin'." Three days in Santa Fe packing boxes wasn't much of a honeymoon, in his opinion.

He did, however, agree to take his evening meal with the family, beginning tonight, which China felt was a victory of sorts.

And yes, she was happy, too. That is, if she didn't think about the real reason she was here; if she didn't think about how easily it all could end in just a week and a half.

Nine days remained before Yance's scheduled surgery. Was he counting the days, too, and the hours? she wondered, and immediately shook her head at the idiocy of the silent question.

Of course he was.

She'd seen the expression in his eyes when he gazed out over the buildings of his ranch, and as he scanned the far mountains. His gray eyes had been quiet, accepting, but aware now more than ever of the heritage to be passed to his son.

When he talked with his cowhands, he really looked at each man, and apart from the business of the ranch, asked them about their lives and that of their families, showing a genuine interest in their answers.

Once, when China was about to enter the kitchen, she heard Yance telling Mabel how much he enjoyed her cooking and how he appreciated the way she kept his house. China had quietly backed from the room, but not before she caught a glimpse of the woman's gratified smile at her boss's words.

Yes, Yance was counting the hours and using them wisely. And China vowed to do everything in her power to help him in any way she could.

Early Saturday morning, China and Mabel packed an enormous picnic lunch to go with the cooking supplies sitting out on the table. Trace and his father had both endorsed her suggestion that they spend the weekend on horseback riding over some of the extensive C3 property and exploring a few of Yance's favorite spots.

Trace met the suggestion with an enthusiastic "Yahoo!" but Yance had merely gazed at China for a long moment before saying quietly, "I think that's a terrific idea."

China basked for hours in the memory of the slow, knowing smile that followed his words.

After handing over the lunch and supplies to Yance so he could pack them on the horses, she went to pull a sweater on over her T-shirt before heading for the porch to see them off. They would take the truck as far as possible before switching over to horses; the pickup with a horse trailer behind it was parked in front of the house.

It was a beautiful fall morning, cool and crisp. But the day promised an equally pleasant warmth later. In the way of mountain days at this time of year, it might even turn out hot later.

The two were standing on the porch. "Ready?" Trace asked, heading down the steps. Yance followed.

China fought the urge to tell them both to wait so she could kiss them goodbye. Get real, she said to herself. "Have fun," she called brightly.

Trace stopped in his tracks. So did Yance. Both turned to stare back at her.

"What do you mean, 'have fun'?" Yance asked in his quiet, low-key, but definitely boardroom voice.

"Chiiii-naaaa!" Trace said incredulously.

She stared at them. "But I didn't plan on going," she said. "This weekend is for the two of you." She laughed. "The little squaw just packed food for the big strong warriors. Don't plan on her making a habit of it, however. This is a one-time-only thing."

"But it won't be no fun if you don't come," Trace said plaintively.

"Of course it will. Your dad knows the ranch like the back of his hand," China said, full of adult reason. "You just think you know all the good spots, Trace. But your dad knows places you've never dreamed of. He told me so. Isn't that right, Yance?"

"That's right," Yance said agreeably. "And I want to show them to you, too, China Dare."

From the set line of his jaw, China knew he wasn't going to budge without her, though why he should throw this clanger in the works was a puzzle. Hadn't he realized she'd planned this so he could spend some time alone with Trace?

But by now she'd counted the horses in the trailer. Besides the packhorse, there were three wearing saddles with sleeping bags tied behind. Yance had always planned on her going. It was an intoxicating thought.

"This is the C3," Yance said quietly, reading her mind

in that way of his. "I want three. Trace and I will share our sandwiches with you if you didn't pack enough," he added, and winked at his son, who winked back at him, both of them wearing identical smug expressions of males who knew they were going to get their own way.

And China couldn't help but give in to them, in spite of feeling this trip should be for father and son alone. "There's enough food on that packhorse," she said, "to feed a small army. Wait while I get my hat and put on my boots."

They drove until they ran out of ranch road and even a ways beyond, before stopping the truck and backing the horses out of the trailer. By this time China had shed her sweater, and Yance and Trace their jackets, as the morning lost its chill and the October sun had a field day without a cloud in the sky to impede its exuberance.

"We need rain," Trace said, echoing a thousand Western men over a good century and a half.

Yance grunted assent. They did, indeed, need rain. But not today, he thought.

Today he wanted to show Trace the spring, high on Wishbone Mountain, that was origin of Madrone Creek whose waters were the original lifeblood of the ranch. It had never run dry, he wanted the boy to know, though it had shrunk to a mighty slim trickle a couple of times.

Today he wanted to show Trace the Indian rock paintings near the creek and hidden in a nest of boulders forming a crude shelter; the same pictographs that his father had shown him when he was a couple of years younger than Trace.

Today, Yance thought, he wanted his son and him to smell of horse together, to smell of leather and sweat and wood smoke together; to be together like men of the land.

And today, at some just-right time and in a just-right place, he wanted to kiss China Dare again.

So please, no rain today, he thought.

They rode silently and carefully through cactus and cat-claw, Mormon tea bushes and cholla, and miniature forests of lechugilla and century plants, living and skeletal. The trail rose with the land, sending them past scrub juniper and on around juniper that took itself more seriously, into the thicker welcome shade of madrone and oak and pine.

Yance breathed the strong clean scent of the pine deep into his lungs, tasting it, savoring it as another man might a good cigar.

About halfway up the mountain, they met the creek. After that, with the three of them going up and it coming down, the music of its descent blended with the sound of the horses' hooves on the rocky trail, the rustle of the wind in the branches overhead and the birdsong piped on occasion to let them know they were not the only creatures stirring.

At one point Yance led them away from the creek and off the trail a ways to a place where they could dismount and tie the horses.

"Is this where we eat, Dad?" Trace asked, swinging his elbows and stretching his back to get the kinks out.

"Partner," Yance replied with fatherly patience, "you ate a breakfast that would do credit to a stevedore not three hours ago."

"Three hours! A kid can starve to death in three hours," Trace exclaimed as if his father had lost his mind.

Without a word, China put an apple into the boy's hand, handed one to Yance and bit into one herself. Riding was hungry work.

"I knew there was a reason we needed you to come, Mom," Trace said around a mouthful. "You understand a guy."

China just looked at him and raised an eyebrow.

"This isn't a lunch break," Yance told them, halfway into his own apple. In spite of his sore body and vague feeling of tiredness, he was enjoying this trip. "I want to show you something." And he led the way through the trees until he came to a clear spot.

Before them was nothing but sky.

"Oh," China said, and walked forward to stand at the edge of a sheer drop and look far out over an earth made of sky and distance and vast reaches of land.

"Wow," Trace said on a long breath of awe.

But Yance said nothing at all. He gazed over the vista that was Chisolm property as far as one could see, but felt no pride of ownership, only a deep appreciation that the Great Power had allowed him stewardship of it for a while.

Thank you, he wanted to say. And did, in his heart.

"Wow," Trace said again. "Look, Dad. Those tiny brown dots are the ranch buildings. And see, there's the creek looking like a piece of yarn from here. And that line over there must be the highway. Wow, Dad. Cool."

"Cool," Yance echoed softly, and placed a hand on Trace's shoulder to survey the vista with the same awe-struck wonder as his son.

China stood beside them but slightly apart as she, too, gazed at the view, the wind teasing her braid and pulling a few strands loose around her face.

But she no longer saw the land and sky before her. Her eyes had tuned out so that her ears could better tune into the boy and man standing so close to her, as if the least sound of their breathing was the most important thing on earth.

And it was, she thought. Because if either of them stopped breathing, a part of China would die, too, and forever.

She was in love with Yance Chisolm, had been from the moment he thought she was a horse.

Two weeks gone. Six days to go.

Chapter Five

They ate their lunch beside the spring, each sitting on a boulder munching a thick sandwich while watching the water bubble forth in joyous release from the heart of the mountain. It flowed into a small pool, which Yance's grandfather had created by removing a few rocks and strategically repositioning others, before it was allowed to meander on down the mountain and out onto the flats, bringing life to the desert lands it found there.

Eventually it flowed on out of the county, Yance told his son, and ceased to be when it emptied into the Pecos River, which emptied into the Rio Grande, which emptied into the Gulf of Mexico, which emptied into the Atlantic Ocean.

"So if I put this soda can in the water up here it will sooner or later bump into an ocean liner. Cool," Trace commented, following this geography minilesson.

"You put that soda can in the water up here," Yance

replied, "and you're dead meat. Pack it in, pack it out, Trace."

Trace looked at his father and gusted out a heavy sigh before shaking his head. "Aw, Dad, you're almost as easy to tease as China," he said. "I know, I know. You and Grandpa drilled that into me at birth. 'The earth is our home,'" he quoted in long-suffering singsong. "'No creature in its right mind pollutes its own nest.'"

Yance grinned back at the boy mockingly, but China saw the veiled pride in his eyes. "Just testing," he said.

His son groaned and tossed the empty soda can under discussion at him, Yance deftly catching it to place it with his own in the nearby plastic bag.

"Why is this mountain called Wishbone?" Trace asked, starting in on a banana. "It's not shaped like a wishbone. It's just a plain ol' mountain."

"That's the same question I asked my granddad," Yance replied. "He didn't know, either. Somebody finding the wishbone in their picnic lunch a long time ago, maybe. Who knows?" He left his seat on the boulder to sit on the ground in front of it and use its hard surface as a backrest.

China, sitting on her own rocky throne with her legs folded in front of her Indian-style, watched him tip his hat over his eyes and get comfortable. A plant stem protruded from one side of his mouth. In moments, the long casual grace of the man was lined out in the sketchbook in her lap.

"Names are funny things," Trace commented ruminatively. "Like my name, Trace. It's really supposed to be *tres,* Spanish for three," he told China seriously, "but everyone pronounces it like its English. I'm Steven Yance Chisolm III. Three, get it?"

"Interesting," China said, and Trace found his way into her sketchbook, as he sat holding his knees on a flat stone slab looking like a cowboy monkey with his hat pushed to the back of his head and a half-eaten banana in one hand.

"Where'd you get your name, China?"

The pencil stopped so China could lift her head and grin. "From a ship," she said. "My real dad was a merchant marine, but he was killed in a car accident not long after my mother found out she was expecting. Blackjack said there was a print of a clipper ship...you know, the kind with the tall white sails," she explained to Trace, "hanging on the wall of their apartment. The ship's name was *China Dare*. He named me, Blackjack said, to honor my father."

"And do you feel a kinship with the sea?" Yance asked her.

"Sometimes. But perhaps its just the sky. There's so much sky over water, but there's a lot of sky out here, as well. I miss it in the city. Things always feel not quite right when the sky is narrow somehow. But," she added slowly, "sometimes I miss the city, too."

"I know what you mean," Yance said.

"Me, too," Trace piped in. "I could play baseball when I spent summers with Dad in Midland. I *like* living on the ranch an' all, especially now that Dad's here. School's better here, too, an' I get along with all the kids. In Midland after Grandpa died, school really su—uh, wasn't all that great, but there's lots to do in the city for summers. Malls and movies and stuff like that."

The age old "grass is greener," Yance thought. How many city kids would love to spend their summers on a ranch? But he understood exactly what the boy was saying, just as he'd understood China. The three of them wanted it all.

The three of them.

After all these years, the words had a nice ring.

He showed Trace the pictographs, faded stylized paintings of elongated men and unidentifiable animals fleeing before a hail of arrows. The drawings covered the ceiling of a shallow overhang protected for centuries from the weather. Soot from ancient fires partly obscured painted figures even older. There were also a dozen or so faded red handprints among the objects depicted there, some of them child-sized.

Trace breathed his favorite tribute, ''Wow,'' and was about to lay his hand on top of one of the prints when his father stopped him.

''The oil from your skin causes them to deteriorate,'' Yance told him. ''Do you see the black prints over there in the far corner?''

At his son's nod, he went on. ''One of those is mine, the smallest one. I was about eight, I think. Your grand-dad's print is there, too, and your grandmother's, and there's one of my grandfather's and grandmother's that were put there before I was born.''

''Cool. Can I put my hand there, too? It's a family thing, right?''

''Right. Tomorrow before we leave, we'll use the wet ashes from the fire and you can place your autograph up there with the rest.''

''Cool,'' Trace repeated. ''Do you think the Indians who painted these pictures had a family thing, too, Dad?''

''Maybe. But those arrows have a pretty businesslike look to them,'' Yance commented from his kneeling position, gazing at the paintings where they flowed from the ceiling onto a portion of the upper wall. ''Perhaps they were just depicting the hunt, and the smaller handprints were of the boys who were along on the hunt learning the way of things.''

''I think they were families,'' China said softly. ''The prints are a way of saying thank-you. The spring is here, you see, and it must have seemed magical, bubbling up in just this place. It *is* magical. This was a holy place and the people hoped to transfer some of the magic to the hunt to feed their families in the same way the spring gave them water.''

She stopped, becoming aware of the two staring at her in amazement.

''I like that,'' Yance said quietly.

''Did you ever find any arrowheads around here, Dad?''

''I've found a couple. There's a nest of piled rocks over a ways that I think the Indians might have used as a surround. I'll show you.''

As the two wandered farther into the trees, China made her way back to the campsite at the spring. All those Chisolm handprints had shaken her badly.

She didn't think about her inability to have children very often. It was painful, yes, but it was a fact of life she'd lived with since she was thirteen. Yet on rare occasions, like now, it was brought home to her that she was the last of both her mother's and her father's line. If her family wall had a gallery of handprints there would be no small prints following hers.

Though Yance might not come out of the operation facing him, and that was a thought that made China's blood run cold, there was a part of him that would yet live on in Trace and in Trace's children.

Just as Melodie lived on in Trace's sunny disposition, and in the dusting of freckles that lay across the boy's nose. Melodie had not lived long enough to place her print on the overhang ceiling, but when Trace placed his there tomorrow, his mother's would be in its shadow.

Did Blackjack ever feel the lack of a blood child of his own? China wondered. She knew her stepfather loved her deeply, but why had he and her mother never had other children? Neither he nor her mother had said, and China never asked. Nor would she. There was a story between Blackjack and her mother that she knew the old man would take to his grave.

But in the same way Blackjack had China to love, she

had Trace. Yance had given her his child; if not in the womb, then in a Prenuptial Agreement. And Trace, as she'd told the boy's father, was an easy child to love. She loved him as her own already. If tomorrow by some bit of magic, she herself gave birth to a child, she didn't think she could love that birth child more.

For long moments China allowed herself to daydream about having Yance Chisolm's child, a child conceived in her womb and carried for nine months next to her heart; a child whose birth would be heralded by a proud papa and a delighted older brother.

She laughed ruefully to herself.

Now wouldn't that just play *hell* with the Prenuptial Agreement? There wasn't a single clause in the damn thing to cover it!

Trace and China found out that evening that Yance Chisolm was a first-rate camp cook. A rich stew chock-full of vegetables and tender ranch beef bubbled in an iron pot over the fire, and when the ashes were removed from the top of the dutch oven, he opened it to reveal a wheel of golden biscuits.

"Yance," China said at last, with an empty tin bowl in front of her following her second helping of stew, "you are a master. This is…was…delicious. But I'll never be hungry again."

"I will," Trace said. "That was good, Dad, but is anything else hidden in the fire for dessert?"

"Have an apple," Yance replied, and tossed one to the boy. "And except for fruit, tonight's feast used the last of the fresh stuff. An ice chest small enough for ol' Becky to pack doesn't hold much, so tomorrow morning it's powdered egg burritos."

"As long as you're cooking," China said with a sigh. "I don't suppose you have any instant coffee in your pack somewhere?"

"What a city slicker you are, China Dare. Of course I don't have any instant coffee. Does this look like civilization to you? What I have, darlin', is real coffee. Some," he added deadpan, "might even call it...Colombian."

China sat back with a sigh and fanned the area above her breast. "Be still my heart."

"But there's a catch," Yance said. When she met his gaze, and by this time Trace was gazing at him expectantly too, he added gently, "The cook doesn't clean."

"I don't drink coffee, Dad," Trace said, blithely smug.

"And you don't eat breakfast, either," his father replied.

Trace accepted the inevitable. "Gotcha."

It didn't take him and China long to have things shipshape again. While the coffee brewed, Yance saw to the horses and made sure they were securely picketed for the night. By the time all of them were finished with their chores, the first stars were out, the coffee sending an aroma to die for and the water boiling for Trace's hot chocolate.

Yance poured coffee for himself and China into two tin cups and made up a cup of cocoa for his son. He then took a seat next to China on the log rolled next to the fire for that purpose. Trace sat on a rock nearby.

Yance's seating was strategically planned. Sitting next to China, unless he turned his head, he couldn't see the firelight playing in her hair or flickering over the strong lines of her face. And sitting next to her, he could see his son's features very well, as the fire's illumination alternately shadowed and brightened the young face that sometimes reminded him of Melodie's and sometimes of his own before life had drawn in lines of experience.

"Trace," he said, "Thursday I'm going into the hospital for an operation."

Beside him, he felt China grow still. Trace's cup halted just short of his mouth.

God, Yance thought. He hoped he was doing this right.

He didn't want the telling to be melodramatic. Would another setting have been better?

"Why?" his son asked, as he'd known the boy would.

"I chipped a piece off my skull in that plane accident," Yance said quietly, telling the thing in the simplest way he knew, "and the doc wants it out of harm's way."

"*Head* surgery? But that's dangerous, Dad. Even I know that."

"Maybe, maybe not, partner. The doc's good. I'm strong. The piece of bone is small. Come Saturday I could be right as rain again."

"Is that what the doc says?" Trace asked bluntly.

Yance made his reply matter-of-fact. "He says he won't really know anything until it's all over."

"That's why we made this trip today, isn't it?" Trace said accusingly. "I'm PO'd, Dad, really PO'd that you didn't tell me before now."

"So you could do what, son? Worry? If I thought it would do any good I would have told you before now. I guess I really didn't know when to tell you. On this trip, and out here under the stars seemed as good a time as any. I'm...sorry if I didn't handle it the way I should have."

"Did China know?"

"She had to know, partner."

The boy's accusing gaze swung to confront China. "And you didn't tell me, either?"

"It wasn't my place," China said quietly.

But it was easier for Trace to be mad at China than to be mad at his father. "Well you shoulda," the boy said fiercely. "You shoulda."

"No," Yance said, his tone going into boardroom mode, "she shouldn't. It's my business, not hers. You're my son, not hers. It was my place and I told you as I saw fit."

"But, Dad," Trace began, not willing yet to give up his anger. Then he hung his head. "I'm just surprised, I guess. And scared, maybe."

"The doc says don't be scared until Saturday morning," Yance said reasonably. "I, for one, am taking his advice. And I brought you and China up here because it may be a while before I'm up to it again. Make sense?"

Trace looked into his father's quiet face for a long moment. "Yeah," he said slowly, "I guess it does."

The boy stood, and using some of the still-hot water rinsed out his cup and hung it on the branch stuck in the ground near the fire for that purpose. "I'm tired, Dad. Think I'll go on to bed."

But before he spread out his sleeping bag, Trace went to his father who had risen with him and hugged Yance hard for a long moment. "I love you, Dad," he said.

Yance wanted to bend over his son and protect him bodily from all the hurts and blows yet to come in his young life, for no life ever really escaped them. But he couldn't protect his son in this with anything but the woman who sat before his fire with tears running over her face.

Would it be enough?

"I love you, too, son," he said.

After leaving Trace in his sleeping bag, Yance was grateful to find when he returned to the crackling, sweet-smelling fire, that China had somehow cleaned up her face. He'd had all the emotion he could stand tonight, he thought. In all his sometimes extremely sticky business dealings he'd never pulled off a more difficult confrontation than that which he'd just had with his son.

He felt "wrung out and pegged on the line to dry," as Blackjack would say.

"You certainly know how to ruin a good cup of coffee," China said lightly as Yance folded himself onto the log beside her. She knew exactly why Trace had opted for his sleeping bag. She'd like to crawl into a dark place and huddle for a while herself.

"Don't I just."

"Do you think he's all right?" she asked keeping her tone noncommittal, and watched as Yance threw out his cold coffee and reached to pour himself another from the pot warming on a stone in the fire ring. With the pot still in his hand he sent her a questioning look and she too tossed the coffee in her cup and held the empty vessel out for a refill.

Aware that his son's bedroll was positioned just out of the fire's light, Yance knew Trace was probably listening to every word. "I think so," he replied. "He's tough."

"So are you," China said quietly, also aware of the listening boy.

"Us Chisolms are a mighty tough breed all right," Yance drawled, deliberately slowing the words to a rich John Wayne Western cadence, and China echoed his chuckle.

"Who like their coffee Colombian," she added teasingly, "their beer from Mexico and their shirts made in England."

He laughed softly in acknowledgment, before turning and bending his head to place his face close to her own.

"So we do," he drawled in a low silky whisper, "but us Chisolms like our women all-American."

China's heart stopped as the warm breath carrying the teasing words brushed against her ear. She should have a witty comeback for this, she thought; she couldn't think of a thing to say.

She wanted to lean away from the face so close to her cheek. She wanted more to lean right into it and turn her face just so....

And found that she had.

And that his lips were there to meet her.

She held her tin coffee cup in both her hands. He held his in one and used the other palm to cup the side of her face.

Yet they sat bound as surely as if locked with chains by the soft bonding of their lips.

Until slowly, reluctantly their mouths parted for each to exhale a long shuddering sigh.

"Trace," Yance finally said in a whisper from the depth of his gut.

"Trace," China echoed softly on the last of a shallow breath.

But even so their mouths met for one last pairing, in tender farewell to what might have been, in another place, at another time. In it was not a promise of things to come, but an acknowledgment of what was now, which was wonderful.

Which at this time was complete.

Which was over.

They drew apart slowly and each turned to face the fire, yet they remained for a moment leaning shoulder to shoulder, as if each would hold the other up.

Finally Yance reached forward and tossed the cold coffee in his cup into the fire where the flames hissed and snapped in angry protest. This time he did not pour himself another but stood to rinse his cup in the warm water left there and hang it on the branch with Trace's.

Without speaking, China did the same.

Then Yance used the remaining coffee and water to douse the flames, leaving only the center coals glowing softly. With nothing to feed on, ringed by stones and with the immediate perimeters cleared of vegetation, there was no danger of a runaway fire, a West Texas rancher's nightmare.

From her sleeping bag, China watched Yance do these things, his economy of movement showing how familiar he was with the task. She had no trouble envisioning the man in the frontier world of a hundred years ago...but knew that all she really wanted was to have him in her world tomorrow.

She closed her eyes to touch her mouth with the tips of her fingers, and holding them there, drifted into sleep.

Yet still aware that Trace had not spoken to her again or told her good-night.

And still aware that Yance had reminded the boy in no uncertain terms that China was not his mother.

In the morning the boy was subdued through his breakfast, not given to his usual teasing chatter, but he laughed at his father's dry admonishments and helped return the camp to its natural state. When they finished, the only sign remaining that they'd camped in this spot was the fire ring, left for the next time a Chisolm visited the spring, that was built by some past Chisolm and had been there as long as Yance could remember.

Before they left the site, Trace gooed his hand in the wet cold ashes of their fire, and he and his father went to the ancient overhang so the youngest Chisolm could also leave his print.

China stayed behind, busy, she said, sketching a family of jays who were arguing and fighting with each other in a nearby pine in the way of many human families, however close-knit. But when Yance and Trace disappeared from view, she put down her charcoal pencil and sat there doing nothing at all. Thinking nothing at all.

But feeling lonelier than she ever had in her life.

Life slipped back to its usual routine on Monday, so that in the race to get outdoor chores done, eat his breakfast and grab up his books, Trace lost some of the wary look he'd worn since his father told him of the upcoming operation. Things surely must not be as bad as he thought, he reasoned, or his normal routine would have changed in some way.

But as he pelted toward the door to hop into the waiting

truck so Yance could take him to the bus just as usual, China stopped him.

"You forgot to make your bed," she said.

He hadn't forgotten. Trace looked at her, wanting to defy this woman who had received his dad's confidence first and thus made Trace feel for the first time in his life as if he were taking second place. There was also the fact that he was scared, and he'd rather be mad than scared.

Yet open defiance just wasn't quite in him, and though he resented it, he returned to his room to throw his bed into some kind of order before dashing out the door again.

China held out his lunch bag and he grabbed it on the fly, but he deliberately didn't thank her for it. Why should he thank *her?* Mabel had made the lunch, just as she had since Trace started kindergarten. As far as he could see, China had no function on the ranch whatsoever. All she did was draw, and anybody could do that.

In the truck he had his father to himself, and they talked as they always did as Yance drove him to the highway. So far today, everything was just as it always was. Trace watched the yellow school bus approach with satisfaction. It was his week for cleaning the classroom fish tank. Cool.

But before he left the truck, he kissed his father on the cheek in farewell for the first time since he started third grade.

Sometimes a guy just had to do it.

China watched Trace hop into the waiting pickup with a small rueful smile. The honeymoon with Trace was obviously over. This morning was the first time he hadn't made his bed since she'd told him the chore was now his. She had no doubt at all the omission was deliberate. It had been written all over the boy's expressive face.

Trace had hardly spoken to her since they'd left the spring on Wishbone Mountain; actually since Yance had told him about his scheduled surgery. She had the feeling

Trace thought his father's surgery was all China's fault in some obscure way. Children found various ways of dealing with fear, not all of them making sense. Being angry with China was probably how Trace was handling his.

Even so, it hurt a little.

It hurt a lot.

Not once over the next few days did Trace make his bed without being reminded to do so, and each time China reminded him he threw her a look of belligerent dislike. The bed was made, but daily with less care until it was hard to distinguish that it had been made at all.

On Thursday morning, China didn't so much as glance into the boy's room. She rode with Yance in the Lexus to take him to the bus that morning, but sat in the back so the boy could sit in front with his father.

Trace was subdued to the point of not opening his mouth the whole eight miles to the highway.

"Nothing happens today, partner," Yance finally said. "They'll just put me in a nightgown without a back to it and stick me in a bed so I can watch soap operas flat on my back. I suppose I'll have to pee into a jar a couple of times so someone can look at it under a microscope, but that's about it."

The boy giggled. When the bus lumbered into view he gave his father a huge bear hug, but all he said was, "Better not bend over, Dad. See ya tomorrow."

"Right," Yance replied, hugging his son back just as hard. He stayed parked by the side of the highway until the bus carrying his son to school was out of sight, then, with China now beside him, pointed the car in the opposite direction and headed toward Midland.

Under Yance's careful planning, Trace would remain on the ranch with Blackjack, who would bring him to the city on Friday afternoon after school and after Yance was out of surgery. Should there be any complication, Blackjack would check Trace out of school and bring him to the hospital at once. Trace had only to remember that no un-expected news was good news.

While Yance was in the hospital, China would stay at the family apartment in Midland, and Blackjack and Trace would join her there over the weekend. Everything was organized for her, down to the phone number of his Midland housekeeper.

When Yance and China arrived in the city, Yance took her to the Chisolm apartment to show her where it was, where to park and what elevator to take. They stayed only long enough for China to take a quick look around and leave her bag inside the door. By then it was time for Yance to meet his doctor at the hospital and check in.

China remained with Yance at the hospital that after-noon, and they did indeed watch a little daytime television and talk sporadically of nothing much. Yance had several tests involving more than just urinating into a small vial and was frequently wheeled in and out of the room until he was clearly exhausted.

Between Yance's detailed planning and the hospital's smooth efficiency, the day had gone like clockwork, and China found she didn't like it a bit.

For one thing, she shared some of Trace's unfounded resentment. This was Thursday, after all, and she felt robbed of a day. Somehow, she'd thought Yance would go into the hospital on Friday, the day scheduled for his operation. It had come as a small shock when at the spring he'd told Trace otherwise.

And she also found herself wishing superstitiously that something in Yance's careful and seamless planning would develop a major hitch. Her artist's instinct knew the situation screamed for contrasting drama, and she would rather that drama come from any place but the operating theater.

She got her wish. That evening, as she left the hospital for the apartment to spend the night, she was carefully backing Yance's Lexus out of its space in the hospital parking lot when a car rounded the corner one space beyond and ran into her back fender.

The elderly man driving the ten-year-old Chevy jumped out and shouted at her for being a woman driver who didn't look where she was backing out, and China, choked up and shaking with nerves, yelled back at him for not looking where he was driving.

Finally they both calmed down enough to exchange names and insurance companies, examine each other's vehicles and breathe a sigh of relief that the damage wasn't worse, each leaving the scene feeling righteously not to blame.

In addition, China felt much better.

Once at the apartment, located on the top floor of the Chisolm Bank building, she wandered around for a while getting a feel for Yance's city persona. The place was huge and sleek, with a decor relying on the clean lines of modern furniture and excellent but indirect lighting. A couple of paintings hung on the walls, done by still-living artists whose names were already the stuff of legend. Objets d'art were displayed discreetly on various tables.

Yet for all its reflection of wealth, the place was comfortable, China thought, and touchable, and probably easy to live in.

She peeped into Trace's room and found that it looked like him, but in a different way than did his room on the ranch.

And she peeped into the master bedroom, an inner sanctum of black silk duvet and gleaming chrome bed frame and, China thought with a soft smile, the three-dimensional embodiment of Yance's boardroom voice.

As she walked farther into the room, the possibility of spending the night in Yance's bed crossed her mind. He'd never know and it would bring him somehow closer to her.

But as she approached the bed to sit on it for a moment and try it out for size, she saw the framed photograph on the nightstand.

Picking up the photograph was merely a token gesture to strengthen her immediate reality check, because she'd recognized it at once. It was the same one the couple sent to the papers announcing their engagement. At the time, China was still in art school in New York, but her mother clipped the announcement and mailed it to her.

Then, as now, she thought it a good likeness of Melodie, who'd been born beautiful and laughing and with a personality to match, whom the photographer had captured very well. Yance looked handsome and happy and just a tad smug, as well he should.

Replacing the photograph where she'd found it, China left the room to find a guest bedroom, choosing one at random. It looked comfortable. In shades of blue and green, it was restful and attractive. It reflected the personality of no one she knew.

When the alarm went off early the next morning, China was already half dressed. She arrived at the hospital to find Yance awake but slowly sinking into the oblivion administered to him moments before her arrival.

He grinned muzzily at her as she came through the door, and to her surprise, held out his hand. Since the episode at the spring, he'd avoided touching her.

Walking forward, she took the brown sinewy hand in her own, but didn't find the vibrancy in it that was so much a part of the man's personality. Her heart began a slow chug.

"Mornin'," he said. "Did you find everything all right? Did you call Lilly?"

"I found everything just fine," China assured him. "It's a beautiful apartment, Yance." She didn't tell him that she'd deliberately not called in the housekeeper.

"I've always liked it," he said, the words rolling around his mouth a little. His lashes fanned slowly down to rise again as slowly.

China wanted to kiss them as she'd done beside the spring. She knew exactly how the soft spikes of this man's lashes felt against her lips.

"China," Yance said, gazing dreamily into her face, "did I ever tell you how grateful I am for what you're doing?"

She smiled. "I know. And no matter what happens, Yance, everything's going to work out as you planned it. I promise," she said, in much the same tone he'd used to make promises to his son.

"I know," he said. His lashes closed, rising again only to half-mast.

Before he drifted away from her, there was something China wanted to know. "Yance," she said, bending forward a little to hold his quiet heavy eyes with her own. "Why me? Why not some other woman?"

He smiled slowly at her then, a hint of mockery entering the sleepy gray gaze as he summoned up enough energy to lightly squeeze her hand. "Because Blackjack was as close to my father as I could get," he said with the brutal honesty the question demanded, "and you were his daughter."

His eyes were already closing, not to open again until after what was to come was over, and the tail of the sentence came from his lips in a long sigh.

Yet just before the hand in hers went completely slack, he added in a slurred mumble, "Because...you know... cloud...pic...shuurs..."

China bent and kissed Yance's closed lashes and rested her icy cheek against the warm side of his face. Within moments he was wheeled from the room, and she left to trail behind as far as they let her go.

The next hours were spent in a waiting room, where she

drank endless cups of coffee, not Colombian, from a hot plate where it was kept fresh by a candy striper, and paged through this month's magazines covering every interest from sports to politics. This was, after all, a very up-to-date hospital.

There were others in the waiting room, as well, some sitting as quietly as she, and like herself, keeping one eye on the door, watching for anyone who might know something to bring them news. Others talked among themselves, a few laughing as though their world didn't hang by a bone fragment floating in a place where it had no business being.

For six hours China waited, until finally the doctor she'd spoken with briefly yesterday came to find her, looking tired, but also looking triumphant. Before he even approached her, he sent her a thumbs-up sign.

"Got it," he said. "Had to chase it around a bit, but we got it. Yance came through everything just fine. But..." he said.

From that one word to the next, time slowed almost to a standstill. An eon passed in the time it took to blink.

"But," he said, "we won't know until he wakes up and takes a few tests if chasing the thing left any kind of trail in his brain. We're hopeful it didn't. We're actually pretty sure everything's fine. But we can't be one hundred percent certain until he wakes up and proves it."

Just what the heck was that supposed to mean? China wondered.

"Whatever," the doctor continued, "I promise you it is no longer a life-and-death situation nor do you have any need to worry that he'll be a living vegetable. In my opinion," and he grinned, taking a decade off his middle-aged face so that China realized he was, after all, a fairly young man, "Yance Chisolm is someone who can handle anything yet to come—and with one hand tied behind his back, brain trails or no."

He chuckled at his own witticism, and China laughed

with him with far more vigor than the joke was worth, wiping her cheeks repeatedly as she did so.

When the doctor left, she used the waiting room phone to call Blackjack, who was just leaving to pick Trace up from school. He promised to relay the good news to the boy at once, saying the two of them would be at the hospital in a couple of hours.

As soon as they allowed it, China went to sit in the Intensive Care Unit with Yance, the white bandage around his head throwing the strong lines of his face into prominence. Though he lay quiet and still, his vital signs made blips and bleeps on various pieces of equipment and drew jagged lines or straight ones on others.

When Trace and Blackjack arrived, China went into Blackjack's old arms and cried, just the way she'd been doing all her life; and Trace, forgetting for the moment that he was mad at her, came into China's arms and did the same.

Then the boy went in to see his father for the five minutes allotted to him but came out of the room looking more frightened than when he'd entered.

"He's still under the anesthetic," China told him, "but he'll be awake in the morning. Tomorrow is Saturday, remember, and your dad will tell you himself that the scary part didn't happen."

Trace stuck up his chin. "Us Chisolms are a mighty tough breed," he drawled with a touch of pride.

"Dang right ya are," Blackjack said, and placed a hand on Trace's shoulder. "Where's a good place to get a hamburger, boy? I'm hongry," he said, turning the situation into as much normalcy as could be found in it. First Things First was Blackjack's motto, which had a way of easing drama and sending tension flying out the window.

"You comin' with us, China?" the old man tacked on. "Might as well, you know. No sense just watchin' the man sleep with your stomach growlin'."

And before she knew it, China was hustled out of the hospital to put in her stomach the only food it had had in it all day.

When she returned, leaving Blackjack and Trace to go on to the apartment, she sat and watched Yance sleep, her stomach remaining nicely quiet, until she was thrown out for the night.

The bone "left no trail," as the doctor put it, and within two weeks Yance was back on the C3.

He had life in front of him. It was glorious.

He still possessed his full mental faculties. When it came to him while he was in the hospital that Southeast Asia might be ready for a branch of the Chisolm Bank, he knew he could still do long-range planning. And when he met a young man on the patient sunporch who had an interesting concept for a car run on electromagnetism, he had no trouble at all following the math and science involved in the telling. The kid, he thought, just might have something.

And he had his full physical faculties, with every limb, organ and muscle working just as it should. In the coming year, he would take his place in the spring gather just as a Chisolm should.

Most important, he had a new wife. She'd dented the back fender of his Lexus, but what the hell. When he asked her about it, she laughed, then burst into tears, as if denting the damned fender amounted to a hill of beans.

Fascinating woman, his new wife.

The fact remained, however, that therein lay the dandelion in his otherwise weedless lawn.

He had a new wife, but he didn't know what the hell he was going to do with her.

Chapter Six

Though Yance was unaware of it, China didn't know what to do about him, either.

Events had left her reeling. The high drama of a life-and-death situation had literally come to an end within six hours. Poof! Things were back to normal.

But as with Alice or Dorothy, normal was something completely unfamiliar.

When she'd gone into this thing, China had to acknowledge, her thinking had never truly gone past the scheduled operation. The fear of his dying far outweighed wondering about her place in Yance Chisolm's life if he didn't. Or his place in hers, for that matter. Where before Yance's surgery she'd known exactly what she was doing, after the success of it she hadn't a clue.

She knew she loved him, but they hadn't married for love. Yance married her to secure Trace's inheritance, a security the boy no longer needed. And now Trace was saddled with a stepmother he clearly resented, for the antipathy that surfaced before Yance's surgery had since remained in all the boy's dealings with her.

And she married Yance to secure Blackjack a familiar place to live out his life, a security assured with the Prenuptial Agreement. Blackjack was far more comfortable on the Chisolm ranch than she. He worked at whatever chores came along that suited him; or not, if that suited him. The C3 might have been his home for years, so easily did he fit in.

So where did that leave her? China wondered.

She was a wife. Well, sort of.

She was a mother. Again, sort of.

Sighing, she rolled the top down on Trace's lunch bag. Fixing the boy's lunch was a chore she'd taken over from Mabel soon after Yance returned from the hospital.

Putting Trace's lunch together made her feel...motherly, she supposed, and she made sure the boy was always surprised by what he found in it. Sometimes it was a funny face drawn on his banana, or a purple cabbage leaf wrapped around his carrot sticks to make them into a surprise package, or a joke written out on a narrow three foot long strip of paper and rolled tightly so that it had to be unrolled to be read little by little.

Trace never mentioned his lunch findings to her, and she wondered if he even noticed.

Today the boy was dawdling even more than usual, and she heard Yance give a short impatient honk. When Trace went hurtling toward the door, snatching his lunch from her as he did so, she stopped him. "You haven't made your bed," she told him quietly.

He threw her the same look he might give a dead rat but returned to his room, yet within seconds Yance was at the boy's bedroom door. "C'mon, Trace. You're going to miss the bus."

"I have to make my bed," Trace said, glancing accusingly at China.

"You don't have time for that. Mabel will do it. Now get a move on." Yance turned away to head back to the still running truck.

Trace sent China a triumphant look as he quickly poked his arms through the sleeves of his jacket. Then he grabbed up his books and trotted after his father.

Knowing there was no time to make an issue of it now, China let him go. One for Trace, she thought ruefully, but promised herself to have a talk with Yance later. She wasn't sure Yance was even aware that Trace was supposed to make his bed now. The subject had never come up.

But the talk didn't happen as planned, mainly because China, immersed in a project with a looming deadline, forgot.

When Yance returned, she was on the back porch taking advantage of the light and putting the finishing touches on a small watercolor of a squirrel climbing up the old pecan tree.

Yance himself spent most of the day down at the pens. He'd bought a new bull that had to be thoroughly discussed with Jack Fergus, his ranch manager, and Chad Chadwick, Mabel's husband and the ranch foreman...and any other male in the near vicinity, he found, from the bull's former owner to the cowhands who unloaded it, to a couple of neighboring ranchers who'd heard of the purchase and wanted to get a look at it for future reference.

The men stood around for the better part of the morning, on through a bunkhouse lunch and quite a while after that, arguing the bull's merits, its considerable physical attributes and its equally considerable studly reputation.

It could be said that a lot of bull of every kind was a part of the general discussion, Yance thought with a touch of humor. At such gatherings, there was also an abundance of masculine laughter, lewd, crude and coarse and highly enjoyable to all concerned.

A city man might take those jokes home with him to share, he mused, but a Western man never did. Such humor was enjoyed only in the company of men, which made those gatherings special in a way that those with more urban tastes would never understand. It pointed to a certain amount of Western male chauvinism, he supposed, but most cowboys didn't give a damn.

Later that afternoon, Yance ambled back to the Big House, the sun beating at his back and a sharp north wind in his face in the way of the high desert with winter rapidly approaching.

God, life was good!

It was a familiar thought. If his brush with death did nothing else, it brought Yance a daily appreciation of life that bordered on awe. He knew now just exactly how much he'd been blessed and he thought he'd never take those blessings lightly again. At least he hoped not. It had been six weeks since his surgery, and he'd never felt better.

As he approached the house, he saw China sitting in the front porch swing with a cup and saucer in her hand. She was a woman who liked a cup of afternoon tea, he'd noticed; Earl Grey, not the herbal kind, and taken with cream and sugar, unlike her coffee, which she took black.

China Dare.

What was he going to do about this fascinating woman who'd become his wife in every sense but the most enjoyable one? He had only to look at the woman to want to haul her off to the bedroom.

So that her tea wouldn't spill, he lowered himself carefully into the swing beside her.

She smiled a greeting and moved over a bit to give him room. But as usual, her eyes were wary.

Her eyes had been wary a lot since his operation, Yance reflected. This woman whose warmth and generosity of spirit had seen him through the most trying time of his life now acted like he'd popped into her world when she wasn't looking. Around him, she seemed to hold herself aloof in an indefinable way. Had she perhaps hoped he would die?

It was a lowering thought.

When Yance awakened in the hospital following his surgery, he'd known almost at once that his mind still worked, and within a few short moments that his body still worked; and he'd known as well in those seconds that he wanted to make a real marriage with China Dare. She had more than proved her worth to him.

And he liked her; truly liked her.

For one thing, she wasn't boring. Everything about the woman fascinated him, from her penchant for drawing whatever crossed her path to the way she sang under her breath as she painted. Yet the fact remained that he hadn't heard her singing lately, and she and Trace didn't seem to play anymore.

A real marriage could make them all more comfortable, he thought now, watching his wife out of the corner of his eye. More normal.

The kiss they'd exchanged up at the spring had had a lot of promise in it, promise he'd been counting on now that he knew life was his again. But as he'd recognized before, pity could be a powerful aphrodisiac; and on China's part, apparently that's all it had been that night beside the campfire. There was also the indisputable fact that he'd originally promised China, if only by implication, to keep their relationship asexual in exchange for her remaining his wife in case Trace ever needed her.

He hadn't counted on needing her himself.

Yance put his arm along the back of the swing to give himself the illusion that China sat under it, and placed a boot on the porch railing. By making himself comfortable next to her, he knew he'd probably disturbed China's comfort.

The knowledge filled him with perverse satisfaction.

He'd like to place his lips on hers and his tongue in her mouth and make her more uncomfortable still. Sitting here on his chilly front porch, he'd like to make her not just bothered, but hot.

Gazing past his scraggly front lawn to the far mountains beyond, Yance picked out Wishbone Mountain, hiding its lushness by looking brown and withered in the distance. Damn.

"Would you like a cup of tea?" China asked. It was the only thing she could think of to say. The man's body next to hers was warm as breakfast toast and she'd like nothing better than to turn her cold face into his neck and warm herself at his fire.

He switched his attention from the mountains to look at her briefly, and what she saw in the gray gaze made her catch her breath. But she also saw a subtle withdrawal there before she dropped her lashes to take a swallow of cold tea dregs.

"No, thanks," Yance said politely. "I've been drinking bunkhouse coffee all day. One more drop of caffeine and I'll zing."

"Blackjack told me about the new bull," she said. "Is he all you expected?"

"And then some. We ought to have plenty of calves down the line."

And that exhausts that topic, China thought. Odd that they'd had no trouble talking before, and now every conversation had to be chiseled from stone. Thank goodness Blackjack had dinner with them in the evenings. The old man kept the conversational ball rolling during the only meal the whole family had together.

Whole family, hah! Two families, really, sitting down to eat together, but she was the only one who seemed to be the outsider.

"Well," she said brightly, and stood. "Think I'll go and, uh, take my cup to the kitchen."

When Yance courteously dropped his boot from the porch railing she felt obligated to pass in front of him instead of taking her original planned route behind the swing, When she did so, he touched her arm.

"China," he said seriously.

Reluctantly she brought her gaze to his, but raised her chin a little so he wouldn't know she'd been feeling sorry for herself.

He dropped his hand. "I just wondered," he said, "what's for supper?"

China regretted not talking to Yance about Trace keeping his room when again the next morning the boy went to sail past her leaving his bed looking like a tornado roared through it. The bed wasn't made the day before, either, so it'd had two days to get in the state it was in.

"Whoa, kiddo," China said, cutting him off at the pass.

"I don't have time," he said and walked on.

"Make time."

He stopped, caught between an overwhelming desire to ignore her and the respect for adults demanded of most ranch children and drilled into him since birth. "Dad'll be mad," he said sullenly.

"Then work fast," China countered.

"At you, not me," Trace flared. "You're the one making me late. Mabel's supposed to take care of my room."

China's voice was quiet. "Not anymore. If you don't do it, then it doesn't get done."

Wrong word choice.

"Then it'll just not get done," Trace said, triumph in his eyes.

"Yes, Trace Chisolm," China said, her gaze holding the boy's until his lashes fell, "it will."

Muttering under his breath, Trace returned to his room and flipped the bedspread up so that it covered the heap of sheets and blanket beneath it. Then he stomped toward the front door where his father waited for him in the truck. When China handed him his lunch he refused to take it.

"I don't want the stupid thing," he snarled and passed out the door, slamming it behind him.

Yance's head jerked when he heard the front door slam and he saw his son hurtling down the walk, every livid inch of him radiating anger as he approached the truck. When he climbed in, his face, too, was a mask of youthful rage.

"What's the problem, pard?" Yance asked quietly, putting the truck in gear.

Trace took a deep breath, aware that his father just might not see eye to eye with him in this. "China wouldn't give me my lunch," he said. And swallowed. He didn't think he'd ever lied to his dad before. But sometimes, he thought righteously, sometimes you just had to lie when the real truth didn't make sense but you knew you were right anyway.

"Why not?" Yance asked reasonably.

"She was mad at me because I didn't make my bed."

Yance stilled. That didn't sound like China.

"Doesn't Mabel make your bed?"

"Not anymore," Trace replied bitterly. "China won't let her. She says I have to do it now."

"Well, I make mine and I've not grown a second head yet," his father said with grin. "It's no big deal, Trace. Just make the bed."

Put that way, it didn't sound like much of a deal to Trace, either. In fact, he was beginning to feel a little silly. He didn't like the feeling. "She's on my case all the time, Dad. And I think it's mean not giving me my lunch."

Yance didn't say anything. He didn't want to side with the boy, but he thought the issue of the lunch was kind of mean, too. Trace put in a long school day, the bus ride into the small town of Fort Davis taking forty-five minutes each way. And the school offered no hot lunch program.

If Trace had no sack lunch it was a long, hungry time till supper, especially for a ten-year-old.

He fished in his pocket for some bills. "Go to the drugstore," he said, "and get yourself a hamburger." Unlike most metropolitan schools, this rural district didn't mandate a closed campus and the kids wandered all over town at noontime, all six blocks of main street. Yance had done it himself. "Tomorrow," he added, "make your bed."

Going to the drugstore was a treat for Trace. A lot of kids did it but he didn't get to very often. His eyes lit up. "Hey, thanks, Dad."

"No junk," his father said, but being a realist added, "or not much, anyway. And Trace."

The boy looked at him, delighted with the day, delighted with the outcome of his bout with China.

"What, Dad?"

"If you slam a door again in anger, slam anything at all for that matter, I'm gonna tan your hide, boy."

Trace's euphoria dissipated into thin air. His father meant exactly what he said. "Yes, sir."

China was in the kitchen fixing herself a piece of toast when Yance returned. She breakfasted erratically and didn't expect Mabel to prepare a morning meal for her as the woman did for Trace and Yance.

Yance went to pour himself a cup of coffee from the pot next to where she stood waiting for the toast to eject. "Trace will be making his bed from now on," he said. "I understand he's been falling down on the job."

"Well, it's become a battle," China replied with a sigh. "At first, he did it without being told, but then he started slacking off." She shrugged a little. "The new worn off, I suppose. It's all right that he keeps his own room, isn't it, Yance? I mean, everyone else does."

"Trace isn't a baby anymore," Yance agreed. "Probably he should have been doing it a long time ago, but no one thought of it.'' He glanced at the sack sitting on the counter. ''Is that his lunch?''

''Yes. I know he's going to be hungry, but when—''

''I gave him money to get something at the drugstore,'' Yance said tersely.

China removed her toast from the toaster and began spreading it with butter. ''Good,'' she said. ''I was worried about him.''

Without replying, Yance took his coffee and headed for his office while China sat down at the table to spread jelly on her toast. She was glad Yance made sure the boy would have lunch, of course, but another part of her wondered if Trace having to go hungry for one day might prevent the episode from happening again.

However, parenting wasn't her strong suit, as Frank had so often pointed out, and Yance had done an excellent job so far. And Yance would back her in seeing that Trace kept his own room.

But another niggling, rebellious part of China's mind wondered why the heck she should need his backing.

Yance turned on his computer monitor and stared at it until the screen-saver pattern came on. Arbitrating between China and Trace wasn't his idea of beginning a bright new day.

This should be between his son and China, he thought. But, hell, he couldn't have Trace going hungry. Should he talk to China about this? After all, for all she knew children's books, she didn't really know children. She'd said so in the beginning, and her first husband hadn't been too impressed, either.

But in the beginning, Yance had been impressed with things other than China's methods of discipline. He'd been impressed with her laughter and her love of life and her ability to play; things that he wanted for himself at that time, and things he wanted for his son. Still did.

The reality, however, was that one couldn't laugh all the time, or play all the time. Sometimes what was needed was a strong dose of common sense, and withholding lunch wasn't it.

Perhaps, though, he'd be better off to let things sit for a while and see what happened. Doing nothing was frequently the best way to handle an issue.

If this were a real marriage, he thought, he and China could discuss it in bed, in the dark, after they'd made love; that special window of time when the most difficult problems could be worked out in the languorous harmony brought about by physical satiation.

He pictured China lying in the moonlight, her honey colored hair spread over his pillow, lying in the crook of his arm with her cheek pressed against his heart, limp with his lovemaking. He imagined himself, also limp with his lovemaking, lying in that same moonlight with China cradled up next to him, his hand possibly caressing one of her ripe breasts. They would talk then, until idle finger play stirred banked coals into flame again; and then they would talk some more, but about a different subject and without words.

Whooshing out a breath, Yance made a mental grab at the thoughts tearing through his imagination. Dammit to hell.

Hitting a key at random, he got his screen back. Time to see what the stock market was doing.

In fifteen minutes, Yance knew all he needed to know. Then he aimlessly surfed the net for half an hour, not really interested, before leaving the PC to wander back into the kitchen for another cup of coffee.

Looking around for China, he didn't see her anywhere so plopped himself down on the couch in the den and flipped on the television. It came on in the middle of a talk show with a couple screaming at each other over who the father was. Swearing under his breath, he turned the thing off.

For the first time in his adult life, Yance didn't have anything to do. Before his surgery, he'd deliberately removed himself from the direct running of his various businesses. Nor was he sure even now that he wanted to pick up those reins again. He liked living on the ranch. It was his home. He wanted Trace raised here and he wanted to be a part of his son's life in a way that he hadn't felt the need to be while his own father was alive and looking after the boy during the school months.

But the ranch, too, could run itself in many ways. Before his death, Steve Chisolm had essentially retired, leaving Fergus, the manager, and Chad, the foreman, to make the day-to-day decisions, the men only consulting Yance or his father when unforeseen or unusual circumstances needed the owners' input.

The trouble with a well-oiled machine, Yance now thought ruefully, was it needed so damn little maintenance. He'd had the uncomfortable feeling lately that he just might be driving Jack Fergus crazy. After all, the man had been hired to do a job and, so far as Yance could determine, he was doing it and doing it well.

Still, as owner, Yance hadn't looked at the ranch books in a long while, so Jack shouldn't object to him going through them now. It was, after all, the prerogative of the boss.

When he entered Jack's office, the man stood and came around his desk to greet his boss pleasantly and with an outstretched hand. The man's face, however, stayed carefully expressionless, and Yance felt about as welcome as a bad cold. He stated his purpose and when Jack obligingly handed him the ledgers, then offered him his own chair behind the desk, he declined, saying he would take the books with him to his office in the Big House.

He could almost hear Jack's sigh of relief.

But after an hour and a half, Yance was back. "I don't see a damn thing wrong here," he said abruptly, placing the ledgers on Jack's desk. "You do meticulous work and a hell of a job, but keeping these up-to-date must take you quite a while." He glanced at the state-of-the-art computer sitting on Jack's desk. It was the man's own and not C3 property.

"Are you aware there are software programs that would cut your reporting time in half?" Yance asked quietly. "The C3 is more than willing to purchase them to make your work easier as well as get you an office PC to run them on, if you don't want to use your own."

Jack Fergus was twenty-eight years old with a Master's degree in range animal science from Texas A & M. He'd been hired by Yance two years ago for an expertise he was extremely well paid for but had seldom been given the chance to use. "I know about the software, Mr. Chisolm," he said.

When Yance looked at him questioningly, Jack added, "Mr. Chisolm—uh, Mr. Chisolm, Senior—wasn't familiar with the, er, programs." He cleared his throat. "When I mentioned putting some of the ranch statistics into a computer for ease of retrieval he, uh, said ledgers was the way it had always been done and he wasn't interested in changing it."

Yance could imagine what else his father had said. He looked Jack Fergus straight in the eye. "I'm interested. For what it's worth, my father didn't run the C3 the way his father did, either. I remember some of the arguments." He laughed a little. "Every generation knows a better way of doing things than the last one, and every generation thinks the one coming up behind it is too damn modern for its own good."

He pulled up a chair before Jack's desk and sat down.

"If you've got ideas, I'd like to hear them. Your degree is in agriculture. Mine's in business. Between us, we ought to be able to bring this ranch into the nineties. I don't want a cattle company, mind you. Guess I'm not that modern, either. Or that needy, since I have other financial interests. But no cowboy worth his salt likes paperwork. Let's see if we can get rid of some. Wouldn't hurt to build a file on each of the bulls, while we're at it.''

"I have files on them, but over there," Jack said dryly, nodding toward a set of metal drawers lining one wall.

Yance shook his head in commiseration, but was secretly relieved to find at least a few cogs in the ranch machine that still needed his oiling.

And by the time he left later that afternoon, Jack Fergus had finally stopped pussyfooting around and was calling him Yance. Which was a relief. Time enough for being called "Mister Chisolm" when he was an old man.

He grinned. Not a bad thought.

Trace now made his bed every morning. After all, it only took him twenty seconds. Flip the spread up and over everything underneath and he was through.

He also took his lunch. For one thing, opening the bag every day had become something of an event in the classroom. Kids gathered round to find out what was inside. Even the teacher came to look over his shoulder sometimes. Yesterday, for instance, there had been one of Mabel's cookies for every kid in the class.

Also, Trace knew his father well enough to know he wouldn't buy China denying him his lunch if he used that excuse too often.

Clothes left on his floor didn't get washed anymore. China said they had to go in the dirty clothes hamper, but Trace had better things to do with his time. The only thing was, he had a couple of favorite shirts that he liked to wear often.

Funny, how lying once made it so much easier to do again, Trace thought, as he sat on the bus thinking about the conversation he'd just had with his dad and feeling a little smug. Telling the literal truth without all the details, however, sat easier on his conscience.

When the two of them were halfway down the road on the way to the highway, his dad noticed Trace's shirt showing through the opening in his jacket and asked him why he wasn't wearing a clean one. It was the easiest thing in the world to say, "China won't let Mabel wash my clothes no more." It was a statement of exact truth.

His dad didn't say anything, and they didn't have time to turn around, but Trace could tell his father wasn't too thrilled with him going to school in a shirt with a jelly stain down the front of it.

But it wasn't *his* fault, Trace thought. His dad paid Mabel to wash dirty clothes period, not just those in the hamper. She'd never had any problem with it before China arrived. Why should China get to pick and choose what clothes Mabel washed?

He didn't mention that fact, of course, but he was sure his dad was getting the picture. China wasn't so wonderful.

Just as Trace thought, Yance was getting the picture, and he didn't like it.

China was in the extra bedroom that had become her storeroom, setting up a canvas when he came in. The morning sun poured through the room's one window and picked up the golden highlights in her braided hair. She was in a white, turtleneck, Aran fisherman's sweater and wore her Apache moccasins that covered the calves of her faded jeans almost to the knee. Turquoise earrings of Navajo design swung at her ears.

She looked, he thought briefly, like a lot of woman, but he didn't give himself time to dwell on it.

"Trace went to school in a dirty shirt today," he said.

China stilled. She recognized that tone. "I didn't notice his shirt," she replied, setting her hands to their task again.

"He usually changes when he comes in from the barn. When he left with you he had his jacket on."

"Does he have a clean shirt to put on?"

"A couple, but I imagine he's down to the ones he doesn't really like by now."

"Why?"

"Because most of his clothes are dirty," China answered quietly.

"Why?"

"I don't like your tone," she said. "Are we having a conversation, or is this an inquisition?"

"I'm trying to find out why the hell my son went to school in a dirty shirt," Yance said tightly.

"Then why don't you ask me in a tone that says you really want to know?" China shot back, "instead of using a tone that says you already know and don't like what you're knowing. Better yet, why didn't you ask Trace? I thought we agreed he would keep his own room from now on."

Yance paused and reminded himself yet again that China had never mothered a ten-year-old boy. "I did ask Trace," he said, trying to keep the brusqueness from his voice and sound merely reasonable. "China, are you seriously expecting him to wash his own clothes? I think he's probably a little young for that. He's only ten."

"If washing his own clothes is what it takes, yes," she replied stiffly. "I was washing mine at his age. At a washeteria, mind you. But perhaps kids without the Chisolm conglomerate behind them are taught to be more self-sufficient."

"You think Trace should be more self-sufficient? Is that what this is about?" Yance asked slowly. Perhaps she had a point, he thought. Seemed like he'd been washing his own clothes at ten, too.

That was the year his mother left and he and his dad had to learn how to do a lot of things they'd never done before. Finally his father solved the problem by hiring a housekeeper, who'd served them until she moved away when Trace was a toddler. Then Mabel took over, the Chadwicks needing the extra money to put the last of their sons through college.

"Yance," China said, her tone cold as a Siberian lake, "I don't know *what* this is about, other than you think I've overstepped some kind of boundary. I'm not trying to be a big bad stepmother in this, but I didn't know how else to get Trace to pick his clothes up off the floor. If you'd rather the whole thing be dropped, then fine and dandy. Frankly, I'm beginning to be sorry I ever brought it up. It just seemed like the thing to do at the time."

She'd lost him. "The floor?"

China stared at the man who was looking back at her blankly. Oh, Lord, she thought. She was not only the big bad stepmother, she was going to be the big bad tattletale, as well.

"Come with me," she said.

Opening the door to Trace's room, she let Yance enter first. Ordinarily, the bedroom doors were kept open during the day, but the boy's room had become such a disaster that she and Mabel kept it closed in self-defense.

Yance entered a room knee-deep in dirty clothes, snack wrappers and dirty dishes. The closet door stood open, the rack looking half-empty with much of its usual contents littering its floor. Bureau drawers were pulled open and left that way, what was left of their contents spilling over the edges.

"Wow," Yance said softly, borrowing Trace's favorite expletive.

"I told Mabel not to wash any clothing items left on the floor," China said, "because Trace is supposed to pick them up. The cleanest item in this room is the dirty clothes hamper. As I said, if you'd rather we drop the whole thing,

I'd be just as happy to go back to the way things were before I came."

She looked at him head-on, then continued, "The implication I'm hearing is that this is none of my business. I'm more than willing for that to be true."

"It is your business," Yance said quietly. "And I'm at fault if I implied otherwise. Trace didn't see fit to tell me the whole story. I'll talk to him tonight and this won't happen again."

China didn't budge. "If it's *my* business, why are *you* talking to him about it?"

"Because Trace is my son and I'll take care of it," Yance said, then got a whole different take on his words when China's head angled up to battle stance.

"And what am I?" she asked, far too gently.

She had a point, he knew. Again.

"You're right," Yance said ruefully. "Tell you what. Since you're the one who was disobeyed, why don't you take care of that part? And since I'm the one who was half lied to, that part's mine. Agreed?"

"I suppose that's fair. But you're sure you don't want to just drop the whole thing? I'm willing, you know."

"Not on your life. You started it." He grinned at her. "Live with it, partner." Partner, he thought. He liked the sound of that, too.

"And what am I?" China had asked, and Yance hadn't answered. He was supposed to have said, You're Trace's stepmother, with *mother* being the word she most wanted to hear.

He was supposed to have said, You're my wife and a part of our family now, and Trace should do as you say.

He was supposed to have asked, What has Trace been up to that he's going to school wearing a dirty shirt? not,

What have you done to my son that he's wearing dirty clothes to school?

Not "my son," China thought sadly.

He was supposed to have said, "*Our* son."

Chapter Seven

Instead of Blackjack picking up Trace that afternoon, as had become the old man's custom, Yance sat in the truck at the highway, waiting for the bus to drop off his son.

As the yellow vehicle drove away, Trace hopped in the pickup with his usual exuberance. "Hi, Dad. Where's Blackjack?"

"I didn't have anything better to do this afternoon," Yance replied with more truth than he liked, "so I came today. I thought it might give me a chance to talk to you."

The boy sighed inwardly. There were talks...and then there were talks. He'd barely passed his last spelling test, for instance. "Sure, Dad," he said without enthusiasm.

"I want you to tell me again why you wore a dirty shirt to school today."

Hot dog, Trace thought in satisfaction. His dad didn't like him not having clean clothes to wear. And today he'd discovered his dad might have a point.

Usually dirt didn't bother Trace, but his favorite shirt

hadn't seemed so cool once he got to school this morning. Leticia Esquivel, the prettiest girl in his room, made a point of commenting on the jelly stain. And he couldn't let her get away with it, so he had to say something back. Trouble was, he didn't like saying mean things to Letty. She was…pretty.

"I told you, Dad," he said now. "China won't let Mabel wash my clothes no more."

"That's right, you did say that," Yance replied slowly. "Seems an unkind thing for her to do, don't you think?"

"Yeah, but China's always doing things like that to me. Mabel's supposed to wash my clothes, isn't she, Dad? She always used to. An' she still washes yours and China's things." He hung his head, assuming a pose of sad dejection. "China just doesn't like me, I guess."

His father's "Hmm" was noncommittal as he took his time negotiating a particularly bad rut in the dirt road before picking up the conversation again.

"I'm sorry to hear that China doesn't like you, son. There for a while, the two of you seemed to be good friends. Did China by chance say *why* she won't let Mabel wash your clothes anymore?" Yance asked with every appearance of sympathy. "Surely she gave you some kind of excuse."

Trace hesitated. That was a sticky question. "She said Mabel wasn't supposed to pick them up for me," he said at last. "But Mabel's *always* picked up my clothes, Dad, you know that. Ever since forever. That's what you pay her for, right? It's her job."

"In other words, China told Mabel not to wash any clothes of yours that she had to pick up off the floor," Yance said, sticking to the point. "China's new rule is that you keep your own room, like she and I both do. That means keeping your clothes up off the floor and put away. If your dirty clothes are in the hamper, Mabel washes them—if they're not, she doesn't. Do I have that right, Trace?''

Staring at his father's implacable profile, Trace swallowed.

''I said, is that right, Trace?''

''Yes, sir.'' The young voice could barely be heard.

''You don't seem to have explained the situation very well the first time,'' Yance said.

''No, sir.''

''In fact, the first time you explained things it sounded like something else altogether, wouldn't you say?''

''Yes, sir.''

''Seems to me, not explaining things completely borders on the dishonest. Would you agree to that, as well?''

Trace's head drooped in earnest now. ''Yes, sir.''

''What do you think I ought to do about it?''

Sighing, the boy brought his attention from his knees to the far horizon. ''Whup me, I guess.''

''Maybe. Maybe not. I'll have to think about it. It's a hard thing for a man to hear his son lie, even when the lie is just skirting around the truth. But if the whole truth is not spoken, then the lie is there by implication. You know that, son. I shouldn't have to repeat it.''

''Yes, sir, I know it.''

''Trace,'' Yance said slowly. ''China is my wife. You need to come to terms with her, because she's going to be with us a long time.''

His son mumbled.

''I didn't hear that.''

''I said,'' Trace repeated defiantly, but keeping his tone respectful…he could argue with his father, but he'd better not sass… ''that China's not really your wife. Not a real one, I mean. I'm not stoopid, Dad. You sleep in Grandpa's room now and China sleeps in your old one. I oughta be sleeping there, not her. If she was really your wife, she'd be in with you.''

"You're coming too close to things that are none of your business, Trace. And I'm telling you now, partner, that wherever China sleeps and whatever room she sleeps in, she's my wife. You will give her respect, if for no other reason but *that* one, or you will suffer the consequences. Do you understand me?"

"Yes, sir," Trace replied sullenly. But, he thought, his father had not ordered him to pick up his clothes. He was leaving that to Trace to handle. Fine. He could handle it very well. He'd show China he could wear his clothes till they rotted off his back and he didn't care what Letty Esquivel thought. She wasn't that pretty!

Yance dropped Trace off at the front door and drove around to put the pickup in the garage.

In one respect his son was right. A real wife would be sleeping in her husband's bed. And no one else's. Wherever and in whatever room, he'd told Trace.

The hell of it was, he'd put in contract form that China Dare could sleep wherever and with whomever she wanted. Just went to show how "stoopid," as Trace said, a desperate man could be.

China had made no mention of wanting to roam, as she had every contracted right to, but it was early days. They'd no sooner married than he had his surgery, so she'd had no real time to get bored. Hell, he'd just seen the doc for his final checkup last week. The element of romance inherent in marrying a possibly dying man hadn't had a chance to wear off.

Perhaps, like many newly wealthy people, China hadn't yet figured out how much freedom her new wealth gave her. She hadn't, for instance, done much spending.

Pretty soon, he'd bet, she'd want to set up an apartment of her own again. She had a look of discontent about her. Would she have had that same look if she'd been left to raise Trace on her own?

Somehow, he didn't think so.

He was about halfway to the house, the cold gray afternoon quickly darkening around him, when his thinking backed up. *Romance?*

Maybe he'd better give that word some further thought. That was something else he and China had had no time for. Originally, it hadn't been an issue, but the idea of romancing China Dare was becoming more and more important every day.

China waited until Trace finished gobbling down the afternoon snack she always had waiting for him when he came home from school. And she waited until he finished his chores in the barn. But when the boy went to settle himself into his favorite spot in front of the television, she stopped him.

"Before you get comfortable," she said quietly, "I think we need to have a bed-making lesson. Will you come with me, please?"

"I already know how to make a bed," he said, and flipped on the television.

Walking to the set, China turned if off again. "I hadn't noticed. Since you already know how, then I think you better go make your bed. You didn't make it before you left this morning."

"That's the way I make it," Trace said belligerently, throwing China a look of acute dislike.

Standing out of sight beyond the doorway and listening to his once-polite and well-mannered son use a tone of voice that the boy knew better than to use to any adult, it was all Yance could do not to go in there, yank the kid up by the collar and haul him out to the back porch.

But China had said she wanted to handle this, he thought, so let's see how she handles it.

"That's not how I want the bed made," she replied. "Time for a lesson I think. Let's go," and she turned toward Trace's room as if completely certain the boy would follow her.

She saw Yance but didn't stop, and he stepped back into the kitchen without Trace, who was following behind her in high dudgeon, aware that he was being observed.

In Trace's bedroom, China walked over the dirty clothes covering the floor like a ragman's carpet, acting as if she didn't hear the snack wrappers crackling beneath them or feel the harder outlines of who-knew-what beneath her feet. At the boy's bed and without comment, she pulled back the spread, blanket and top sheet, and lay the pillow aside.

"Pay attention," she said. "There's a test later. First you smooth the bottom sheet, like so, after swiping off any crumbs you spent the night with. You might also want to check for ants at this time so they won't be checking you out at midnight."

Trace frowned even harder to keep from half smiling.

"Then you pull up the cover sheet, level the hills and ridges with a few strokes of the hand like this...magic, huh?...and make sure it's straight. This one being striped, that shouldn't be a problem. All you have to do is keep the lines lined. Once the top sheet is straight, you pull up the blanket and swipe out the wrinkles in it. If you go in the Marines someday, they'll make you bounce a quarter off it, but I'm easy. Just so long as it bounces a penny."

She fished a penny from her jeans' pocket and flipped it expertly so that it rotated several times before landing on the bed. It didn't bounce. China stared at it as if in consternation for a moment, then shrugged. "Heads. Good enough."

Reaching for the bedspread, she flipped it over the blanket. "This part's tricky," she said instructively. "It has to be even to the floor on this side. I don't care how uneven it is on the other. After all, that side is next to the wall and your walls don't talk."

Trace's grin quirked up before he could stop it.

"Make sure the top is smooth, though, and the bottom end also even to the floor," China continued. "Then fold the top part back like so. Toss on the pillow, cover it over with the spread, and voilà, you're finished. Now. Think you can do that?"

The boy changed his unwanted expression of humor into a roll of his eyes and said in a tone implying extreme but patient boredom, "Sure, China. Who couldn't?"

"I told you there was a test," China replied, her voice bright as a gold tooth. She reached down and deliberately tore apart the coverings on the newly made bed and handed him the pillow. "Now you do it."

"Hey," Trace cried in surprise. "That's not fair!"

"I think it is," she said evenly and there was no humor at all in the reply. "Call me when you're finished and I'll check it out. If you still don't have the hang of it, I'll show you again."

Leaving Trace mumbling behind her, China exited the room and made a beeline to the front door. Once on the porch, she dropped her face into her trembling hands, not even noticing the dark or the cold dankness of the early evening. Nor did she hear the door open behind her.

Two strong arms wrapped around her shoulders.

"You're not crying?" Yance asked quietly, concern in his voice.

She turned in his arms to press her face against the breast pocket of his shirt. He hadn't stopped for a jacket, either. "No," she said. "I'm not crying, but I hate doing things like that. And Trace hates *me*. I didn't want that to happen, Yance."

"I don't think it has happened, honey." He used his thumb and forefinger to gently squeeze and massage the top of her neck under her braid. "Trace is just having to make some major adjustments, that's all. And as the new kid on the block, you're getting all the flack. Give him time, China, and I think he'll go back to being his old even-tempered self again.''

Lifting her head, China smiled ruefully. "I hope so. We used to get along really well, you know.''

Yance stared down into the strong-boned Nordic face of the woman in his arms. It was, he thought, the first time they'd ever stood like this, with his arms wrapped fully around her. She wasn't a small woman, and was tall—made, he thought, as he so often did, like a queen.

And she fit into his arms as if custom-built for their encirclement.

"I know,'' he said softly, staring into her eyes and having no idea what he was agreeing to.

China's lashes slowly drifted downward, all the invitation he needed to lower his head....

"Chiiii-naaaa!''

Trace's shrill voice drifted out to them, coming from around the back of the house where he was probably yelling out the back door.

"Chiiii-naaaa!''

Yance groaned audibly and China looked up at him and blinked, as if not quite sure where she was. Then she seemed to pull herself together and stepped out of his arms.

"Guess he's finished with the bed.'' She smiled faintly, then shivered. "Good grief, it's cold out here,'' she said in surprise, and led the way into the house.

"Chiiii-naaaa!''

"I'm right behind you, Trace. Is your bed made?''

Trace, with his head half out the back door, visibly jumped then turned to look at her accusingly. "Where were you? I couldn't find you anywhere.''

"I was on the front porch,'' China said calmly, "uh, talking to your father about the weather.'' She deliberately changed the subject. "Finished?''

Now that he knew where everyone was, Trace's mouth

dropped into a sulk. "Yeah." He saw Yance standing behind her. "Yes, ma'am."

"I like good manners," Yance commented and behind the boy's back he winked at China when Trace led the way to his bedroom.

The bed was remade, perhaps not as neatly as China had made it the first time, but effort clearly showed. Since to China only effort counted, it was good enough.

"Looks nice," she said. "You did a good job. That's the way I want to see it before you leave for school in the morning."

To avoid misunderstandings later, she added gently, "If you think you don't have time to make it this well, since I know you also have outside chores, I'll be glad to call you a little earlier in the morning if you need it. I wouldn't want you to miss the bus."

Trace looked at the woman standing beside him and fought back the niggle of admiration that was interfering with the "mad" he'd felt for so long that he'd come to expect it to always be there. She had him on this, he thought. But she couldn't boss him around completely. He'd show her.

But at her next words, he almost forgot to be mad again.

"On Mondays," China was saying, "you don't have to make your bed. That's the day I strip the sheets in everybody's room and put on clean ones. So to start off the week, maybe you can get a ten-minute extra snooze." She smiled at him and turned away, touching his shoulder lightly as she did so.

Trace stood for a moment looking at his bed, the only neat object in the room. It did look pretty good, he thought.

When he went back to the den, he found his dad sitting on the couch watching the evening news. Before the boy could settle into his usual spot, Yance lowered the volume.

"I've given our discussion this afternoon some thought," Yance said quietly, "and I've decided your punishment for lying to me will be the absence of everything electronic for a week. That's a seven-day week, Trace, not a five-day one, and it begins tonight. No television, no videos, no computer games, no Internet, no CD player or radio. And not at Blackjack's or at the bunkhouse, either. Do I make myself clear?''

"Ah, Dad. There's nothing to do. A guy's gotta do *somethin'!*''

Yance gazed at his son levelly, but a smile hovered. "Well, there's homework,'' he suggested. "Maybe your spelling grade will come up this week. And you could read. You've not been doing much of that, lately. Or there are puzzles and board games. Tell you what. If you get really bored, I might find you a few extra chores, if you like.''

Trace was clearly not amused. "Ah, Dad.''

He left the room, dragging his feet, and went to sit at his desk and spread out his homework, since China and Mabel were putting the finishing touches on supper and the kitchen table was not available.

But in the process of opening a book, he knocked over an empty glass and it hit the floor, shattering. He looked at the pieces, debating on whether or not he wanted to pick them up, then decided that he might as well. After all, he walked around the room barefoot sometime.

Besides, you never knew about his dad. He didn't come into Trace's room often, but sometimes he did. And while Yance might forgive dirty clothes on the floor, shards of glass might be another matter.

How was it life had gotten so complicated lately?

The following morning, when Yance returned from taking Trace to the bus, he found China standing at Trace's bedroom door, surveying the transformation.

"I don't know how you did it,'' he said quietly, "but

Trace either cleaned the place up or the shoemaker's elves snuck in during the night.''

"I don't know how I did it, either. Trace just came in yesterday afternoon and picked up all his dirty clothes. Next thing I knew, he'd cleaned up the rest, too.''

Yance grinned. "I can explain part of it,'' he said. "I told him he couldn't go to school wearing dirty clothes. He was down to nothing clean to wear but a plaid shirt his grandmother gave him that he claims is 'dorky.' It was get his own clothes washed or start wearing mine.''

China's heart sank. So it wasn't her doing at all, she thought. It was Yance's maneuver that had Trace turning over a new leaf. The wicked stepmother was being obeyed, but only because Real Dad said so.

She turned away, heading toward her makeshift studio, her pleasure over the neat bedroom now gone completely.

Yance ambled after her to stand in the doorway in his turn, watching her gather her supplies. "China,'' he said quietly, "are you happy here?''

Deliberately she kept her tone flip. "What's not to be happy? Blackjack's settled. You're well. I'm rolling in green.''

Standing in front of a small canvas, Yance studied a view of mountains and sky. If one looked carefully, there was a face subtly showing through the crags and outcroppings of the mountain. A child would delight in finding it. It had delighted him when he'd first found it, too. He loved China's work.

Keeping his eyes on the canvas, but his attention on the woman standing at her worktable, he said softly, "You don't always look...content.''

"I just get restless sometimes, I suppose. Remember, I grew up moving around.'' But in her heart of hearts, she'd also always yearned for a permanent home, China thought. How she'd wanted to find it on the C3. Instead, she felt like the odd one out.

She'd been hired...the most polite word for it...to be a security guard, only to find there was nothing to guard after all. For the life of her, she couldn't seem to find a purpose for herself now. At least not here.

Anywhere?

"After Melodie died, Yance," she asked on a hesitant note, "why didn't you marry again? Not right away, of course, but later, as Trace got older?"

He laughed ruefully. "Honestly? It didn't cross my mind. Never met the right woman to make me think of wedding bells, I suppose, and was too busy to go looking. There were women, but none who made me slow down and think of growing additional family instead of growing additional corporations."

One of China's city scenes caught his eye, and he gazed at it for a moment. There was delight in the small painting of autumn in an urban setting, the season somehow as glorious on the city street as in the country.

"A place is a place," China had once said. She saw beauty everywhere.

"My dad and I always shared the raising of Trace," Yance continued, picking up the thread of their conversation, "so in many ways I never felt the need of a parental partner. After the accident, of course, with Dad no longer here to look after Trace and when life for me was a big question mark, I can't tell you how much I regretted not remarrying and how much I regretted not having more children. And all because I just never thought of it."

And because I never found a woman who could live in two worlds, he added to himself.

Until now.

The hell of it was, he hadn't even been looking for himself, only for Trace. He'd made all his plans for his son and never truly looked beyond his surgery to what those plans would mean for himself if he recovered.

Now, finally, here was a woman who could comfortably

walk beside him whichever world he traversed, and he'd signed away his right to have her exclusively, and had verbally promised not to touch her.

And he wanted to touch China quite badly.

All over.

China stuck a couple of brushes in the hip pocket of her jeans and picked up her easel to carry it out on the back porch to work in the morning's rapidly warming sunshine. "Guess I'd better get busy," she said brightly. "I have a deadline."

Plucking the easel from her, Yance stood with it under his arm and watched her gather her paints before following her out onto the porch. "Wish I did," he muttered to her back.

"Wish you did what?" China positioned the easel to her liking, hoping the man would leave her soon so she could stare off at the horizon, think glum thoughts and do nothing to her heart's content.

Content. There was that blasted word again. Heart's content. A knife in the heart, surely.

"Had a deadline. China," Yance said abruptly, "I'm bored stiff."

China stopped her restless fiddling so she could stare in surprise at the man now leaning against a support post gazing out over the barns and outbuildings of his ranch.

"Bored? Yance, you're head honcho of one of the largest ranches in West Texas and who knows how many businesses and corporations. How can you be bored?"

"Sounds strange, doesn't it? But the truth is, before the operation, I delegated myself out of the picture, and now I'm left with everything so arranged that it works just dandy without me."

He frowned. "It's damned difficult carefully doling out responsibility, then going in and taking that responsibility away from someone as if it were nothing but a whim. The men and women I chose to run things are good at what they do. I can't in good conscience demote them now."

"I guess you can't, at that," China said slowly. "But the ranch? Chisolms have always run the C3, Yance. You grew up on a horse, and I'll bet Uncle Steve made sure you know everything there is to know about this place."

"Don't forget, Dad retired two years before he died, and in that time I was handling the business end of Chisolm, Inc. For the past two and a half years, the C3 has been run by the ranch manager and the foreman. Dad was the boss, just like I'm now the boss, and I have a final say, but Jack Fergus wouldn't take kindly to my stepping all over his managerial toes or Chad to me superseding his authority with the men."

Yance turned to gaze at China ruefully. "I could let Jack go, I suppose, and take over completely myself, but Jack just went and got himself engaged. Seems kind of unfair to dismiss the man for no reason when he needs his job to make a living and I want his job only for something to do. It makes the ranch sound like nothing but a rich man's toy."

He used the side of his boot to sidekick a small stone off the edge of the porch.

"The truth is, even if I were running the ranch I'd probably be just as bored. I love this place and if it were a choice between here and the rest of the world, I'd take the C3. But I'm a man who will always need more than just the land, I think. Sounds greedy, doesn't it?"

"I don't think so." China placed her canvas on the easel and took the brushes from her hip pocket. "Some people see small intense visions, others see broader ones, that's all. Seems to me you should just find yourself a new venture that has no one but you to set it up."

Yance stared back at her. "I'll be damned," he said slowly. There was the boy in the hospital with the idea for an electromagnetic car. He still had the kid's name and address somewhere.

"Now why didn't I think of that?" he asked himself aloud, turning again to gaze at the far horizon, his mind already beginning to churn. "Too busy trying to readjust to actually being alive, I suppose," he answered himself absently.

When China looked at him in surprise, he grinned back at her. "Did I ever tell you about the kid I met in the hospital?"

And he'd been thinking about a Chisolm Bank branch in Southeast Asia, too, while lying in that hospital bed recuperating.

Hell, why not mainland China? Might be difficult. Might be impossible. But nothing ventured, as they say. A dare.

A China dare.

The thought had romance written all over it.

"China," Yance said slowly, "how would you like to see your namesake?"

Chapter Eight

Yance had to postpone his trip to China. Thanksgiving was almost upon them, and he, more than most, had much for which to be thankful.

It was the custom for the Chisolms to go to Midland for the holiday. Mabel chose to make Thanksgiving dinner for any on the ranch who had nowhere else to go, but had a holiday from any duties pertaining to the Chisolm family itself. Steve Chisolm and Trace had always gone to the apartment in Midland to join Yance, and the three of them then went to a restaurant for dinner.

When Yance asked China if she would like to do this as well, she agreed. Blackjack would come with them. Ever since China's mother died, she and Blackjack had been making the restaurant holiday circuit themselves.

However, after arriving at the apartment on the Wednesday before Thanksgiving, Blackjack and Trace dug in their heels.

"Since there's four of us," Trace said in his best whine, "I think we ought to eat at home."

"Seems kinda strange for a *family* to be eatin' in a rest'ernt," Blackjack agreed.

China stared at him balefully, yet in her heart agreed with this man who'd never before quibbled over where they ate their holiday meals. Both of them had known that holidays were not the same with China's mother gone. Yet even so, her stepfather knew China couldn't cook and certainly hadn't the foggiest notion how to go about baking a turkey.

"You make good salads, darlin'," Blackjack said as if reading her mind.

"Even restaurant food sounds better than turkey salad for Thanksgiving dinner," she replied drily.

"Did I ever tell you I was a dab hand at corn bread stuffin'? I'm purty good with giblet gravy, too," her stepfather added, his tone turning wheedling.

"I can make instant pudding for dessert," Trace said eagerly. "An' I can mash potatoes."

Even Yance turned against her. "Vegetables and cranberry sauce come in cans," he said, "or we can have a raw vegetable tray."

"Both," said Trace excitedly. "And we can buy a frozen pumpkin pie, China, and fake whipped cream."

China gazed around at the males who thought instant, canned and frozen would make a just dandy Thanksgiving dinner. "Turkey?" she asked faintly.

"Just buy 'er smoked," Blackjack said promptly. "Your ma always did. All you have to do is heat 'er up. Or get a precooked ham, if you want, and do the same thing."

"Ham *and* turkey," Trace decided. "That gives everyone a choice. C'mon, China. It'll be easy and we'll all help. We'll have a *real* Thanksgiving."

On Thanksgiving, running only about three hours late

to the initial noon they had aimed for, the four of them sat down to a dinner that was truly a communal affair.

As Trace decreed, there was a small smoked turkey, so he could have a drumstick, and a small ham that China found no trouble decorating with the traditional pineapple slices, cherries and cloves before reheating it in the oven. There were sweet potatoes from a can and white potatoes that only boiled over once before Yance came to their rescue. Trace then mashed them enthusiastically.

Blackjack really did have a knack for making giblet gravy, though his corn bread stuffing was questionable. Yance, it turned out, made delicious deviled eggs and had a strong suit for rescuing anything on the stove before it burned. A talent he'd picked up in corporate life, he explained solemnly.

China made a tossed garden salad and a fresh fruit salad. She also stuffed celery with store-bought pimento cheese to go on a tray with raw broccoli, green and black olives and tiny sweet pickles because Blackjack liked them.

The pumpkin pie was not frozen, though its crust was. Between them, she and Yance managed to follow the directions on the pumpkin can and Yance made sure the thing didn't burn except for one little spot in the center. Canned whipped cream covered it up.

All agreed the table was beautiful. Melodie's china, crystal and sterling made lovely place settings, and China made a centerpiece of dried corn, gourds and fall flowers and leaves flowing down the table from a tipped-over silver urn. Trace had picked out the pilgrim and turkey candles at the hobby store, and China added a couple of tall yellow ones to actually light and grace the whole.

While Blackjack asked the blessing, they held hands around the table and China, before raising her head at its conclusion, had to surreptitiously wipe her eyes. From her peripheral vision, she caught Blackjack doing the same.

Yance lifted his head and surveyed his family. Odd that

until this moment he'd never thought of the four of them in that way, as if they were a unit. Yet he'd deliberately brought China and Blackjack into his life to be just that; but for Trace, not himself.

Well, I'm damned, he thought again. A family.

Then he corrected himself with an inward smile. Better make that, I'm blessed.

As it had so often since the operation, joy in the gift of life swept over him. He looked down the table at China, passing the bowl of heated, canned green beans to Trace. She glowed with life, his China Dare. He watched Trace giggle at something she said. Even his son was forgetting these days to be surly and was slowly being charmed back to the way he used to be.

China may not be much of a cook, but she sure had a way for making all that she touched come together.

Yance found himself hoping this dinner would become a tradition. A *family* tradition. Canned, frozen and packaged as it was somehow made it unique, and he liked the idea that all of them had pitched in to make it come together.

How long had it been since he sat down to a holiday dinner with family? Not since Melodie was alive, when they had dinner with her parents. But not since he was a child and his parents were still married had he enjoyed a family holiday meal in his own household.

It was, he thought, a damned good feeling.

It was, China thought as the four of them cleaned up the disaster in the kitchen, the nicest Thanksgiving she'd spent since her mother was alive. She handed Yance a handful of washed silver to dry, which he in turn handed to Trace to put away.

Trace had learned today that the silver was a wedding present given to his parents by his mother's family. He'd been fascinated by the knowledge, and China realized how little of Melodie was actually a part of the boy's life.

Knowing that, she'd made a point of using Melodie's china and crystal. Trace needed things like that.

But she hoped someday he'd need her, too.

Wise Blackjack decided to stay at the apartment, but at Trace's insistence, China, Yance and the boy visited the city's largest mall the following afternoon to wade through its splendor of Christmas decorations. It didn't take long before they caught the spirit from those around them, who, like themselves, were lured by Christmas while still full of Thanksgiving turkey. The mall's assault soon turned Trace into a jumping bean of excitement.

China understood the boy's enchantment completely. Line and color; depth and texture. Her favorite things. Add to it, sound. Music, laughter, the hum of a thousand people talking, an occasional overly tired child crying, a Salvation Army bell dinging…and cash registers ringing up profits for worried but ever-hopeful store owners.

Trace walked with them, agog and hypnotized by commercialism.

"Look, Dad. See this cool video game. That's what you can get me for Christmas. And look at these bad action figures. If you run out of gift ideas, remember I showed 'em to you.

"Hey, Dad. How 'bout getting me a ferret for Christmas? Look at 'em, Dad. Aren't they cute?

"Dad, I sure would like to have…

"Dad, see…"

"What would you like for me to give you for Christmas, Trace?" China asked at last.

The boy looked at her blankly. "I dunno. A shirt, I guess. That's what Gramma always buys me. But not plaid," he added hastily.

I'm not your grandmother, China wanted to say. "Well, show me the kind you want," she said instead, "and I'll see what I can do." *In your dreams,* she added silently. No way was she getting this boy clothes for Christmas.

Actually, shirts were slowly becoming a real issue with Trace, and pants, and just the right tennies. Walking from store window to store window, he found himself discussing this seriously with China, who, unlike his Gramma, actually seemed to know what he was talking about. But then, China always seemed to know what he was talking about.

Always had.

Funny, he'd forgotten China in his Christmas thinking. What would he buy for her? he wondered suddenly. It had to be something different because China was…different.

Hey, maybe they'd have a Christmas as cool as Thanksgiving had been. A real one, like other kids, with another dinner and everything. Wow!

Watching the boy's animated face as he called her attention to clothes that he found "cool" warmed China as much as his earlier one-sided conversations with his father had chilled her. It made her feel…motherly…that he would discuss items of apparel that he liked and didn't like with her.

It also made her aware of how quickly he was growing up. Eight years was not after all the eternity it once seemed.

"What do *you* want for Christmas, Yance?" she asked quietly when Trace's interest in clothes waned for the more dramatic attraction of a huge electric train display set up in a toy store.

"You're asking the man who has everything," he said with a grin. "Literally. Except a deadline, but I'm working on that myself."

He watched China smile in immediate understanding and wanted to hug her right there in the middle of the toy store, right there in the middle of half of Midland. Right there in front of God and everyone.

I want you, he wanted to say. *I want to wake up on*

Christmas morning with you lying beside me, naked, with your cheek on my chest and your unbound hair tickling my nose. And I want the felicity of waking you with a kiss and having you give me just the smile you're giving me now.

That, China Dare, is what I want for Christmas, he wanted to say.

"And you, China? What do you want?" he asked.

She shrugged. "Actually, I think I have it all, too," she said.

You, she wanted to say. In every way, you, Yance Chisolm. Always you. And Trace. I want to be let in. I want not only the Chisolm name, but the Chisolm hearts, she wanted to say.

"Wow! Did you see those trains, Dad? Come see, China. Look at the little houses—even little haystacks and barns and everything. Check out the bridges, Dad. Cool, huh? I want a train. A big one, like this. We can set it up in the den. That's what y'all can give me for Christmas."

"Y'all." In Western parlance, you…and always in the plural.

The day after Thanksgiving, standing in a toy store in the middle of a crowded mall, China received her Christmas gift from her stepson.

And that same day after Thanksgiving, standing in the middle of a crowded video rental store, China had her Christmas gift taken back.

Each of them had picked out a video for an orgy of movies and popcorn that evening and were headed toward the checkout line when China took a good look at the selections she carried in her hand. She stopped, causing Yance, walking just behind, to bump into her.

"Problems?" he asked mildly, putting his hands on her shoulders to steady her.

China handed the video in question to the boy. "Not

this one, Trace. You need to find another. This one's R-rated and it's extremely violent. I've seen the ads.''

Trace glowered. "I want to see it," he said mutinously. "Nobody cares about violence anymore. Ever'body's used to it. Right, Dad? You'll let me watch it, won't you? You've let me watch Rs before.''

"Not intentionally, I haven't. Put it back, Trace, and get another.''

"Dad, it's not that bad. China doesn't know. It's a good movie, Dad. People just killing each other, that's all. A little cussing, but nothing I haven't heard before. This is the nineties, Dad.''

"Put it back, Trace, and get another." And when the boy opened his mouth to argue further, Yance added, "Or don't get one at all. Your choice, partner.''

Throwing China a murderous look, Trace stalked back down the aisle to return the offending video and find another. He came back with *Cinderella* and a chip on his shoulder a mile wide.

Once more, China thought, she'd drawn a line only to have it enforced, not by herself but by Yance. To Trace, she was the wicked stepmother, the outsider, whose rules his father upheld and which he was expected to obey, but only because his father said so.

China hadn't won this argument; she hadn't even been a part of it. She'd only been to blame for it.

But the evening was peaceful. After a supper of Thanksgiving leftovers, Yance popped up microwave popcorn and they settled into the apartment's family room. Blackjack lowered his old bones into the recliner, Trace lounged in a beanbag chair, and China and Yance took opposite ends of the couch.

"Cinderella?" Blackjack commented, studying their selections. Since he hadn't picked, he got to choose which video to watch first.

"It's a stupid movie," Trace said. "I don't know why

I got it. We don't have to watch it, Blackjack, if you don't wanna.''

"Hmm. I dunno, boy, 'bout it being stupid," the old man drawled. "I kinda like them mice. Last time I saw it, China was about your age. I liked the mice, she and her ma liked the prince." He chuckled. "No taste a'tall, them wimmen."

Trace laughed. "Let 'er rip then, B.J. I'd forgotten about the mice."

As the old man and the boy settled in to watch the Disney movie, Yance shifted his position on the couch so he could say softly, "So you liked the handsome prince, did you, China?"

"Umm-hmm. But you know what? I liked the mice just as much as the prince."

Yance chuckled. "Now why am I not surprised?"

But he had achieved his objective and was now at China's end of the couch, and before the evening was over, the two of them were shoulder to shoulder, just as he'd planned.

Romance, he thought. With enough romance maybe he could get around the prenuptial agreement and his promise of no intimacy. After all, he wouldn't be bound by a promise if China herself absolved him from it. To have a real marriage with his wife he was going to have to court her.

He couldn't think of anything he'd enjoy more.

But the family room, Yance soon discovered, was crowded with…family.

If he hadn't been so aware of his son and Blackjack in the room, he would have put an arm around China and drawn her to him. And he knew for a positive fact, that without Trace and Blackjack in the room, he would have taken what came next as far as China would let him.

As it was, the two of them sat shoulder to shoulder and shared only a large bowl of popcorn; Yance occasionally shifting with the discomfort of suppressed fantasy and

China gripping the popcorn bowl as if it contained her heart and soul, buttered and salted.

On Saturday, Lilly, Yance's Midland housekeeper, came in to make supper for Trace and Blackjack, and China and Yance had their first evening out alone.

The two of them were invited to what had to be the first Christmas party of the year by one of Yance's executives, who'd only learned Yance was in town when Yance called him on another matter.

Just the thing to get him and China away from family for a while, Yance thought, accepting the invitation immediately. Romance.

"A Christmas party?" China echoed when he told her about it.

Oh, Lord. He hadn't asked. He'd just told her. "We don't have to go, if you'd rather not," he said quickly. "I can easily call Max back and cancel. China, I'm sorry. Sometimes I forget there's now more than myself to consult."

And there's a truth if ever she heard it, China mused, caught between the humor of the thought and its sadness.

"To have a Christmas party so early, they must be trying to get rid of Thanksgiving turkey," she said aloud. "I'd like to go, Yance, but I didn't bring party clothes with me."

"But my dear China," Yance proclaimed, looking down his refined nose. "You have a gold credit card, the ultimate accessory." He then spoiled the effect with a wink. "Use it."

China laughed. "So I do. And so I will. And you might be sorry."

He wasn't.

When Yance walked into Max Henderson's November Christmas party, he walked in with a queen on his arm.

He hoped to hell he was a handsome enough prince for her because if she found another he'd strangle the guy. To hell with the prenuptial agreement.

China was lovely. Tall and statuesque, her wheaten hair worn in that magic style she somehow achieved that was both confined and loose, she was a study in white and gold.

Her white dress was off the shoulder, draping her full breasts enticingly but without being blatant about it, with a loosely pleated skirt that flowed sensually around her calves whenever she moved. The white of the dress offset her natural tan, giving her skin a luminous golden color. Her sandals, with their three inch heels, were gold, too, and put her at a height that came within an inch of matching his.

With his dark hair and suit and her fair hair and white dress, he imagined they made a striking couple. China, he thought, would love the contrast. He kind of liked it, himself.

Reluctantly, after he'd introduced her to their host and hostess and then to several other people, he released her so that each of them could mingle. But he kept her in constant view so he could watch her slow progress around the room and observe the easy way she had of meeting strangers.

There was nothing shy about China; but then, he thought, Norse queens were seldom shy. But neither was she overbearing, and the various groups she was a part of could always be heard laughing. Yance found himself resenting not being a part of those groups.

As soon as he could do it without the maneuver being obvious, he rejoined his wife so they could mingle as a couple.

Somehow, however, he was cut from the herd by a business acquaintance who hadn't the wit to know Yance had no interest in talking business at a function that was his first major outing with his new wife. The man didn't stand a chance, yet Yance no sooner was free of him and was about to rejoin China after scanning the room quickly to find her, when a low voice spoke at his shoulder.

"She's striking," Elaine Brisbane said.

Yance smiled at the petite redhead. "Hello, Elaine. I saw Gavin a few minutes ago. I thought you and he were making New York your home now."

"We're only in town for the holidays. Gavin's daughter and her husband live here, you know. I understand you've been busy since I last saw you. Or not busy, as the case may be. Semiretired and a very sudden new wife."

She laughed up at him, her eyes sparkling with the sultry mischief. "But I imagine a new wife keeps you much more busy than a few corporations. Who is she?"

"She's China Dare," China said, tucking her hand into the crook of her husband's arm. "Hello."

Yance covered China's hand with his, liking the feel of it there. "China, this is Elaine Brisbane. I think you met her husband, Gavin, earlier. Elaine, my wife, China."

The two women smiled politely at each other, both knowing instinctively what they had in common and not liking it.

"Old girlfriend?" China asked, when Elaine drifted off after a few minutes.

"Yes. Before she married Gavin a couple of years ago, of course."

"Of course," China murmured. "She's beautiful."

"That's what she said about you."

China looked at him and quirked an eyebrow.

"She really did," Yance said. "Cross my heart," and he crossed his chest, keeping his face straight with an effort. Hot damn. His China was jealous!

"I'm sure she did, Yance. No need to swear. And your heart's on the other side," China replied and took a last sip of her wine.

He chuckled. "I was testing you. Want some more of that?" indicating her wineglass.

"Just a swallow or two," she said. She didn't really want more alcohol, but she badly needed a few minutes alone.

When she handed the glass to him, Yance left her to get it refilled at the small bar in a corner of the room. China then pretended an interest in a painting so that her hostess wouldn't think she'd been abandoned and needed rescuing.

What she needed, China thought disconsolately, was a sense of purpose, a reason for being at her husband's side. Maybe no one else knew they weren't really a couple, but she herself had been aware of it all evening.

Being Trace's guardian didn't make her Yance Chisolm's wife. Not really. And she'd never been more aware of it than when Elaine Brisbane approached Yance and every instinct China possessed went into red alert. The woman's interest in him was obvious to any but a fence post, whether Elaine had a husband or not.

Mine, China had wanted to say, just as Yance proclaimed it to the cowboys when they'd first returned to the ranch from Santa Fe. But Yance had staked a claim to protect her, he said. And now she had staked a claim to protect herself, as well, however a sham that claim might be.

As Elaine said, Yance was not that busy anymore so it was only a matter of time before he realized how empty his and China's relationship was and do something about it. However good life was for him now, he still didn't have eight years of it to lose to a hasty Prenuptial Agreement.

Now that the idea of marriage had entered his thinking, *real* marriage, he'd want to consider it far more seriously than he had when he thought there was little time to spare. And this time he would want marriage with someone he loved, someone who could give him additional children.

Appearing at her elbow, Yance handed her a glass with

only a splash of wine in it and leaned close to whisper in her ear like a conspirator. "I passed the hors d'oeuvre and canapé trays," he said. "Guess what I saw mingling chummily with the cheeses, pates and caviar?"

She chuckled. "Turkey."

"Bingo." And he ran the tip of his tongue slowly over her ear's outer shell to briefly nuzzle the gold loop in her lobe.

China dropped her wineglass.

"Thank you," Yance said with a great huffing sigh of relief and eyeing with satisfaction the stain trailing into the folds of China's skirt. "Now we can get the hell out of here. Let's find Max and make our polite goodbyes."

"It would've been easier," China said, once she had her heart back, and joining Yance in dabbing at the small wine stain on her skirt, "to just say you were ready to leave. I've now ruined a very expensive dress."

"It'll wash. Where's Max?"

"Just across the way, watching us with a knowing leer," China replied. She retrieved the glass, miraculously unbroken, and saw there was no stain on the carpet, since the contents of the glass were on her.

"Ah. A good man, Max. And what with that leftover turkey, also very frugal. I like that in my executives. Let's go."

He took her hand, but in the act of heading across the room to confront his host, stopped suddenly.

"Oh, Lord, China. I did it again. Did you want to stay? The dress isn't that bad. Most of the damage is hidden in the folds and it was white wine." He grimaced. "Forgive me."

It was China's turn to lean in close, so close that her lips and Yance's ear were only a molecule apart. "I've been to parties like this before. In about half an hour, they get out the lamp shades."

A great area for lips this year, she thought, liking the almost-feel of the ear's arcs and ridges against her mouth.

Making sure her breath trickled lightly over and through all the right places, she added in a throaty whisper, "Let's get out of here."

"What did you say? I mean, hell, yes. Let's go."

For the first time, Yance hated the fact that his Lexus didn't have a front bench seat. Like the randiest teenager, he wanted China next to him, as close to him as he could get her as he drove back to the apartment. Instead they were separated by a state-of-the-art console that he would gladly have torn out and dumped in the nearest trash bin.

The best he could do was chastely hold China's hand in his and use his other hand to drive.

He concentrated on the feel of that hand, unconsciously stealing China's ever-present awareness of the senses. Her hand was warm, firm, clasping his larger one lightly.

Slowly he threaded their fingers together, savoring the brief undulation of China's knuckles as they slid sensuously against his own, and the slender roundness of her fingers as they pressed intimately against his, locked with his.

Just, he thought, as her body would lock with his.

Her legs would clasp him as hard, as soft as her fingers did now; her abdomen, her breasts would push up against him just as the pad of her palm now pressed against his palm, its firm hills and valleys joining his, skin to skin.

The stunning fit of her to him was a constant miracle of craftsmanship, he thought. Their hands, their lips, their bodies.

Soon, soon the most intimate parts of them would fit together as closely as their hands did now, and they would lock into each other, rock with each other, absorb into each other in perfect matching rhythm.

Unconsciously, slowly, rhythmically he rocked their

joined hands back and forth, back and forth, and heard China give a little moan of pure sexual frustration. Her fingers held his tightly, almost painfully, and he knew that whatever he was feeling, she felt as well.

The atmosphere in the luxurious automobile thickened with suppressed longing, with the almost audible throbbing of expectation.

When he parked the Lexus in the parking garage, Yance jerked his door open to hurry around to assist China, but found her already out of the car.

He didn't so much as check his forward movement, but continued headlong to sweep her into his arms, wrapping them around her to hold her as close to him as he could get her, and at the same time lowering his mouth to her lips as if they were an oasis and he was dying of thirst.

Somewhere in the dim recesses of his mind, he felt her arms around him, holding him as tightly as he held her, as her lips met his with matching hunger.

Gradually, gradually he became aware of her breasts thrust up against his chest. Reaching between their annexed bodies, he ran his palm over the closest one's fullness, savoring the firm weight of it, resenting its thin covering.

He felt China's supple fingers now in his hair, tugging a little in the same rhythm he'd unknowingly set up as he gently massaged the breast beneath his hand.

His mouth left hers to find her cheek, her closed eyes, her wonderful ears, while another part of him went rigid with the feel of her lips trailing over his face, exploring up under his chin, limning his jaw.

When their lips met again it was a homing in from a long journey, tongue caressing tongue, reaching, supping, trying to go deeper, deeper, pushing.

"Oh, China," Yance finally gasped, and took her face between his two palms to rest his forehead against hers, breathing heavily.

China reached up and touched Yance's hot cheek with her fingertips. "Oh, my," she whispered dreamily. "Oh, my," and heard his soft laugh just before he lifted his head.

"Oh, my, indeed," he said, but his voice still rasped. "Oh, my China Dare."

Taking her hand he led China to the elevator, but once inside its plush interior, he lowered his head to kiss her again. A gentle kiss this one, a series of little kisses actually.

Oh, she loved the feel of his lips, China thought, savoring them with her eyes closed, meeting them with blind instinct. Hard. Soft. Silken. Supple. A wondrous banquet of touch against her seeking mouth.

And the smell of him. Aftershave. Soap. A whiff of Scotch. Perhaps a sniff of the wine she had spilled.

When the elevator door opened, she opened her eyes slowly, her lashes feeling weighted, as if reluctant to exchange touch and smell for sight.

Ah, but what a sight. Eyes of gunmetal gray stared into hers solemnly but with the merest touch of gentle laughter.

She loved that laughter. Yance had so much of it—a gentle humor that managed to in no way impair his authority. And he looked so handsome tonight, at home in his evening suit, wearing it with the same ease he wore jeans and a Stetson. He was easily the most handsome man at the party. He was easily the most handsome man China Dare Smith had ever met.

China Dare Chisolm.

She kept forgetting that. After tonight, would it become more real?

As if sensing her sudden disquiet, Yance took her two hands into his and gently pressed his mouth to hers again in a soft, lingering kiss. Only a gentle touching of mouth on mouth, no tongue, no eroticism, but for China it might have been soul on soul.

Their mouths pulled apart slowly, reluctantly, so that for a long moment each could examine the face of the other in unsmiling search.

And what they found was enough.

Hand in hand, shoulder against shoulder, head tipped to head they slowly drifted into the apartment to rediscuss their honeymoon…

…and found Blackjack waiting up for them.

They jerked apart as if they'd been scalded, and neither could have said why.

"County sheriff called," Blackjack said. "Somebody tried to steal your new bull, Yance. Chad caught 'em redhanded. They're in the clink. Since Fergus is gone for the holiday, the sheriff wants to know if you, as the owner, will come in and check with him about it. You havta sign somethin', he said."

Yance ran a hand through his hair, trying to get a grip and still his outraged libido. "Tonight?"

"Whenever," Blackjack replied laconically.

"Then to hell with him. We're headed back to the C3 tomorrow. I'll check with him then. Was the bull damaged?"

"Not in any way that matters, Chad said."

"So all right," Yance repeated. "Tomorrow's good enough."

China slipped from the room and Yance watched her go, still feeling like he'd been poleaxed.

"Sounds reasonable," Blackjack said. "Just thought y'might want to know t'night, is all."

Rubbing a hand over his jaw, Yance sighed quietly. "Yeah. Thanks, Blackjack. Sorry. It just came out of left field. I'm glad you told me."

"About China," the older man said carefully.

Yance stiffened.

"I've, uh, noticed since I been here, that you an' China don't, uh…that is, you each have your own room. Trace says that's the way it is at the C3, too. I wasn't pryin', Yance. It just come up. But I'm remindin' you,'' the old man said sternly, gathering steam after stumbling around a subject that went against his old-fashioned sensibilities, ''that I told you I expected you to do right by her, boy, and I meant it. What's between you is your bizness, but what's right is right.''

''What is between China and me is certainly our business,'' Yance said evenly, ''as are our sleeping arrangements. But I'll say this, anyway. I won't force her and I'd cut off my leg at the knee before I'd hurt her.''

Blackjack cleared his throat. ''Good enough,'' he said abruptly, and left the room.

For the first time in recent memory, Yance walked to the whisky decanter and poured himself a stiff drink, downing it in one slug.

The old man had rattled him. What did he mean, ''right is right''? Had China discussed their personal relationship with him? She'd said not, initially, but had she later changed her mind?

Was Blackjack warning him against sleeping with China, since he'd promised her there would be no intimacy between them, or was Blackjack saying he expected their marriage to be a whole one?

Yance didn't know. More important, he didn't know where China fit in all this. She wanted him, that he knew. You could've cut the lust between them with a knife tonight. And he damn sure wanted her.

But, he'd learned, in the middle of that Thanksgiving Christmas party, if not in the middle of a crowded mall, that he wanted all of her. Body...and heart. Most of all, her heart.

He loved her. Had loved her for a long time, maybe since he'd first met her. Definitely since he'd kissed her at the spring.

He wanted marriage with her: a real union where they

slept together in one bed and neither of them shared that bed with anyone else.

China was a passionate woman, and he knew they would be good together. But would she, in spite of their prenuptial agreement, be willing to give that passion only to him?

Would she be willing to renegotiate their contract?

When Yance tapped at her bedroom door and called her name softly, China wanted to weep, wanted to open the door and fling herself into his arms and let Yance reweave the wonderful sensual spell he'd created earlier.

She didn't. "I've gone to bed, Yance," she called quietly through the closed door.

He didn't answer for a long moment and she couldn't blame him if he was angry and disgusted. "Can we talk for a little while?" he asked at last, keeping his voice low.

"No. No. I'm...tired." And it was true. Suddenly she was exhausted. "Too much wine, perhaps. I'm...I'm not used to it." Would he think that was why she'd been all over him like moss on the north side of a tree?

Probably not. Yance Chisolm wasn't stupid.

And something in his voice made her realize he, too, had cooled down. He really did just want to talk, perhaps find a common ground for what happened tonight, or make excuses for it. After all, he was a healthy man and to her certain knowledge he'd been a long time without a woman.

But tonight China didn't want excuses, or explanations, or anything that said he'd thought better of it, or hadn't meant it, or wanted to continue it, or wanted it never to happen again.

She just wanted to go to bed and pull the covers up over her head and shut the world out. Somebody could wake her next spring.

Seeing Blackjack had made her feel guilty as a teenager, coming in tousled and flushed from a hot date. It would be different if she *felt* married, and not just Yance's live-in— Live-in what? Companion? Security blanket?

"Good night, Yance," she said clearly.

"Good night, China," he replied, and she thought she heard him sigh, but perhaps it was just the sound of her own.

Chapter Nine

They left Midland the following morning for the two-hour drive back to the C3. There was little conversation in the car, the four of them subdued, as if at once relieved and disappointed to be returning to the ranch.

Blackjack and Trace sat in the back seat, talking quietly for a while before each rested his head in a corner and went to sleep. China sat in front with Yance. They talked hardly at all.

They did not hold hands.

Once at the ranch, Yance dropped them off and left again to meet with the county sheriff.

Blackjack and Trace drifted off on their own pursuits.

China went to her room to unpack. And repack.

Last night she'd decided she wanted a break; in the almost-silent car on the ride back to the ranch, she'd confirmed it. Freedom of movement was in her contract, she thought briefly. Yance had very carefully provided her with that freedom; now she was going to use it.

She told him later that evening. "I'm going to Santa Fe for a few days," she said when Yance returned to the den from telling Trace good-night.

Yance, who'd envisioned an entirely different scenario for this quiet time together, paused in midstep, then continued slowly on into the room to take a seat on the couch across from the overstuffed rocker where China sat. His original plan had been to take her hand in his and lead her to the couch where they could sit side by side and talk.

Maybe, hopefully, do more than talk.

For a moment he didn't know quite what to say. There was that damned agreement, for one thing. What *could* he say?

Why? Certainly not. What the hell for? No.

That last was the word he most favored. No!

"Oh?" he said at last, as if it didn't matter, as if something in him hadn't died a little.

"I have friends there," China said into the silence, after she accepted the fact that Yance wasn't going to tell her he didn't want her to go. "I thought I might combine a little visiting with some early Christmas shopping," she added, when he still didn't say anything.

Finally, he spoke. "When did you want to leave?"

"Tomorrow."

"Tomorrow." He repeated the word slowly, as if it held great portent. Just like that, he thought. Tomorrow.

Last night might never have been.

"Did you want to fly? The jet's available," he offered courteously. "Or if you want to drive, you can use the Lexus. Or the Suburban."

"I think I'll drive. And if you don't mind, I'll take the Lexus." She smiled a little. "This time I promise not to let anyone run into me."

"That's something you can't guarantee, honey," Yance said seriously. "Just call me when you get there, please. Promise that, instead."

"I promise," she said, understanding him completely.

Honey, he'd called her. Unlike many Western men, Yance didn't use endearments often or easily. And when he did, as he occasionally did to China, each was a small treasure. She knew, however, that to Yance the endearment had no special significance, but still it warmed her for a moment, like a sip of smooth brandy.

But he hadn't said he didn't want her to go.

True to her promise, China called Yance when she arrived. She made the long trip in one day and told him she was tired, but glad to see her friend, Essie Somerfield. She asked about Trace and Blackjack and Mabel. She asked Yance if there were any new developments in the attempted theft of the bull. She told him that if anyone needed her, she'd left Essie's name, address and telephone number on the memo pad kept near the kitchen phone.

I need you. Come home. *Now,* Yance wanted to say. But didn't.

Over the next few days, Yance had reason to be grateful for the army of carpenters he'd called in. He'd made up his mind to run his new operations out of the ranch.

With the kind of exploratory interests he was now in the act of developing, he could work on the C3 as well as anywhere else. Modern global technology allowed him to set up an office wherever there was an electric outlet, and he saw no problem in bringing New York, London, Tokyo and Shanghai to the West Texas mountains via the Internet.

But however busy he was during the day, there was always something missing. He knew it. So did Trace.

The first full day after China left, Trace didn't make his bed before he went to school. Yance discovered the fact later in the day and promised himself to crawl all over the boy for it that afternoon. Yet when he finally got around to tracking his son down when Trace came home, he found him in his bedroom in the act of making the bed. Quietly leaving without the boy knowing, he'd stood in the doorway for a moment, Yance left him to it.

The next morning the bed was made.

When before daylight Yance drove Trace to the bus a couple of days later, his son asked casually, "When's China coming back, Dad?"

"I'm not sure," Yance replied, keeping his eyes on the road. He found the words depressing.

"She makes good lunches," Trace said. "Mabel's aren't any fun."

Yance chuckled a little, enjoying a discussion in whatever capacity of the woman closest to his thoughts. "Is China's cooking getting better?"

"You don't cook sandwiches, Dad. I guess China puts in the same stuff as Mabel, but she always adds somethin' extra, you know? Somethin' different. Know what she put in the day she left? A snake," he said enthusiastically, not giving his father a chance to reply. "A green rubber snake. It was bad. I chased Letty Esquivel all over the playground with it."

"I'm sure Letty loved that," Yance replied with a grin.

"Hasn't China called or nothin'?" Trace asked, returning to the subject at hand.

"No, no she hasn't, son."

"Mabel doesn't leave me a snack for when I come in from school, either," the boy said, his tone aggrieved. "Why don't you call China, Dad? Ask her when she's coming home."

"You sound like you miss her, son," Yance commented, pulling onto the side of the highway to await the bus.

Trace sighed mightily. "I guess I do. She makes me mad sometimes, that's okay, isn't it, Dad? The kids at school get mad at their moms, but they still like 'em."

"Being mad at someone doesn't mean you don't like

them, son. Or don't love them. It just means you're mad at them for a little while is all. No big deal.''

The boy nodded sagely. "I guess.''

But that afternoon, Trace took matters into his own hands. Before supper he went clomping into Yance's office, his brows twisted into a horrific scowl.

"You gotta call China, Dad. I can't find my ZZ Top shirt and I want to wear it next Wednesday. Ever'body's supposed to wear their favorite clothes, 'long as its decent, Ms. Chambers said, and then we're supposed to write about 'em. That shirt's my favorite and I can't find it. It's a classic. Mabel says she hasn't seen it. I gotta have it, Dad. Can you call China an' ask her where it is?''

Yance stared at his son, who stared back at him earnestly...and innocently. Yet if Trace had been the picture of guilt, Yance knew he'd have still bought the story.

"I suppose I can do that. You need it by Wednesday, you say?''

Trace nodded.

In the act of picking up the phone, Yance realized he didn't have the number. The two of them made the trek to the kitchen for the memo pad where China said she left it. Backing up a page from the current grocery list, he found her neat handwriting.

And took a deep controlling breath to keep from slamming a fist against the refrigerator.

"I think,'' he said, and then had to repeat himself, because the first time his words came out as a rasping growl. "I think,'' he said, after clearing his throat, "instead of calling her, son, I'll just go get her.''

"All riiiight! Way to go, Dad,'' Trace said, his face lighting up.

"Run and ask Blackjack if he minds taking you to the bus in the morning,'' Yance instructed, already beginning to organize his departure. He headed to the bedroom to throw a change of clothes into a bag, China's note balled tightly in his fist. "If he's busy I'll get one of the hands to do it," he threw back at his son.

Trace stared after him, openmouthed. "You're going now? Tonight?"

"I'm going tonight," Yance replied tersely. "I'll call you tomorrow sometime and let you know when I'll be back. Blackjack will stay in the house with you so I'm expecting you both to hold the fort."

"Wow. You miss her too, huh, Dad?"

But Yance, pulling a small case from the top of the closet, didn't answer.

S. E. Somerfield, he thought savagely. Not Essie Somerfield. *S* period, *E* period Somerfield.

No way in hell was Yance Chisolm sharing his wife with any S. E. Somerfield. He'd written that blasted contract. He could damn sure break it.

To hell with the thing.

His wife wasn't sleeping with anyone but him, dammit! And if she didn't want to do that, she could damn well sleep alone, just as he was doing.

He wished he was a cussing man. A few piddling *damn*s and *hell*s just weren't cutting it.

Striding over to the phone beside the bed, he picked up the receiver and punched in his pilot's number.

Four hours later he stood at the front door of a small Southwestern-style house in one of the older parts of Santa Fe, ringing S. E. Somerfield's doorbell and more than ready to ring the man's chimes.

When the door opened, however, he paused a hair. The man who stood before him was easily a good six foot ten, maybe even seven feet tall, and had the brawn to match his height.

Yance had to tilt his head up a bit, but he looked the man right in the eye. "S. E. Somerfield?" he asked, his tone cold enough to freeze water pipes.

The man just stared back at him for a long moment, not the least intimidated, in spite of an incongruously gentle face. "No," he said mildly. "And you are...?"

Though a part of him was relieved this wasn't the man, Yance's tone was no less aggressive. "I'm looking for S. E. Somerfield. Is he here?"

"*She's* here," the man replied. "Perhaps," he added, in a voice so soft it almost purred, "I can help you instead." Menace radiated from the giant's very pores.

Yance didn't notice. He blinked. "She?"

"My wife," the big man replied briefly, warningly.

But Yance had begun to smile. "Wife," he repeated. "I'll be damned."

"And who wants to speak to my wife at nine o'clock at night?" the man asked again, after raising an eyebrow.

"Sorry," Yance replied. "I'm Yance Chisolm, China Dare Chisolm's husband. It's actually not your wife I'm looking for, but my own. Is she here?"

A knowing laugh as big as the man who uttered it boomed out into the night. "S.E.'s here, but China isn't. She's having dinner with friends. Male friends and female friends," he added with a twinkle.

"But she said she'd be in early. Why don't you come in and wait for her, Yance, and meet the family. I'm S.E.'s husband, Reginald. I know, I know. Dumb name for a man my size, but my mam didn't know how big her little darling was going to grow. I'm Reg, to my friends."

He led the way into a living room, cluttered with toys and reading material, its disarray unpretentious and inviting.

"S.E.'s giving our two-month-old a feed, but she'll be here in a minute. And this doll baby is Sandra, up past her bedtime." He swung a little girl of about five into his arms, where she perched on his forearm in her nightgown.

"Say hello, Sandra," her father said. "And say goodnight."

"Hello and good night, Sandra," Yance said, smiling at the beautiful child beaming down at him.

"'Night," she said as her father carried her from the room.

"I'll be right back," Reg said. "Make yourself at home. Ah, here's S.E. This is Yance, darlin'. China's Yance. He thought you were me. Or I was you. Whatever. He's looking for China." And the big man left the room.

"Hello, Yance," S.E. said, coming forward. "I'm glad to meet you at last. China's missed you."

She has? Yance thought. Good.

When China let herself in the front door an hour later she heard voices coming from the living room and paused. It sounded like—

It was.

As if by instinct, Yance looked in her direction just as China appeared in the doorway. He stopped in midsentence, rose from his place on the couch, and in four strides was across the room and sweeping his wife into his embrace.

Start as you mean to go on, he thought. He'd known it was a good plan from the very beginning.

And this was exactly how he meant to go on. And on.

Lowering his mouth to China's, he let it sizzle. And when he lifted his head and looked down into her startled green eyes, he smiled. And his smile sizzled, too. He knew it because he read it in those dazed eyes of hers. And that was just the way he meant to keep her. Dazed. Dazzled. And his. Only his.

Reg cleared his throat. "Guess who's here, China," he said and laughed. "And guess who's leaving? We are. Good night, children. Say good-night, S.E."

His wife giggled at this joke her husband had been using since he'd first met her. "Good night, y'all," she said in her best Texan, and the two of them left the room hand in hand.

"Hello, wife," Yance said.

"Hello, Yance," China replied, gazing into his face as if it told her secrets.

And perhaps it did, he thought. He hoped so.

"You're supposed to say, 'Hello, husband,'" he instructed quietly.

"Am I?" Her gaze clung to his. "Hello, husband."

And her mouth was right there waiting when his came home.

"I missed you," Yance said, some time later. They still stood, just inside the living room door where he'd met and greeted her. China still wore her jacket.

"I missed you, too," she said, not realizing she still wore it. Her arms, like her heart and mind, were full of Yance Chisolm.

"I'm glad. I want you to miss me, China." He kissed her again, because he'd had the thought and as if she'd heard it, she raised her face.

"I understand you're sleeping on the sofa," he murmured.

"Yes."

"Come with me to a hotel?"

"Yes."

"Bag?"

"All packed. I was going home tomorrow."

"Yes."

Leaving a note that was probably unnecessary, China promised the Somerfields she would see them in the morning before she left for her return to Texas.

She'd have to, Yance told her with a laugh, because he'd picked up a rental car from the airport and wherever they were going tonight, they were going together, leaving a car in the Somerfield driveway.

And, he added, the rental car had bench seats; had been

chosen for that very reason. They were using it tonight and leaving the Lexus.

China, in the act of gathering any belongings not already in her bag, looked up at that. And found Yance's gunmetal gray gaze waiting, laughter lurking in it. But also something else.

Something old as time, old as Adam who first looked on Eve and liked what he saw. Something hot; primeval.

But it was also gentle and just for her.

She wanted laugh. She wanted to weep.

She wanted to strip then and there and take Yance Chisolm to the floor.

Swallowing, China dropped her eyes to fumble with the catch on her suitcase, until Yance's hands brushed hers aside and latched the thing.

Then he swung it up with one hand and took her arm with the other. "Ready?"

"Oh, my, yes," she said on a long sigh, at which point he put down the case and deliberately kissed her again.

"If we don't get out of here now, we're never going to," Yance said at last, coming up for air. "Walk in front of me, darlin', and don't look back. I'm not a pretty sight. But you are, and if I keep looking at you, I'm going to peel off every garment you're wearing right here in the Somerfield living room."

"Oh, my," China said, liking the idea if not its location, and thinking Yance was a pretty sight himself, bulge and all. She turned, though, and led the way out the front door after locking it from the inside.

Standing on the front steps, however, Yance decided to take the Lexus after all. "Or we'll never get to the hotel," he explained ruefully.

Once in the car, he didn't hold her hand, either, but deliberately allowed the rolling boil to cool to a low-level simmer. They still had the desk clerk to face.

He headed for the Hilton because he'd passed it on his

way to the Somerfield's and knew where it was. And, standing at the desk, he realized that one of life's small pleasures was signing the register as Mr. and Mrs. Yance Chisolm. It was the first time he'd ever linked himself and his wife together in writing.

The thought sobered him. Before anything, he and China had to talk.

Yet once in their room, they stood for a moment and just looked at each other, both smiling; each content, for the moment, just to look.

Finally, China shrugged out of her jacket.

Yance, instead of helping her do it, shrugged out of his. They had to talk.

He wondered how the hell to begin. "Would you like anything?" he asked. "Coffee? Something stronger? I can call room service."

China shook her head, beginning to feel awkward.

Room. A nice one. Certainly up to Hilton standards.

Bed. A big one. Probably also up to Hilton standards.

She'd never been alone in a bedroom with Yance. What moments before had seemed so elemental, now didn't seem quite so simple. "Nothing for me, thanks. But order for yourself, if you want."

"I can't touch you right now, China," Yance explained quietly, in that way he had of reading her mind. "Because if I do, I won't let go of you till morning, and maybe not even then."

Not giving himself time to think, and so touching her after all, he plunked himself down on the side of the bed and gently pulled her down beside him, rubbing his hand up the inside of her arm for a moment, the backs of his fingers brushing over the side of her breast.

Suddenly becoming aware of what he was doing, he let go of her arm as if it scorched him.

"I want a real marriage," he said abruptly. "You and me, together. Man and wife, in the true sense."

Turning toward her, he stared fully into her face. She found no laughter in the now darkly serious gray eyes gazing into her own.

"I find I can't share you," he continued, "no matter what I put in that contract we both signed. I'm not, after all, a man who can share his wife, especially if you...if we...become truly married. And I want that, to be truly married. But if you can't see yourself with only me over the long term, then now is the time to say it. I'll bide by the contract, if that's what you want, but we'll have to live apart. I don't think I can stay in the same house with you anymore and keep my hands off you."

He smiled a little before dropping his gaze to his boot tips. "As an only child," he said ruefully, "I never did learn to share. Guess it's a little late for me to learn now."

His gaze slanted back to her. "Do you need some time to think this over?"

China sighed. This man knew her so little, even though at times he seemed to live inside her head. "Yance," she said slowly, "it's just not in me to violate a marriage vow. It never has been. I signed your contract only because it was what you wanted, what you insisted on."

Were contracts all he understood? she wondered sadly.

She took a deep breath. "I suggest you delete your permission for my extramarital affairs all together," she said quietly. "I'll gladly initial the cross-out, or whatever one does in such cases. I want a real marriage, too. You and me, together, just as you said. But," she added, her eyes meeting his levelly, "I'm also an only child and nor did I ever learn to share."

It was a warning that pleased him.

His slow smile warmed her all the way to her belly, and all the way down from there.

"C'mere, wife," he said.

And she came.

* * *

They had lunch with the Somerfields before heading out of town the next day. Reg was a metal sculptor and S.E. a potter, Yance learned. He liked the couple, and their children; even held their two-month-old son for a little while, liking the feel of the small bundle in his arms, and the baby, milky smell of him.

Yance also liked the sight of China holding the baby, who even now looked as if he might grow to some of his father's size. China held the wriggling infant up to her shoulder and crooned in his ear, and the baby immediately stilled and seemed to listen. Yance loved the way China's face softened…and hated the way her eyes saddened.

She should see a gynecologist, he thought. It had been years since her accident, and medical research was always making new discoveries. He had mentioned it before they were married but maybe he should talk to her about it again.

"You're good with babies," she said, after they dropped off the rental car and the two of them were in the Lexus heading south toward Texas. "You burped little Regie like a pro—even thought of the towel on the shoulder before-hand and everything," she teased.

"I learned on Trace," he said, grinning. "It's like riding a bicycle. You never forget. You're pretty good yourself, darlin'."

"I learned on Leanne, though she was several months older than Regie when Frank and I first married. But still a baby," she added softly, "and so beautiful. I miss her terribly sometimes."

"Have you checked with a doctor recently, China?" Yance asked. "They're doing some miraculous stuff now, you know. If you want children, they might be able to fix things that couldn't be fixed when you were young."

China gazed at Yance's profile as he easily negotiated the highway. "I haven't seen a doctor in years," she confessed. "Just got used to the idea of not ever being able to have children, I guess."

She fingered her wedding band for a moment and watched the bright, afternoon sunlight stream through the car's window and warm the gold. "I'm sorry I can't have children for you, Yance."

Reaching across the console, Yance covered her two hands with his one. "I'm sorry you can't have children for yourself," he said quietly. "Why don't you see a doctor and get yourself checked out? For your sake, honey, not mine. As far as children are concerned, we can adopt, if you like. I don't have any problem with that. I doubt Trace would, either, once he got used to the idea."

China turned her hand so she could thread her fingers through his. Adoption? she thought. She'd love to.

"Trace missed you, by the way," Yance continued. "He likes your surprise lunches, he says. Something about a green rubber snake. You're a woman after his own heart, it seems. Oh, and he insisted I call you so you could tell him where you put his ZZ Top shirt. I, uh, decided to come get you instead."

China gazed at him in surprise. "But it's in his T-shirt drawer, on top. He wanted to wear it for a favorite-clothes day they're having at school, so I made sure it was clean before I left and told him right where I put it."

"Apparently he forgot," Yance replied and laughed. "Thank you, Trace," he murmured to his absent child. "You're a good son."

Since they'd made a late start, it was long after dark when they entered the Davis Mountains. Yance called the ranch to tell them they wouldn't be in until the following day and pulled into a motel. But after receiving the key to their room, he got back into the car and drove down a side road to the edge of the small community, away from the lights, then found a spot on the empty road to pull over.

Leaving the warmth of the car, China joined him in the chill night. They stood close to the front of the car, however, to absorb its heat, and close to each other for other reasons. But Yance hadn't brought China to this deserted spot for lovemaking.

They stood front to front, arms locked about the other, both looking up.

A thousand stars glittered above them, their dancing points of light a surprise of silence, as if an accompanying mighty orchestra had just been abruptly cut off. The spangle of lights was so vibrant with life, with message, with the utter joy of being that surely there should be a matching crescendo of sound.

No place on earth, China thought, had the skies of West Texas, and there was no one on earth with whom she'd rather share them than the man who held her clasped lightly against him.

They were a gift, those stars, in air cleaner than in any other part of the country. They were a reminder of what was lost and a hope for what was to come.

And she knew that she would never look at such skies again without thinking of Yance Chisolm and this night and her own hope for what was to come.

Slowly Yance turned her about so that her back was to him, and locked his arms around her shoulders and chest, not in embrace but in the united joining of a man and a woman who each stood separately, yet together, and looked up.

"I love you, China Dare," he said softly for the first time.

The words were a part of the night, a part of the great cosmos above them.

Nor was there need to seal their meaning with a kiss, and China didn't turn around. In this place and at this moment, a kiss was far too small. Their locked bodies, fully clothed and facing outward, surely forged the strongest bond in the universe.

"I love you, too, Yance Chisolm," she whispered.

They stood quietly then, not speaking, as the stars glittered with a melody they couldn't hear but felt to their beings; until a shooting star, quick as thought, slow as eternity, streaked across the sky and ended their awe with its flash of surprise.

"Ah," Yance said. And turning China toward him, he slipped the ring he'd bought so long ago onto his wife's finger so that it took its place next to her wedding band.

"I think we've earned this at last," he said. "You can take it off when you paint," and he kissed her.

"Did you make a wish?" he whispered, after a while.

"I couldn't think of anything to wish for that I don't already have," she answered with a small laugh, her thumb brushing lovingly over the diamonds and three emeralds of the C3. "Did you wish?"

"Nah. Let someone who needs it have it tonight. My wants will be answered as soon as we get back to the motel. It's cold out here, wife. Let's go get warm."

Trace barreled out the front door as soon as he saw the dust cloud drawing the meanderings of the ranch road with the precision of an Etch-A-Sketch.

"They're here," he yelled at the top of his lungs.

Blackjack ambled out the door behind him and was standing on the front porch when the Lexus pulled up into the front drive. "Looks like it," the old man drawled.

Though Yance hadn't asked for it, Blackjack had silently given the younger man his full approval when he'd decided to go get China and bring her home where she belonged.

China hadn't been happy lately. Blackjack knew it instinctively, but didn't know what to do about it. He did know, however, that she needed to be here.

Leavin' never did solve anything.

But when he saw his stepdaughter's radiant smile as she stepped out of the car, he had to revise that opinion. Somethin' had been solved.

His China was bloomin'.

"Hey, Mom," Trace said, cannoning into her and wrapping his arms around her waist. "Where's my ZZ Top shirt?"

China hugged him back. It was the first time Trace had teased her this way since before Yance went into the hospital.

"Hmm," she said, giving the question some thought. "Let me see now. That's the blue one, right? With the big ZZ concert schedule on the back? I think it's in the ragbag. It being too small for you and all, I thought it would make a good dust cloth."

He wasn't fooled. "You dare," he said, and laughed.

"Got one of those hugs for me, boy?" Yance asked, grinning at his son.

"Always got one for you, Dad," Trace replied, who'd been brought up expressing affection, and he embraced his father.

China hugged her stepfather. "It's good to be back, B.J.," she said. "Is everything here all right?" She knew better than to ask him how he felt.

"Right as rain, darlin'. You look happy," the old man replied, fighting emotion and winning except for his gruff voice.

"I am, B.J." Over the old man's shoulder, she took a good look around for the first time. "Good grief. What's going on?"

"Didn't Yance tell you? He's addin' on."

"With what? A second house?"

"Two more bedrooms with their own baths, another office, another garage, and I'm, uh, modifying the back porch. I'm also enlarging the living room,'' Yance said, joining them and placing an arm around China's shoulder.

She gazed up at him, puzzled. "Why?"

"Because I'm taking your advice and going into a couple of new areas where I don't already have people running things,'' Yance said, guiding her up the steps and through the jumble of wood and carpentry tools now strewn about what used to be the living room..

"Electromagnetic cars, for example. Remember me talking about that boy I met in the hospital and his ideas? I think he's onto something.''

They arrived in the kitchen, which China was glad to see remained untouched, and Yance went to the cabinet to take down a can of Colombian coffee. He spooned grounds into the basket and poured water into the automatic brewer as he talked, then flipped the switch to get it going.

"I like living on the ranch and don't want to go back to offices in the city, nor do I see why I should have to, at this stage. The bedrooms are for any business guests, the second office is so I don't have to modify the current office into a high-tech mode. Dad would croak,'' he said as an aside and with a grin.

"The garage is for research, and the living room enlargement is so that it will hold more people in case we want to give parties that don't call for barbecue. Redoing the back porch is, uh, because I want to.''

"But the C3 Big House has always looked like this,'' China said, trying to take in the enormous changes Yance planned.

"No,'' he said gently, "it hasn't. My great-grandfather started out with two rooms, then added a third when he made a little money. My grandfather added to that and put in indoor plumbing. When it became his, my father knocked out a wall and made a master bedroom, added another bathroom and added the den.''

He smiled a little, hoping China would understand, but

also knowing that moving from place to place all her life had probably given her a sense of displacement.

"It's only a house, China. Our home. It isn't an inviolate antique, it's a place for living…comfortably. And I'm alive."

She reached up and took three coffee mugs from the cabinet. "Don't I know it," she said softly, and with her back turned to her stepfather and Trace, shot Yance a wicked, mischievous glance that said more than that.

But it wasn't the changes in the house that made her nervous, China thought later, taking a long, soaking bubble bath before going to bed. It was the changes Yance was obviously getting ready to make in his life. He was returning to the world of big business, whether he conducted it from an office in the mountains or an office in Hong Kong.

And it was a world in which China had never fit well.

Yance opened the door to the bathroom wearing nothing but his skin and without a word, stepped into the bathtub with her…which caused China's thoughts to stop completely.

She then entered a world of the senses where she fitted very well indeed.

Chapter Ten

Carrying her coffee mug, China wandered about the house, stopping now and then to watch the various carpenters and craftsmen hammer, saw and measure.

Sounding much like a child's rhythm band, the place rang with the cacophony of construction, sometimes blending together for a period and sometimes far out of tempo.

The noise didn't seem to bother Yance. He sat in what had been his father's office with a phone attached to his ear, listening while scribbling on a yellow legal pad, talking while scrolling with the speed of greased lightning through his computer, murmuring while standing at the window looking out at the far mountains.

And he laughed often with whoever was on the line at the time, China noted, with all the excitement and enthusiasm of a Boy Scout planning a camping trip.

She smiled herself, just listening to him.

Wandering out the back door, she stepped onto the porch, her favorite place to set up her easel. There were even more workmen out here, closing in half of the formerly open area, and extending walls farther into the backyard. Thank goodness all her current projects were completed, leaving her free of deadlines until mid-spring.

China ran a fond hand over a remaining post, enjoying the rough feel of its sun-cracked paint against her palm. Whatever Yance had planned, the new room was going to be large, but she was sorry to see most of the porch go to accommodate it.

The old pecan tree was nearby, leafless now, but revealing the flow of line and harmony in its bare limbs and branches. The ranch outbuildings clustered just beyond, their once bright paint faded over the years to earth tones, and so providing wonderful contrast to the vast West Texas sky. Corrals and fences and several natural upthrusts of boulders added texture to the whole.

Yes, she was going to miss this porch.

The north wind was sharp, however, the porch's one disadvantage, and she didn't linger.

But after reentering the house and heading down the central hall she came face-to-face with a stunning young woman wearing the feminine version of a Madison Avenue business suit. The woman's vivid blond hair was cut in the currently popular messy style and without a strand out of place, her makeup understated but for her bright red mouth. She looked, China thought, as though she'd stepped straight from the pages of *Business Woman's Magazine.*

They saw each other at the same time and both stopped.

"Hello," the woman said easily, putting out a hand. "I'm Brenda Duchen."

China shook the manicured hand, automatically noting how the fingernail color exactly matched the woman's lipstick. "China Chisolm," she replied, at a loss.

"I'm getting Yance's coffee," Brenda Duchen said, and

for the first time China saw Yance's favorite mug in the woman's other hand.

She looked at the mug, then back to the woman's beautiful face.

Brenda smiled ruefully. "You haven't the faintest idea what I'm doing in your house, have you, Mrs. Chisolm? Let me begin again. I'm Brenda Duchen, Yance's new secretary. I started this morning. He, uh, said he couldn't stand being called Mr. Chisolm."

Yance hadn't mentioned hiring a secretary, China thought. Yet she supposed he needed one. And this one looked like she could send faxes with flair, and spreadsheets...or whatever one did to them...and dance WordPerfect like a pro. She could probably also make a pot of coffee to rival Starbucks, mix a mean Manhattan and whip up a batch of canapés in twenty minutes flat.

China wondered if she'd ever been a nanny.

"And I can't stand being called Mrs. Chisolm," China replied, lying through her teeth. "Call me China. I'll show you where the coffeepot is," she added politely, and led the way into the kitchen, conscious of her faded jeans and Apache moccasins...only to deliberately bring her green-tinged thoughts to an abrupt halt.

Get real, she told herself disgustedly. If Yance wanted this kind of woman, he'd had ten years after Melodie died to grab one. He was leaving the slick life behind, wasn't he, even if he was once again entering the corporate world?

When Yance walked up behind the two women and placed a hand on each of their shoulders, she was glad she'd had that little talk with herself.

"I see you two have met," he said cheerfully. "Brenda is going to be a permanent addition around here, China. She and Jack Fergus are getting married after the first of the year. I'll have my ranch manager and secretary under one roof."

He dropped his hands from the women's shoulders, but

wrapped an arm around China's before winking at Brenda. "Saves bunkhouse space, Fergus tells me," he said, deadpan.

Brenda laughed and colored the least bit, in a way few Madison Avenue women did, and China realized the woman was young and had probably wanted to impress her new boss. A couple of days walking over the rock-strewn ranch grounds would probably have her leaving her high-heeled shoes in the closet along with her black business suit that would soon show every fleck of sawdust.

In the meantime China would leave these two to wheel and deal. She had work to do herself today, the most important of which was transferring her things into the master bedroom.

And couldn't help a certain cat-and-cream satisfaction just thinking about it.

Before beginning the transfer, however, China stood for a moment in the doorway of the room that had been hers for three months and looked around. Odd that there was so little of herself in it, she thought.

She'd put her stamp on the living room and den, but in this room no personal items sat about to mark her territory. Even her makeup articles were tucked away in the dresser drawer instead of sitting out in the small Peruvian basket she kept them in. Beneath its mirror, the dresser was totally bare, as it had been when she moved in.

No artwork of hers hung on the walls, nor any of the favorite pieces of others' work she'd brought with her. No framed photographs occupied the nightstand, those of her mother and Blackjack still packed away in a box in the bottom of the closet.

Actually, there were several still-unpacked boxes in the closet and perhaps half a dozen full cartons under the bed. It was as if she'd always known she wouldn't be here long.

Or as if she'd hoped.

This move, then, should be easy.

She was wrong. Moving her own things might be easy, but first, she found, she had to shift Yance. He hadn't occupied the master bedroom long either, and his possessions were scattered everywhere and mixed with those of his father's.

Had it been difficult for him to weed out his father's things, China wondered, or had he just not bothered?

When she asked him at noon while they sat companionably at the kitchen table and downed tuna salad sandwiches and potato chips, he said it was a little of both. With the uncertainties before the operation, he'd moved into the bedroom more from Midland than from his old C3 bedroom, yet he'd shied away from putting down roots in it, so to speak. The room still held the essence of his father, and hc hadn't been sure at that time if it would ever hold the essence of himself.

"But I love what you do in a room, China Dare," he said with a leer, giving the words double meaning. "So do in our bedroom whatever pleases you, darlin'."

China batted coy lashes. "Ooh," she said in a demure high falsetto. "What you do say, Mr. Chisolm."

Yance's eyebrows worked. "Ooh. What you do, Mrs. Chisolm."

He rose and bent to kiss her mouth. "Mmm. Tuna fish. My favorite. Save seconds for later, hmm?"

After taking his dishes to the sink, he returned to kiss her again briefly. "Later," he whispered meaningfully, and strode from the room like a man with all his tomorrows in front of him.

China traced her tongue over her upper lip, tasting Yance's last swallow of lemony iced tea. She'd never known lunches to be so delicious.

The afternoon was spent in an orgy of discovering the contents of boxes and cartons, emptying drawers and filling drawers, moving the dresser to a place of better light which then meant having to empty the bookshelf and move it to a location more pleasing to her sense of balance.

China shuffled, folded and hung, loving the feel of her husband's clothing in her hands, finding a few pairs of silk boxer shorts she'd never seen him wear and planning on insisting he model them for her later; loving the idea of Yance's briefs in a drawer on one side of the double dresser and hers in the drawer next to it.

Photographs of her mother and Blackjack, and of Yance, Uncle Steve and Trace, now sat on the dresser and bureau top.

Three generations, China thought, holding one framed snapshot for a moment to study it. A vision of handprints flitted through her mind. She sighed, and placed the picture just so on one side of the dresser.

She also found a picture of Melodie in a drawer. Melodie, laughing, and in jeans and cowboy hat, standing beside a horse that China remembered.

I'll look after them for you, China wanted to tell the laughing, beautiful girl, and knew even as she thought it that it wasn't true. Yes, she would look after Yance and Trace to the best of her ability. But not for Melodie's sake, rather for her own.

Not knowing quite what to do with the photograph, she at last placed it in the bottom of Yance's sock drawer.

With the next day being Saturday, she asked Trace if he would like to move into his father's old room, the bedroom she'd vacated.

The boy's face lit up. "Awriiiight!" he exclaimed delightedly, and trotted down the hall to look into the now empty bedroom as if to verify that it was still there.

"Bed and bureau and everything?" he asked.

"Everything," China confirmed. "You're the oldest son, aren't you?"

"I'm the *only* son," Trace replied dryly, sounding in that moment just like his father. "The only, period."

"You might not want the bedspread," China commented, gazing thoughtfully at the double bed with its covering of blue chenille. After a brief inward tussle over spoiling the surprise, she shrugged her shoulders, coming to a decision. "What the heck. I bought you a Christmas present in Santa Fe, but I think I'll give it to you early. Wait here."

When she returned, she carried a large department store bag which she placed on what was now Trace's bed. "I hope you like it."

Trace opened the bag and pulled out a folded brown and tan blanket. A blanket? "Well...um, thanks, China," he said.

"You might want to open it up before you keel over with enthusiasm," China told him.

She took one edge and the boy took the other and they pulled the folded bed cover open together.

Printed onto the soft fluffy fabric was an eagle, wings and talons outspread and with its beak open in a wild silent scream. Caught in flight just as it spied prey far below, the bird was delineated against a vast sky and above an outcropping of rugged mountains. The whole, in browns and tans and golds, was at once dangerous and majestic.

"Wow," Trace breathed. "Bad. *Thanks,* China."

"You're welcome, kiddo," China said with a smile, gratified. "You can use it instead of a bedspread. Makes the bed easier to make, too," she added slyly. "Ready to move?"

And somewhere in the process of changing rooms, the decor of the boy's bedroom shifted also, going from that of a boy to that of a preteen. It was not intentional on anyone's part, but in the weeding out of clothes that were now too small and toys not played with for years, in the deciding of which baseball posters to hang on the wall, and the lengthy discussion of where to put the CD cabinet and how to set up speakers for maximum resonance, the subtle shift occurred.

Later, as the two of them stood in the middle of the room surveying their handiwork, China wondered if Trace realized what had happened.

"Bad," he said, and she laughed.

And in that instant it occurred to the boy that he'd just moved into the room that China had occupied. "Hey," he said. "Where're you sleep-innng..." His voice trailed off as realization hit. "You're in Dad's room now, aren't you?" he stated, his tone faintly accusing.

"Yes," China said matter-of-factly. "Want to see how I've fixed it up?"

"I guess," he replied without enthusiasm.

China led the way to the master bedroom and stood in the doorway with Trace as he looked it over. "Doesn't look like it did when Grandpa was in here," he commented.

"No. But your room doesn't look the way it did when your father was in it, either."

"How do you know?" There was a touch of belligerence in the question, and Trace was at once sorry for his tone and not sorry at all. It felt odd for China to be sharing a room with his father, and he wasn't sure he liked it.

"Because when he was your age, he loved airplanes he told me, and had models hung all over his room. Just like you have baseball stuff and animals all over yours. That room is your room now, Trace, not your father's anymore. And this is your dad's and my room, not your grandpa's anymore. Someday it will be yours."

"And who gets my old room? Your kid?" Trace demanded aggressively.

"Maybe," China replied, not wanting to discuss her inability to have children with this boy, yet wanting Trace to realize there might be another child someday, whether from adoption or medical miracle.

"I don't know why you come in makin' changes," Trace blurted out, scowling at her. "You're not really family. And Blackjack's not your dad, neither. He's just a stepfather. You don't love him like a real one."

The words came from nowhere, and without thinking China responded to their challenge.

Nobody talked about Blackjack like that. Nobody. "You listen to me, Trace Chisolm. I love Blackjack. He's my father, the only father I have, and I won't let you say things about him. Do you hear me? No one loves me better than B.J. does. He's always been there for me. Always!" she hissed, leaning down and glaring into Trace's face.

"Well, all right!" Trace said with a dark scowl, not knowing what else to say.

"Well, all right!" China echoed, turning her back on him and folding her arms. She was shaking all over.

The boy clumped down the hall to his new room, and China stayed where she was, trying to pull herself together. She'd just quarreled with Trace as if she was ten years old herself, she thought in disgust.

Why in heaven had the boy brought Blackjack into the conversation? She would bet the boy loved the old man. The two always seemed to get along well together, so why had Trace said what he did?

She stared unseeingly at the far wall. Was Trace perhaps thinking of stepmothers instead of stepfathers? They'd been talking about new children coming into the family. Had the boy remotely imagined that another child would somehow replace him in the scheme of things?

Oh, God. Why was she understanding this now? Why hadn't she understood it at once when Trace spouted off, instead of, like a child herself, flying to Blackjack's defense?

Her relationship with Blackjack didn't need defending,

but her relationship with Trace just might need some clarification. She'd have to talk to him.

But when she went to Trace's room, he wasn't in it, nor was he anywhere in the house. China sighed. She ought to be helping Mabel with supper, but at the moment she just wasn't up to it. The family would have to do without salad tonight.

The family. Such a wonderful word. And such a responsibility.

She sighed again and returned to her bedroom to rummage in the bottom of Yance's sock drawer. With Melodie's picture in her hand, she walked down the hall to Trace's bedroom and placed the photograph on his nightstand.

Part of the problem, she thought, was the fact that the boy seemed to have no pictures of his mother, nothing to peg onto. China didn't have any pictures of her own father, either, but she had her name, given to her by Blackjack to honor that father who'd died before her birth.

In some ways, half of Trace's birthright was missing. He saw his grandparents on his mother's side on occasion, usually when they wanted to borrow money from Yance, China had to admit. They brought the boy expensive toys that were for the most part far too young for him, but they seldom asked Trace to spend the night or a weekend with them.

Actually, as long as China had been on the C3, they'd *never* asked their only grandchild to visit. Of course, they were busy and had a business to run. And perhaps they just didn't know what to do with a boy Trace's age.

But the fact remained that Trace was very much a Chisolm, with his mother only peeking out of him in his ready laughter and his usual delight in life in general.

Leaving the house, China headed for the pecan tree. The workmen were gone for the day, so the yard was quiet as she made her way up the nailed boards that formed a rough ladder. The wind had died, but it was still cold and she wouldn't stay long. Yet she desperately wanted private time without four walls for a little while.

However, no sooner did she lie down on the rough platform to stare up at the blustery afternoon sky, thinking of the last time she'd been in this tree house and Yance's proposal of marriage, than she heard movement below her.

Trace poked his head up to eye level from his standing position on a lower branch.

"What're you doin' here?" he asked, scowling fiercely.

"Thinking," China answered. "Want to join me, or do you want me to leave?"

"I saw you come up here," he said, climbing onto the platform. "This is *my* tree house."

"I know it is. I'll leave if you want."

Trace sat down beside her supine body Indian-fashion. He didn't look at her, but he also didn't tell her to leave.

"I'm sorry I yelled at you, Trace," China said at last. "It was a stupid thing to do."

"I'm sorry I said stuff about B.J.," Trace responded, his voice so low she could barely hear him. "I didn't mean it," he added earnestly, glancing at her and then gazing again at his ankles folded into his lap. "I like Blackjack."

"I love Blackjack," China responded. "I think the most important part of the word *stepfather* is the last half of it."

"I guess," Trace agreed.

Neither spoke for long seconds.

"Why'd you put my mother's picture in my room?" the boy asked at last.

China rolled her head to face him, and for a moment he met her eyes before squinting up at the gray sky. "I thought you might like to have it there," she answered quietly. "Your mother loved to laugh, just like you do, and that picture shows her laughing. You remind me of her sometimes."

Trace gazed at her in astonishment. "You knew my mother?"

"We were friends when we were kids." She laughed softly. "Your mother and I managed to get in lots of trouble together."

Returning his attention to his ankles, Trace murmured, "I thought you put her picture there to remind me that you're not my real mother."

"You don't need to be reminded of that," China replied, her voice dry.

"Sometimes I do," Trace said, ducking his head as if ashamed of the statement. "Sometimes I forget you're not my real mom. Do you think she gets mad at me for that?"

China wanted to gather the boy into a hug, but settled for sitting up and hugging her knees.

"I think," she said carefully, "that she's standing somewhere up there with my father, watching the goings on here at the C3. And I think my father is saying, 'Thank you, God, for Blackjack.'"

She turned to look at Trace fully. "And I hope, oh, how I hope, Trace, your mother is also saying, 'Thank you, God, for China,' because I love you very much. I couldn't love you more if you were my very own child, just the way Blackjack loves me. If your daddy and I have a dozen more children, you will always be our oldest son. No one can ever take your place."

Trace swallowed, his lashes batting madly. "I love you, too, China," he said roughly.

"I need a hug," China said.

He sniffled. "Me, too," and he went into her waiting arms.

In spite of the C3's rocky, uneven terrain, Brenda Duchen continued to wear her high heels; not too high, of course, which would have been contrary to current fashion, but definitely dressy in a sophisticated, understated way.

Nor did it appear to bother her that her boss came to work in jeans and boots and open-necked Western shirts

The secretary was always friendly to China, her manner polite and unencroaching. The few times the women chatted, it was also clear that Brenda was very much in love with Jack Fergus.

So why couldn't she like Brenda more? China wondered.

Christmas was rapidly approaching, and China drove into Fort Davis to buy gifts. She always tried to shop locally for such things, aware of what a struggle it was for small-town merchants to keep their doors open when the tourist season was over. She knew many of the store owners and spent freely, not only on gifts but on decorative items for the house and bunkhouse.

China then threw herself into decorating the den for the holidays, since with the living room torn up they would put the tree there this year. But always she was aware of a little niggle of unease...and a sense of waiting, as if she knew something unpleasant was going to happen, but didn't know when.

Placing a bunch of red candlesticks on a side table, she stepped back to admire the effect, and stepped right into Yance's encircling arms.

"Hello, wife," he said, nuzzling her ear from the back.

Turning within his embrace, she snuggled into him. "Hello, husband," she replied.

He hugged her, but only kissed her on the forehead before saying regretfully, "Wish I could stay, but I have a conference in a few minutes."

"Oh? Do we have guests? Should I do something about lunch?" Would executives like egg salad at the kitchen table? she wondered. But if she spruced it up with seven-grain bread, perhaps, and maybe some of the Greek olives Yance was so fond of?

Yance chuckled. "A conference call, I should say. And

you do whatever you want about lunch. I can fix something for myself later. Right now I'm up to my...back pockets in management, so we'll have to skip our usual lunch date. Sorry, darlin'. I'll make it up to you after supper.''

He waggled his eyebrows, gave her another squeeze and was gone.

And maybe that was why she didn't like Brenda Duchen, China thought. The secretary represented the corporate side of Yance that China was never comfortable with; the side of him that in some indefinable way shut her out. When it came right down to it, it wasn't actually dislike of Brenda that she felt at all, but jealousy of the woman's ease in fitting into the schemes and plans Yance was up to his back pockets in.

Would there come a time when, like Frank, Yance realized that China was a possible hindrance to those plans, that she would never truly fit?

She felt a chill run down her arms and rubbed her hands over them to bring back warmth.

But there was the other side of Yance, she reminded herself. The side that was warm and giving, that was full of dry humor; that was at home on a horse and in this old-fashioned room. The side that took his son to the bus every morning and lunched with her at the kitchen table. She fit just fine with that side of him, didn't she?

Yes, she did. And it didn't matter a whit that he had no time for lunch with her today. She could wait and eat with him later.

But it seemed he didn't have time for it later, either, and finally China fixed him a sandwich and took it to his office, where he sat at his desk shuffling papers, talking to the air around him and being answered from speakers in the telephone. Brenda sat opposite him, typing up things on demand or pulling them up on her computer screen.

China returned to the kitchen and fixed the secretary a sandwich, too.

Both Yance and Brenda smiled at her gratefully and mouthed thank-yous, but China doubted either would have time for even a bite before the bread dried out. Feeling like a good little waitress, she returned with two mugs of coffee and placed them strategically, then left them to it.

A week before Christmas, China suddenly realized that most of the foot soldiers in the army of workmen were gone, and only the occasional bang of a hammer rang against the mountains. Its single staccato sounded lonely now that it was without its fellow percussion section. After the first fascination with the craftsmanship that went into it, China had deliberately avoided the new construction, gradually coming in some vague way to distrust what was happening to the old ranch house.

Now, in the unfamiliar quiet, she wandered into the new living room and looked around.

Within moments Yance walked up behind her and placed his two hands on her shoulders, so that they could survey the room together. "What do you think?" he asked, his voice coming from above her head.

"It's...big."

"I thought we'd make it a little more formal than before," Yance explained. "I imagine we'll be doing more entertaining now that my main office is here."

"But you kept the fireplace."

He nodded, and still with his arm around her, walked farther into the large, empty room, widened now to extend beyond the front porch.

"I like the fireplace," he said. "My great grandfather built it. And I like the view of the mountains, so I added more windows." He nodded toward the huge bank of windows that took up most of the front wall. "The porch is going to wrap around in front of them," he said, "to create a deck. But the other half of the porch will remain as it is, swing and all."

"It's a beautiful room, Yance," China said, feeling ice crystals begin to trickle through her veins.

"I also kept the hardwood floors," he continued. "I think the workers matched the old flooring pretty well, don't you? But if you think with the room being larger that it needs carpeting again, we can do that, too."

"No," she said. "No."

Keeping his wife under his arm, Yance walked China to his new office, located just beyond the old one. "Dad's office will remain as it is," he commented, passing through it with a nod to Brenda, working at her desk. "Brenda will use it, and it will still be the office where any ranch business is conducted that Jack Fergus doesn't take care of. But this one," and he waved an arm to encompass a large, paneled room also with a bank of windows, "will be to keep me in touch with the rest of the world."

"Lots of outlets," China commented.

"Lots of equipment," Yance replied with a laugh. "I've put in my own generator to back up county utilities. You know what an ice storm can do to power lines out here, and I don't want to be caught."

No, he wouldn't want to be caught, China thought. Yance was a careful planner. The only time his planning had been shaky was when he'd had to have that operation and didn't know whether he'd come out of it or not. Since then, his life had changed, and changed again. Did he now feel trapped by her?

Each of the new bedrooms was large and spacious, well-lit and airy, with a view of the distant mountains. Each had its own bathroom and a large walk-in closet. Whether from Chicago or Hong Kong, a mover and shaker would feel right at home here, she thought. There was nothing in the new bedrooms that said Chisolm. They were sterile, without personality.

"Lovely," she said, and felt the lie choke her.

"Everything needs furniture and accessories," Yance

replied, apparently unaware. "Can I leave that in your hands? I'm busy as a cranberry merchant right now, trying to get a couple of ideas off the ground before the holidays get here and everything stops. Midland has several good specialty stores, or you can fly into Dallas if you'd rather."

"Dallas," China said shortly.

Yance paused and looked at her a moment, but China faced away from him as she stared around the bedroom. He must have misunderstood her tone, he thought.

"Ever wonder what makes cranberry merchants so busy?" he asked with a chuckle.

"Conference calls," China replied, before she could stop herself.

He chuckled again and, standing in the sun-filled empty room, pulled his wife into his arms and kissed her, wishing he had the time to haul her back to bed, wishing he had the time to go with her to buy furniture and dance awhile in Dallas.

Maybe for New Year's Eve, he thought.

New Year's eve with China Dare in Dallas. Sounded X-rated. Sounded raunchy. He could live with that.

It wasn't until later that China realized they had not toured the room off the back porch. But she didn't care. She had no desire to look at it.

The following day was the last school day before the holidays, and China had promised to send cookies for the fifth-grade Christmas party. She didn't make them, of course. Mabel did. But that afternoon China and Trace decorated them.

Standing at the kitchen table with various bowls of colored frosting, cinnamon red hots, gumdrops, silvered sugar pearls and varicolored candy bits, the two indulged in an orgy of creativity while singing carols at the top of their lungs.

Trace taught China the words to the subversive fifth

grade variation of "Rudolph the Red-Nosed Reindeer" that was full of giggly bathroom humor and would probably cause Gene Autry heart palpitations; and China taught Trace the equally decadent version of "Rudolph" she and her friends had sung at about his age.

Yance entered the kitchen at midchorus. "Is that what the younger generation calls funny?" he asked severely.

"No, that's what my generation called funny," China told him. "Trace's verses are different. Sing 'Rudolph' for your father, Trace. Maybe he'll like your version better."

Trace, delighted to oblige, sang with gusto, really putting his heart into the gross parts and watching his dad with mischievous delight through the whole.

"Nah," Yance said, shaking his head, "that's pretty tame. We had better words than that," and he proceeded to serenade them with the "Rudolph" take-off that had delighted his own fifth grade.

Trace and China judged his version to be okay, but each felt their verses were better.

"Let's do a round," China suggested. "Each of us will sing our own. Ready? I'll start. One. Two. Three," and she began to sing, then pointed to Trace, who chimed in, then to Yance, who added his bass.

But stumbling over words, losing the tune and fighting giggles, they couldn't finish, finally grinding to a laughing, tattered halt.

After making himself a cup of instant cocoa in the microwave, Yance joined them in the cookie decorating, thinking himself the happiest of men.

But there had been that moment with China in the bedroom, he thought suddenly, remembering it now and not dismissing it as he had then.

She wasn't happy with the additions to the house, he mused. Was it because she liked things to stay as they'd always been; was uncomfortable with change? Had moving around in her youth made her now want to cling to sameness?

He'd worked carefully with the architect so that the additions to the house would blend with its former lines, would represent a growth rather than a restructuring. It surprised him when China wasn't more enthusiastic. As an artist, he'd thought her more open to change.

Yet by next year at this time, he decided, the changes would no longer be new. And if China purchased the furniture and decorator pieces for the rooms, they would certainly become more hers and not just extra space in the house.

And there was the surprise he was planning for her as a Christmas present. He couldn't wait to see China's face on Christmas morning.

Reaching into the gumdrop bowl he popped a red one into his mouth.

"Unh, unh, unh," China said, waving his returning hand away from the bowl. "Everyone likes the red ones. Soon there won't be any left. Eat some of the black. We're only using those for snowmen's buttons."

"But I don't like licorice," he whined, mimicking Trace at his best.

The boy giggled.

"Tough," China said.

The three of them were laughing and gossiping easily together when Brenda appeared in the kitchen doorway. "Sorry, Yance. Mr. Jenkins is on the phone, returning your call."

"Damn," he said, rising, and left the room.

China gazed after him. She'd been losing some of her earlier ire, but now felt it rise again. She wanted to throw a spoon at him. She wanted to cry.

She wanted to run.

Early the next morning, she ran to Dallas.

Chapter Eleven

Picking out three rooms of furniture took China exactly two hours and forty-seven minutes, including the time it took to write out explicit instructions so the delivery men could find the ranch. With Christmas in three days' time, however, delivery would not be made until the following week.

She supposed she'd set some sort of speed record, China thought, as she made her way out of the well-known interior specialty store. But with cost the least factor in her choices, the choosing hadn't been difficult.

The pieces she'd chosen were beautiful in design, and elegant.

Think luxury hotel, she'd told herself, pointing out a bureau to the hovering clerk.

Think sleek. Slick. She liked those words, as much as she hated the images they conjured…as much as she hated the new rooms. And pointed out a matching bed frame.

Having completed the reason for her coming to Dallas

in record time, China stood indecisively on the sidewalk in front of the store a moment, the holiday crowds streaming by on either side of her as if she were a bit of flotsam caught momentarily in the flow of an unseen current.

Now what? she wondered. Promising herself she wasn't going back to the ranch until tomorrow, she had the rest of the day in front of her. She turned to drift with the flow of shoppers past holiday-decorated windows, standing at one of them for a while to watch animated elves in Santa's workshop make the same toys over and over.

The scene was colorful and charming, and the little girl standing next to her gripping her mother's hand couldn't get enough of it, but China soon did. She was having a hard time working up Christmas spirit this year.

When she found herself in front of Neiman-Marcus' famous doors, China went in to explore and exited three hours later with her arms full of bags and boxes.

Knowing they would love the sheer absurdity, she'd bought useful but elegant gadgets for Reg and S.E., and imported mechanical toys for the Somerfield offspring, understanding full well it would be the children's parents who'd take the most delight in them. But regardless of what was inside the packages, the Neiman-Marcus label alone would make the Somerfields laugh, just as it would have made her laugh this time six months ago.

And China had bought herself a cocktail dress, then gone a little wild in the lingerie department. She'd gone a little wild in the men's equivalent to the lingerie department, as well. Nor did the boy's department escape her notice.

Shopping, China thought, sitting her weary body down in a nearby restaurant for coffee and an early supper, was the modern woman's panacea for a sore heart.

And there was not a reason in the world for her to be heartsore, her thoughts continued on as she took a fortifying sip of rich Colombian coffee. The richness of taste made her immediately think of Yance.

Could it be that her hormones were out of whack? A woman thing perhaps?

But then she remembered the tiny scrap of black silk she'd found for her husband and her plan for giving it to him in a very private moment as a very private Christmas gift.

Nope. Her hormones were just fine.

So what was wrong with her? She loved Yance. Yance said he loved her. Life should be wonderful.

Yet the fact was, it wasn't.

She found a moderately priced motel to spend the night in, having seen all the luxury-style furnishings she could stand for a while. Besides, all she wanted was a bed and no matter how elegant the room, if the bed didn't have Yance Chisolm in it, it would not meet her exacting standards.

It was still afternoon and she called the ranch to let Yance know where she was staying. But he wasn't there, Brenda said. He and Trace had gone into Midland for last-minute Christmas shopping, but she would leave the message.

Perhaps Yance would call her later, China thought, flipping on the television. Three channels carried *Miracle on 34th Street,* two the old version and one the newer. Two other stations carried *It's a Wonderful Life.* By flipping back and forth, China managed to watch both movies at the same time. She cried in all the right places, and in some places that weren't meant to be sad.

Yance didn't call.

By now more than ready to go home, China boarded the corporate jet first thing the following morning. Yance and Trace were at the runway to meet her as soon as the plane touched down.

They had stayed the night in Midland and gone to a

movie, they told her, and so it was too late to call her by the time they received her message.

She hugged them both and cried, and they hugged her back and teased.

And then it was Christmas. And then she knew why she'd been heartsore and angry and scared.

Yance gave her a studio.

With a flair for the dramatic, Yance wrapped one of his handkerchiefs around China's eyes, and with Trace and Blackjack in tow, led her to the room where half the back porch had been. Then he untied the blindfold.

"Oh, Yance," China breathed. The huge room was filled with light, two walls, corner to corner, made up of floor-to-ceiling windows so that nothing obstructed her view; the same view she'd had from the back porch but without the cold and wind.

There were long miniblinds on the windows, however, raised now to the ceiling, so that she could control the light if she wanted, Yance said, pointing them out to her proudly.

She nodded, still stunned. One wall held a long bank of open shelves already containing the materials she'd stuffed into the small bedroom Yance originally gave her for storing her art supplies. Below them were cabinet doors hiding away additional storage space. In the center of the room was her long paint-stained worktable with materials on it just as she'd left them when the table was in the extra bedroom.

And propped up against the remaining bare white wall were dozens of her canvases.

"I left that wall for you to hang your paintings," Yance said.

China froze.

Slowly she turned to face him. "My paintings?" she asked, her tone holding the same chill as her heart.

"How do you like it, China?" Trace asked excitedly, before Yance could respond. "Bad, huh?"

"Bad," China agreed, smiling down at him.

And meant it to her bones. Her paintings had again been relegated to her studio, not good enough for the upscale life-style this old-fashioned ranch house was beginning to reflect. Would China herself figuratively be relegated to her studio, also, her paint-stained hands and askew vision of the world, as Frank had called it, an embarrassment to the CEO Yance was again becoming?

"I didn't know you were such a good artist," the boy chattered on. "Dad showed me the pictures you did. We have some of the books with your pictures in them at school. I didn't know that. And the painting you gave me of Dad for Christmas is super."

He stared at the white wall. "But I don't want to hang it in here," he said. "I don't havta, do I? I want it in my room."

"No, you don't have to hang it in here," China said, her voice hard. "I meant for it to hang in your room, or in the living room. It's supposed to be a companion to the one I gave your dad of your grandfather."

"Good," the boy said, satisfied. "Do you like your earrings, China?" he asked, going on to his next concern.

China wore the pair of wooden hoop earrings, each shaped like a snake swallowing his tail that Trace had given her.

"Love them," she said.

"They're not your real present," Trace said earnestly. "I'm giving you your real Christmas present for New Year's." He giggled. "An' you'll never guess what it is in a million years."

"A portrait of Blackjack," China said immediately.

"Close," the boy said, and laughed again.

"Giving us portraits of our fathers was a wonderful gift, honey," Yance said before Trace could spill the beans, and wrapped China into his arms. Over her shoulder, he winked at his son. "Just so Trace doesn't use mine for target practice," he teased, then forgot Trace to tilt China's face up to his and stare down into it.

"Merry Christmas, wife," he said.

And it was completely beyond China not to murmur in reply, "Merry Christmas, husband," just before his mouth descended.

"It's gettin' a bit thick in here," Blackjack observed. "What say we find us some cider and fresh air, boy?" and he and a giggling Trace left the room.

"Do you really like the room, China?" Yance asked when they'd gone. "I tried to make it as much like the studio you had in Santa Fe as I could remember. Except that I added more window space. I know how much you liked the view from the back porch."

"It's beautiful," China assured him. That much, at least, was true. "Ready to start Christmas dinner? I think our fellow chefs are getting restless."

And she left the spacious studio that had been Yance's gift to her, that brought the outdoors in so well...but seemed to China to wall her true self off completely.

She closed the door behind her and didn't enter it again that day.

Christmas had been on a Friday, and the following Wednesday the truck from Dallas rolled down the ranch road, a cloud of dust churning in its wake, bringing the new furniture.

China was the only one at home, with Yance and Trace and Blackjack in Midland doing men things, Trace told her importantly, and Mabel having two weeks off for the holidays, as did Brenda.

The men unloaded and China directed them as to the placement of each piece. She was easy to work for, they found. She didn't change her mind once.

By the time they left, the bare living room and two bedrooms were bare no longer. Yance, of course, had furnished his high-tech office to his liking last week, so now all the new rooms had furniture in them, if not heart.

With the dust still hounding the truck the eight miles back to the highway, China went to get ladder, hammer and tacks and then the canvases from her studio, where they leaned against its bare white wall just as Yance had placed them.

When she returned, she hung her paintings, carefully inserting tacks where they would do the least damage to the walls, but otherwise paying no attention at all as to what she was placing where. When she was finished, she surveyed her handiwork with an air of cold satisfaction.

And fought the urge to cry.

It was almost dark when Yance returned. He came in the back way from the garage and found China sitting at the kitchen table eating a bowl of canned soup and with a novel propped up in front of her.

He bent down and kissed her. "Hmm. *Passion's Fire.* Sounds like a book I'd enjoy. Care to act it out for me later?"

"I don't know," China said. "Right now, the heroine's on a ship in a hurricane and is seasick."

"Then we'd better wait till you get to the good parts," Yance said. "Any more of that?"

"On the stove. Peach and mango salad in the fridge. Saltines in the canister. New furniture in its proper places. Where's Trace and Blackjack?"

"In Midland. We're joining them tomorrow. So the new stuff arrived, did it? Good. I can hardly wait to see what the China Dare look looks like this time." He reached to take a soup bowl from the cabinet.

Minestrone, he thought. His favorite. "But in a minute, darlin'. I'm starved."

And only canned soup for supper. China watched him ladle a hefty portion into his bowl, and sighed.

She finished before he did but sat with him while he ate. They chatted, Yance teasing her a little and carrying most of the conversation because she didn't have much to say.

What would he think of her furniture choices? China wondered. What would he say when he saw the living room? What would he say when she told him of her plans?

Yance ate seconds and then a large bowl of fruit salad, his conversation dying in the face of China's lack of response.

Something's wrong, he thought.

But something had been wrong for a long time. Sooner or later he was going to figure out what it was. Or China was going to tell him. It wasn't like her to keep her gripes to herself, one of the traits he liked most in her.

He carried his dishes to the sink, rinsed them and placed them in the dishwasher. "Ready to show me the great makeover?" he asked easily, placing an arm around his wife's shoulder but aware of the watchful look in China's eyes.

"I think you'll be pleased with the furniture," she said coolly, and led the way into the living room.

Yance had taken three steps into the room before he stopped abruptly, and stared around him, feeling as if all the blood had been drained from him.

He'd told China the room might need to be more formal than it was in the past, so she'd made it formal.

And sterile as a hospital waiting room.

The furniture pieces themselves were in impeccable taste, but had all the personality of a plastic bag. Matching end tables bracketed a long couch in a subtle rosy tan, the shades on the new lamps sitting on the tables color coordinated with it. The end tables themselves exactly matched a low-slung coffee table, with a piece of French crystal placed on it for maximum effect.

This from a woman who decreed matching was boring.

There was a conversational grouping of chairs, daring anyone to actually sit in them, with a low round table in their midst looking intimidated.

His eyes traveled to the fireplace that had been the focal point in the room. Now its mantel was bare, somehow giving it a look of elegance that Yance never knew it had. He wasn't sure he liked the discovery.

Nothing in the room was in bad taste. Far from it. With no decorator items but the piece of French crystal sitting on the coffee table, the room seemed to blend with the stark grandeur of the view outside the windows.

Stark, Yance thought; that was the word.

The Chisolms were not in this room.

There was nothing of anyone in this room. It was as aloof from humanity as the mountains it was somehow a part of.

Except for the two interior walls, covered floor to ceiling with China's paintings.

Dozens of them, he saw, arranged in no particular order nor for any bid to eye appeal. They just…hung on the wall, like children's drawings taped to a refrigerator, so many of them in all shapes and sizes their frames touched. There were even a few without frames.

The mass of color leaped out at Yance, so that he felt almost overpowered.

Slowly he brought his gaze from the room and the paintings to fix it questioningly on China's face.

"You agreed that I could hang my paintings anywhere in the house I wanted," she said tightly, and snatched from a nearby table where he hadn't noticed it, the prenuptial agreement they'd both signed. She handed it to him.

"Page six, I believe. About halfway down."

He didn't bother checking.

"I don't choose to hang them in the studio," China added, in case he missed the point.

"I see that," Yance replied dryly. There was a message in this and he wasn't getting it. He'd thought he knew why China disliked the additions to the house, but when she'd frozen into a little ball of distance and long silences after he'd presented her with the studio, he hadn't an inkling as to the problem.

Of course he asked. And China, usually so direct and forthcoming, evaded, as if the subject were too important for her to touch at the moment. So he'd given her time.

And now this.

He looked for something to say, something to give him a glimmer of what was in his wife's mind. "What happened to your couch?" he asked at last when nothing presented itself. "I kind of liked it in here."

"It's still in the storeroom where you put it when the carpenters arrived," China said. "I didn't bring it in because I want to take it with me to Santa Fe. I've decided to set up my own apartment again."

Yance stepped away from her as if she'd hit him. "The hell you are!" he ground out savagely.

"Page three, paragraph five."

"I don't give a damn what page and what paragraph. You're not moving to Santa Fe. Hell, is all this because you think I didn't want your paintings hanging in here? I put 'em in your studio, China, so you could hang them wherever you damn well wanted. Some of them were on your studio wall in Santa Fe, remember? But I love your work. I'm proud for anyone to see it and recognize your talent. They were only placed in your studio for convenience. And I didn't just put your work there, as you should have noticed, but all the canvases I found, including my grandmother's."

"Oh," China wanted to say, feeling silly, suddenly realizing the truth of his words. He hadn't been wanting to hide her work, the very *self* of her, away at all.

But she lifted her head. "It's not just that," she said. "It's everything else, too. I don't belong here anymore, Yance. You have to already know that. I'm not the kind of woman who fits into a corporate life-style. I never have been. Just ask my ex-husband. I don't know how to mix drinks, or cook, or even how to work a computer."

And at last Yance knew they were at the core of the problem.

"You married me when you were desperate to protect Trace," she went on, "the one thing I could have done very well. But you don't need me for that anymore. You don't really think of me as his parent, anyway. It would be best if you found someone more fitting to you. I was only ever plan A, remember? A plan you had to go with because there was no plan B. That doesn't mean you have to be stuck with me for the rest of your life."

"Bull," Yance replied.

"You gave me my freedom, Yance," China said nodding to the contract he still clutched in his hand. "And in doing so, you gave freedom to yourself, as well. I think you should use it."

He deliberately ripped the contract in half, then in half again. "I love you," he said.

"You respect me," China contradicted. "I'm good people. Solid. I can be relied on in a crisis. But the crisis is over."

Yance stared down into her averted face. "You're right," he said. "I think this damned contract has outlived itself. Go into the den," he ordered brusquely, in a tone he'd never before used with her. "I'll be there in a minute."

When he joined her in the den, still decorated for Christmas and with the Douglas fir from Wishbone Mountain giving off its clean tangy scent in the warm room, he found

China on her knees in front of the fireplace, staring into the flames.

"Good spot," he commented and dropped to his hunkers beside her. Before she could stop him, he tossed her ripped-apart copy of the prenuptial agreement into the heart of the fire, where in seconds the paper blackened and curled and was no more.

"And now mine." And he fed his own copy, page by closely written page, to the hungry flames.

"We'll see my lawyer tomorrow and get this straightened out once and for all," Yance then said briefly.

China swallowed. "All right."

By mutual consent, they spoke no more of the thing. Yance turned on the television and they sat side by side on the couch, not touching, and watched programs flicker across the screen that neither one saw.

If she'd been given the opportunity, China would have slept in another room that night, maybe in one of the new ones. But Yance saw to it that she occupied the bed with him, though he did no more than curl her body into his spoon fashion before he dozed off.

And that was the way their marriage ended, China thought morosely, lying awake curled up next to him, with Yance's arm draped over her waist. Not with a bang but a whimper. And she did so want to whimper, but didn't dare, afraid she would wake the sleeping man behind her.

As if he read her thoughts, Yance tucked her more firmly against him and apparently slept on.

She'd been wrong about the studio. When she realized that, in her heart of hearts she'd hoped she was wrong about the rest, too; that Yance would tell her all her fears were groundless. For a moment there, she'd thought he was going to do just that, but then he'd mentioned seeing his lawyer and setting things straight, and she'd known that their marriage was over. He had finally recognized that she didn't fit with him at all.

In the morning they would meet with Yance's lawyer to work out details of the divorce. Blackjack would be angry and Trace not thrilled but they would both get over it. China wasn't sure she would, however.

But hadn't some part of her always known the end would come?

What began with necessity had almost from the first taken on something far beyond the original intent. Yet the almost visible sexual attraction was there from the very beginning. That little detail was an element that Yance, in his so carefully worded Prenuptial Agreement, hadn't accounted for. Making love, forming a real marriage, was never a part of the agreement. And so its fundamental intent had gone awry.

Had they stayed together, Yance would have had to work on it some more anyway, she supposed, maybe adding a clause for the protection of his children by her. She'd seen a gynecologist and things looked promising for putting her reproductive organs back together again. At the time, she'd thought Yance was quietly pleased. Now, children were again a non-issue for her.

In spite of herself, a tear trickled over her nose and into the pillow. China swiped her hand over her face and turned over to place her forehead against Yance's chest and feel his heart beating through her skin and into her mind.

He pulled her close and rested his chin on her bent head and she heard him exhale softly.

Was he awake?

But she didn't ask, and he didn't answer.

The two-hour drive to Midland was made in almost total silence. Once out of the mountains, the land flattened, the sky broadened and the air smelled of the oil and gas industry.

China stared out the window and considered, because she didn't want to think of anything else, how easy it was to imagine this land called the Permian Basin as the ocean floor it had been until fairly recently, in geologic time. It was virtually treeless, its mud-flat look patched here and there with short thin brown grass. Depressing.

"I hate this drive," Yance said. "I'm putting in a chopper pad next week."

Of course, China thought resignedly. A chopper pad. Why not? Trace would be thrilled.

Yance reached for the car phone and called the apartment in Midland, instructing Blackjack and Trace to meet them at the lawyer's office in an hour.

As he replaced the phone China stared at him, aghast. He wanted Blackjack and Trace in on this? Surely that wasn't necessary.

"Do you think that's wise?" she asked quietly.

"Very wise," Yance replied. "We're all in this together, whatever is decided."

Staring again out the side window but seeing nothing of the passing landscape, it dawned on China that it was New Year's Eve. The last day of the year, she thought. The real last day of a marriage that began with instant rice and ended with canned minestrone soup.

Fitting, she supposed. She'd laugh if she weren't so afraid of crying instead.

Yance didn't waste any time. They went straight to the lawyer's office. Trace and Blackjack were already in the reception room, and both rose when the couple walked in.

"Hi, Mom and Dad," Trace said, and grinned, delighted with the words.

"Hullo, kid," China managed to choke out around the lump in her throat.

Blackjack didn't say a word, just looked at them both and smiled.

The old man, China noticed, positively glowed. *Oh, Yance, how could you do this to them? Wouldn't it have been better to tell them later, in private?*

George Goforth, Yance's lawyer, appeared in the doorway, a large smile spread over his seamed, mid-sixties face. "Come on in," he invited, and they passed in front of him into his private office. He made a production of courteously seating China in a large leather chair, at the same time waving the men to other seating drawn up close to his desk.

"The papers are ready and everything's in order," he said with satisfaction, seating himself across from them. As if to put them in better order, he patted the edges of the papers on his desk with the side of his palms. "But then it always is when Yance does the planning," he added jovially, and chuckled.

Fighting the desire to jump out of the chair and physically attack the man, China clenched her fists.

"Shall I give them to her, or do you want to?" the lawyer asked Yance.

"I want to give her mine," Trace said, before his father could answer.

China gaped.

The lawyer gravely handed Trace the top document, and Trace walked over to China with it in his hand, holding the thing with some reverence.

"Merry Christmas, China," he said with a shy nervous smile completely out of character, and handed it to her.

Looking down at the document, China saw her name and Trace's name and a plethora of wherefores and whereases, but her mind, overloaded with sorrow and bewilderment couldn't take in the content.

She looked up at Trace blankly.

"I'm giving you me," the boy said, and grinned suddenly from ear to ear. "These are adoption papers. Dad and I agreed. This gives me two real moms."

"Ohh." China stood. "Ohh," she wailed and, gathering Trace into her arms, burst into tears.

He hugged her back tightly for a long moment before

looking up. ''You're gettin' me wet,'' he said, still widely smiling. ''Blackjack has somethin' for you, too.''

And China found her stepfather standing beside her, also holding a sheaf of papers. The old man cleared his throat. ''We don't havta do this if you don't want it, China Dare,'' he said, looking down at the papers in his hand for a moment before lifting his faded and now diffident blue gaze to her face. ''But it would please me mightily to adopt you as my own daughter, if you agree.''

China went into his arms. ''It would please me very much,'' she said quietly. ''I've always loved you as my real father. It might as well be legal,'' and she laughed a little and snuffled.

''Now, darlin','' Blackjack said gruffly, ''this is my good suit. Can't have you waterin' all over it,'' but he held her tightly, and she heard him give a suspicious snort himself.

''I have a document, too,'' Yance said, after George Goforth handed out tissues and used one himself. Everyone was standing now, and Yance nodded to the blue bound contract in his hand.

China recognized it as their Prenuptial Agreement. She stilled, and turned sick inside.

''This is the last remaining copy of the agreement we made before we married,'' Yance said, holding her gaze with his own. ''What we do with it is up to you. I'll bide by it, if that's what you want. I'll add to it or delete in any way that you want. You decide exactly what you want done with this thing.''

His eyes darkened to the color of gunmetal as his tone turned grim. ''But I won't let you move to Santa Fe or give you a document of divorce, China, without a battle. Unless, of course, you tell me you don't love me.''

He handed her the contract.

With the papers in her hand, China gazed at their blue

covering for a moment in the silence. "I can add anything?" she asked, not looking at him.

"Anything."

"The moon, the stars and a planet or two?"

"Yep." She heard the smile in his voice, and raised her lashes to find the same humor in his gaze, resting on her face.

"I love you, husband," she said.

"I love you, wife," he replied, then added quietly, "you don't have to be a corporate person, China. That's my job. That's who I am, just as the C3 is who I am. Your job is to be an artist—to be only who you are. Because who you are is the woman I love, and want, and need, and no other but you fits me so well."

What a fool she'd been, China thought, seeing his love for her in Yance's eyes; just as, blinded by her own insecurities, she'd been unable to see his total acceptance of who and what she was from the very beginning.

"Mr. Goforth," she said, staring fixedly into her husband's face. "Does your office have one of those gizmos that turns paper into confetti? It's New Year's Eve, you know, and the Chisolms seem to be in short supply."

"Why I believe I do," George Goforth replied expansively. "If you'll just step into the next room," and he led the way, the four of them trooping after him into the outer office and to a machine behind his absent secretary's desk.

"Thank you, sir," China told the lawyer formally when he switched the contraption on for her, and then carefully fed the prenuptial agreement into the shredder's ravenous maw.

In a wink, pieces of blue and white pulp dribbled into the plastic-lined empty bin below it.

"Wow!" Trace said, fascinated.

With Mr. Goforth's permission, China pulled the plastic bag from the bin and handed it to Trace. "We'll need that later, son," she said, making him giggle.

Yance's hands on her shoulders turned her slowly around so that he could gaze into her face a moment before he dipped his head.

With his eyes closed, it was instinct alone that led his lips to hers. They homed in as if China's mouth had been their landing pad for years, just as they had on their wedding day in another office.

Caught up in the moment and in a fit of exuberance, Trace opened the bag and he and Blackjack tossed the now confettied prenuptial agreement until it was all over the floor and decorating everyone's hair and clothing.

But when there was nothing left to throw and the couple still hadn't come up for air, the boy said plaintively, "Ah, c'mon you guys. Can't we go home now?"

His father finally seemed to hear him. "Yes," he said. "Let's go home."

At three o'clock in the morning on New Year's Day, Yance lay stretched out in a long slant across the bed, propped on one elbow that was anchored in the bank of pillows, and watched his wife, who sat cross-legged at the foot of the bed busily sketching his relaxed body.

"And you got this thing where?" he asked, indicating the minuscule scrap of black silk that was all he wore.

"Dallas," China answered, carefully detailing in her sketchbook the scrap in question...and what it did and did not cover. Line, she thought, and form. And umm, that texture. Mr. January.

"That look you're wearing, wife, can change the shape of this model real fast."

China glanced up at him, her face full of mischief. "Promise?"

"Promise. You about finished? I'm tired," he said pathetically, knowing the look in his eye belied the assertion. "All that furniture moving you made us do earlier. What a way to spend New Year's Eve."

"But the new rooms look better now, don't you think?" China carefully sketched in the clean line of Yance's nose.

"Yes, darlin', they do." And they did, Yance thought, once China's unerring eye put the Chisolms and the Kerrigans in them. The new rooms were now like the rest of the house, reflecting two families made into one, the whole somehow magically greater than the sum of its parts.

"But moving furniture around is not quite how I fantasized spending a first New Year's Eve with my wife," he continued. "I was thinking more on the lines of doing Dallas. Dancing maybe." He grinned suggestively. "And stuff. You know," he explained, "the stuff we were doing a little while ago before you got the drawing bug."

"Hmm." China added a couple of light strokes to her sketch of Yance's eyebrows and studied the effect. "Dancing in Dallas," she said thoughtfully, not looking up from her drawing pad, but her mouth beginning to curl into a smile that caused her model's lower parts to change position.

Then, through her lashes, she glanced up at her husband's face. "Did I tell you about the dance I heard was all the rage in Dallas?" she asked softly, putting down her pencil to reach up with both hands and slowly gather her loose hair so that it flowed down her back and left her bare breasts exposed.

Her model came to full attention.

"What dance?" Yance asked, his voice low and husky.

China put her sketchbook and pencil on the dresser near the bed with a long slow sensuous reach that caused her hair to slide caressingly across her bare back and over one shoulder.

"It has complicated movements," she said. "I might have to show you. They say you do it while lying down, and moonlight—" she switched off the bedside lamp "—adds to the rhythm." And China stretched out beside her husband, who immediately gathered her into his arms.

''To really groove, the partners have to be…close,'' she whispered throatily into his neck.

''C'mere, wife, and show me how they dance in Dallas,'' Yance commanded, his voice guttural and his arms already pulling her closer.

And she came.

Epilogue

Yance studied his cards. Hell of a hand, he thought. But perhaps he could bluff.

At a slight noise, he turned his head toward the door, but no one was there, so he returned a small part of his attention to his cards.

Trace looked at him and grinned. "You're lookin' kinda green, Dad," he said. "You just about match the walls in here." The boy's gaze roved over the pale green waiting room walls for a moment, before it returned to rest knowingly on his father.

Someone must have convinced a hospital administrator sea green was soothing, Yance thought. Personally, he found it nauseating. "Mind your manners, boy," he said briefly, with no real heat.

He glanced across the low magazine table toward Blackjack, who stared into his own fan of cards as if memorizing them. He'd bet the old man was feeling as green as he was.

Finally, Yance tossed his remaining two matchsticks into the pile in the table's center.

Scowling, Blackjack added his last one.

Trace, with a whole pile of kitchen matches on his side of the table, carefully selected five to add to the pot.

Poker, Yance thought with an inward smile, had brought him a wife. He'd not played a game since, until tonight. Hadn't wanted to put his winning streak in jeopardy, he thought with a touch of superstition. And he refused to allow this three-handed version of the game, where they'd bent the rules freely, to count.

Good thing, too. After tonight, if he was a smoking man, he'd have to quit for want of a light.

They each put their cards on the table, faceup, and Trace chortled. "It's easy to beat you guys when you don't pay attention," the boy said, raking in the pot before looking up to give the two men a severely patient look.

"Lucky in love, unlucky at cards," Yance said, and the words burrowed into his heart the moment they were out of his mouth.

Well, I'll be, he thought in wonder. He'd forgotten about that.

But a nurse had appeared in the doorway. "Your new son has arrived," she told him at once, smiling. "Whole and healthy Eight pounds, five ounces. Your wife is doing fine. We're just cleaning her up a bit. While you're waiting to see her, you can see your baby in the nursery."

After leaping to his feet the moment the nurse entered the waiting room, Yance couldn't move. "Damn," he said, and blinked. "Well, damn."

Trace tugged at his arm. "What're you waiting for, Dad? Let's go *see!*"

And so the three of them stood at the nursery window and peered at the tiny red infant wrapped tightly in a blue blanket and wearing a blue knit cap.

"I thought he'd be bigger," Trace said at last.

"Big enough," Yance replied, anxious to see China. "You were smaller than that," he told his oldest son, placing a hand on the boy's shoulder.

"Last time I saw a little un like that," Blackjack said gruffly, "was when China was born. The little fella looks like her, don'tcha think?"

"How can you tell?" Trace asked, puzzled. "He's all covered up and his face is all red and squinchy."

"I just can," the old man said grumpily, not liking to be called on this.

The nurse was back. "You can see your wife now," she told Yance. "We'll bring the baby to join you in a few minutes."

Yance left Blackjack and Trace standing at the nursery window to hurry down the hall to China. When he walked in, she was propped up in the bed waiting for him, looking tired but radiant. Her hair was freshly brushed and hanging loosely braided over one shoulder.

"Hello," he said softly, coming forward to kiss her forehead. "He's beautiful. So are you, darlin'."

"Hi, yourself," she replied. "I think he's beautiful, too. He looks just like you, doesn't he?"

"Blackjack disagrees with that," Yance said with a smile. "Are you sure you're all right, honey? He was big."

"Not too big," China said reassuringly. "And *he* is Jacob John, please, after Blackjack, if you haven't changed your mind." She looked a question.

"No. Jake's a good strong name. Can't think why Blackjack never used it."

"He said his mother called him Jacky when he was a boy," China told him with a laugh. "So as soon as he could, he changed it." Her face lit up. "And here's little Jake now," she said, sitting forward so the nurse could place the baby into her arms.

Trace and Blackjack trooped in right behind the nurse. "He's a miracle, isn't he?" China asked of no one in particular. She raised the blue bundle a tad so that it angled toward Trace, who leaned on the side of the bed, braced on his forearms, watching.

"See, little Jake. This is Trace, your big brother. You're going to look just like him, someday."

"He looks like you," Blackjack said, leaving no room for doubt.

China smiled at her father. "Do you think so?"

"Wish your ma was here," Blackjack said, twisting his hat in his hands.

"Me, too," China said softly. She laid the baby on the bed beside her and slowly unwrapped the blanket so they could all count fingers and toes and examine the wondrous tiny body.

With the touch of the cooler air, baby Jake opened his eyes.

"Wow," Trace said softly. "Look at that. Blue eyes."

"They probably won't stay that color," China said. "Babies' eyes change, you know. Pretty soon, they'll turn gray."

"They'll prob'ly be green," Blackjack said, "like your ma's."

"More hands," Trace said abruptly, as China rewrapped the baby. His young voice carried a note of satisfaction.

"You know," he elaborated, when no one seemed to get the point. "At the spring. Another set of Chisolm hands to go on the wall."

"Two more sets," Yance corrected. "Your mother hasn't left her prints there yet." And he took China's free hand in his. "I love you, wife," he said.

"I love you, husband," she replied.

"Hey, Jake," Trace told the infant, who still had his eyes open. "Better get used to it. Things get mushy at our house real often."

The baby yawned and closed his eyes, well satisfied that it should be so.

* * * * *

▼™ SILHOUETTE
SPECIAL EDITION®
AVAILABLE FROM 20TH AUGUST

FATHER-TO-BE Laurie Paige

That's My Baby!
One night of passion with Hunter McLean was all it took for Celia
Campbell to fall pregnant with his child. But was marrying for the
baby's sake really the best solution for this unlikely couple?

THE PRESIDENT'S DAUGHTER Annette Broadrick

Nick Logan had been assigned to *protect* the President's daughter—not
fall in love with her. Lovely Ashley Sullivan seemed to return his
feelings. But Nick was torn between duty and desire…

PRINCE CHARMING, M.D. Susan Mallery

Prescription: Marriage
Nurse Dana Rowan had to admit surgeon Trevor MacAllister was
gorgeous. But she swore to her colleagues she was immune to his
charms. After all, only a fool would fall for the same man twice!

MEANT FOR EACH OTHER Ginna Gray

For Leah Albright, Dr Mike McCall was a life-saver because he'd
helped prevent her brother's death. But were her feelings for Mike
more than just gratitude? And was she ready to trust him with her
family secret?

BABY STARTS THE WEDDING MARCH Amy Frazier

Dallas Parker and Julia Richardson had been friends since childhood.
And when Julia couldn't face telling her parents she was pregnant—
and single!—Dallas offered to pretend to be the baby's father.

UNTIL YOU Janis Reams Hudson

Strait-laced Anna Collins was not well pleased to be playing hostess to
irritatingly attractive stranger Gavin Marshall. But she had no choice,
Gavin held the clue to her missing brother's whereabouts…

Available at most branches of WH Smith, Tesco, Asda,
Martins, RS McCall, Forbuoys, Borders, Easons,
Volume One/James Thin
and most good paperback bookshops

9908

AVAILABLE FROM 20TH AUGUST

▼™ SILHOUETTE®

Intrigue
Danger, deception and desire

NEVER LET HER GO Gayle Wilson
A FATHER FOR HER BABY B. J. Daniels
REMEMBER ME, COWBOY Caroline Burnes
TWILIGHT PHANTASIES Maggie Shayne

Desire
Provocative, sensual love stories

A KNIGHT IN RUSTY ARMOUR Dixie Browning
THE BRIDE MEANS BUSINESS Anne Marie Winston
THIRTY-DAY FIANCÉ Leanne Banks
WILL AND THE HEADSTRONG FEMALE Marie Ferrarella
THE RE-ENLISTED GROOM Amy J. Fetzer
MIRANDA'S OUTLAW Katherine Garbera

Sensation
A thrilling mix of passion, adventure and drama

GABRIEL HAWK'S LADY Beverly Barton
SECONDHAND DAD Kayla Daniels
UNDERCOVER LOVER Kylie Brant
ROYAL'S CHILD Sharon Sala

▼™ **SILHOUETTE**®

36 Hours

When disaster turns to passion

A THRILLING NEW 12 BOOK SERIES.

A town fights its way back from disaster...
Passions run high...
Danger is a heartbeat away...

The rainstorms and mud slides appear from
nowhere in the little Colorado town of
Grand Springs, as does the 36 hour blackout
that follows. The natural disaster causes all kinds
of chaos—the mayor dies—but it may not have been
an accident, a baby is born and abandoned and a bride races
away from the altar with a band of killers on her trail.
But sometimes, even the most life threatening situations can
inspire the most passionate romance...

Look out next month for the exciting conclusion!

Book 12 - You Must Remember This
by Marilyn Pappano
On sale 20 August

*Available at most branches of WH Smith, Tesco, Asda,
Martins, Borders, Easons, Volume One/James Thin
and all good paperback bookshops*

If you enjoyed 36 Hours,
you'll love our new 12 book series:

MONTANA

...where passions run deep and mystery lingers

Passion and romance...

Murder and mystery...

Secrets and scandals...

The mystery begins with:

Book 1 – Rogue Stallion by Diana Palmer

Special Offer

BOOK 1 FREE with selected Silhouette® series
books and book 12 of 36 Hours.

On sale 20th August 1999

Available at most branches of WH Smith, Tesco, Asda,
Martins, Borders, Easons, Volume One/James Thin
and most good paperback bookshops

Sometimes bringing up baby can bring surprises —and showers of love! For the cutest and cuddliest heroes and heroines, choose the Special Edition™ book marked

That's my baby!

▼™ SILHOUETTE
SPECIAL EDITION®